A LIFE LESS LONELY

A quiet English town is home to Dr Andrea Palmer, the young widow of a military hero and mum to little Josh. Focused upon her son and vulnerable mother, she has no thoughts of finding romance. Events conspire to change that, but she wonders how many times a broken heart can mend . . . Keir is the self-styled bad boy of the consultants' dining room. He dislikes his eligible bachelor tag and anticipates meeting Andrea only because her qualifications perfectly equip her to co-present his findings. When Andrea and Keir meet, each feels a frisson. But flirtatious nurse Moira has other ideas, and is determined to have Keir for herself . . .

Books by Jill Barry
Published by The House of Ulverscroft:

DREAMS OF YESTERDAY
GIRL WITH A GOLD WING

JILL BARRY

A LIFE LESS
LONELY

Complete and Unabridged

ULVERSCROFT
Leicester

First published in Great Britain in 2013

First Large Print Edition
published 2015

A catalogue record for this book is available
from the British Library.

ISBN 978–1–4448–2324–0

Published by
F. A. Thorpe (Publishing)
Anstey, Leicestershire

Set by Words & Graphics Ltd.
Anstey, Leicestershire
Printed and bound in Great Britain by
T. J. International Ltd., Padstow, Cornwall

This book is printed on acid-free paper

1

Andrea picked up the call winging from the reception desk of the university where she worked.

'Dr Palmer? Could you come to the main entrance, please? There's someone here to see you.'

'What sort of someone, Cheryl?'

The receptionist hesitated. A little too long. 'My lines are buzzing. I'll say you're on your way.' She cut the connection.

Andrea pushed back her chair and headed for the elevator, gulping greedy mouthfuls of air while the lift lumbered to her floor. She watched the numbers climb from first through second to third before the doors slid apart and she darted forward, anxious to push the button and descend. But someone blocked her way. Someone built powerfully enough to make a significant obstacle.

'I'm so sorry,' said the stranger, shifting to her right.

'My fault.'

She'd mirrored his move. They locked gazes, Andrea frowning as the expression in his slate-blue eyes changed from barely concealed admiration to concern. Did she really appear that needy? His scrutiny unsettled her, and not only because she found him disturbingly attractive. Flustered, she checked for a non-existent name badge. He looked important. Maybe no one dared challenge him when he walked through the building. Although not matching her late husband's height, this man would be able to see over her head in a crowd. Close-cropped dark hair and silver-tinged sideburns plus a charcoal-grey sharp suit distinguished him from the denim and sweatshirt-wearing academics making up her world.

'Are you all right?' The voice lived up to the appearance. Understatement.

'Fine, thank you.' She averted her eyes. Surely he could sense her urgency? She dived past him, hand reaching to punch the Down button.

A twinge of guilt hit her as he disappeared from view. She'd greeted a stranger's civility by offering instant annihilation by automatic door. He left behind an image of eyes the right kind of blue. Eyes capable of recognising the anguish churning inside her. Yet the stranger's good looks weren't the sole cause of her disquiet. The receptionist had been too evasive. Someone as competent as Cheryl would naturally

2

falter if pretending indifference. Something. Was. Up. As the lift descended, Andrea clenched her fists, feeling the sharp bite of nails against palms. Remembering another occasion, the receptionist tried not to be too precise about someone asking to see her.

★　★　★

Keir Harrison, chief psycho-geriatrician at Hartnett General Hospital, strode along the corridor towards Richard Bailey's office. Keir, a man who made a wry face at the sound of his own job title, sought the School of Anthropology's collaboration in testing a new dementia-busting drug. Money talked and Keir needed to get his priorities right when it came to funding.

But the face of the young woman he'd all but tap-danced with at the elevator still tantalised him. The expression in those smoke grey-eyes had hinted of something, or someone, haunting her. He'd seen that look before, for sure. Sometimes it belonged to a patient dreading test results. Sometimes a loved one wore it.

Keir's lips curved into a wry smile. Didn't he have enough to occupy him without inventing cases from random encounters? Not that he'd even left the lift before being ambushed. She'd been very sharp with him too. His lips twitched at the thought of Ms Torpedo's chilly attitude. It made a refreshing change. Ever since he took on this high-profile role, certain staff members treated him as though he walked on water as his prime leisure pursuit.

He'd walked too far. Discomfited by dangerous daydreams, Keir retraced his steps and tapped on Professor Bailey's door.

★ ★ ★

Andrea forced herself to look straight at Reception, anticipating a uniformed police officer waiting to report her mother had taken a tumble while walking and offering a lift to the A & E department. Seeing Rosemary admiring plump white tulips crammed into a square glass vase, Andrea's first astonished reaction dissolved into instant guilt.

She wanted the floor to swallow her. Longed for a giant hand to scoop her up and deposit her elsewhere. If only she could turn back time. Then, Greg would still be with his military unit, sitting down to another plateful of tinned sausages, baked beans and mash and going online to check his inbox for his wife's daily email. Her mother would still be alert, working a few weekly stints in a local charity shop and baking her trademark sweet, fluffy cupcakes for fundraising events. Of course, in this apricot fondant dream, her mum's capabilities still included babysitting her adored grandson Josh. If only.

Andrea felt as though she acted in a soap opera where heartache and hysteria went hand in hand with black comedy. Her mother wore a fuchsia-pink wool cardigan inside-out so its seams protruded like swollen veins. On a chilly, raw day, Rosemary had neglected to wear a coat and beneath black slacks one pale, bare instep cried out for a sock. This petty but poignant detail almost cracked Andrea's fragile self-control.

'Hello, Mum.' She reached for those restless hands, gently grasping what felt like two bundles of brittle twigs wrapped in tissue paper. Looking down, Andrea noticed purple smudges where Rosemary must have damaged her fragile skin while gardening. A surge of compassion overwhelmed her as she raised her mother's hands to her mouth and kissed the fingers. The gesture spoke more than words could say as she mourned the woman who'd once been. It wouldn't be so bad if she could soothe her mother; provide the tender loving care necessary at this stage of her life. But to do that properly, Andrea needed to put her own emotions to bed as easily as she dealt

5

with her little son's night-time rituals.

'I came on the bus,' Rosemary said, voice ringing with triumph. She stood smiling at her daughter, eyes shining.

'Well done,' said Andrea. 'But I'm sorry, Mum; it's impossible for me to have lunch with you today. I just need to speak to my boss, so he knows I'm driving you home.' She clasped her mother's left elbow and gently guided her to a seat. 'You wait here for me. I'll find you a magazine.'

Her mother obeyed without question as Andrea pushed one of the gossip weeklies across the table. Rosemary ignored its colourful cover and focused upon the TV screen above. Easy listening music treacled through the sound system and Andrea saw her mum's eyes light up as she recognised her favourite, Barry Manilow. She walked back to the desk in time with the beat of 'Copaca-bana', anxious to tell Richard Bailey she needed to leave the building for a while. She didn't know the rest of the script but she must keep her cool. With her back-story, she felt as though a ten-mile hike would be a pushover by comparison.

Cheryl, the duty receptionist, handed the phone to Andrea along with a sympathetic glance. 'Professor Bailey's extension's ring-ing,' she said.

Dr Keir Harrison had clicked with Professor Richard Bailey, each respecting the other's professionalism and finding much in common. This, Keir knew, was important in his search for the right team to conduct a high-profile drug trial. He waited, eyes fixed on a glowing watercolour of Cornish fishing boats at sunrise, trying to hide his impatience while the professor took a call.

'Sorry about that, Keir,' said Richard, replacing his phone. 'I was about to say I think some of my colleagues would bite your hand off to join this trial. I especially have in mind a junior research fellow.' He grinned. 'Although she has a distinct wariness of the drug culture in general.'

Seeing Keir's expression, he held up his hand. 'This is a woman who's been lecturing in anthropology for a while now. I'd like to involve her in this project because she's passionate about community medicine. Be warned, though.' He steepled his fingers. 'She's sure to play devil's advocate. I shouldn't say this, but my colleague also has an excellent personal reason for wanting to learn more about Dimaribon's street cred.'

'Whoever she is, she sounds perfect. I know I'll be heckled at the seminar. Tinkering with vitamins always winds up certain people. Your colleague will provide me with some sparring practice.' Keir hesitated. 'What's her name?'

'Dr Andrea Palmer. I'm afraid I can't introduce you at the moment because she's, um, taking a couple of hours off. She's had a wretched time lately.'

Keir watched Richard drum the fingers of one hand on the pristine blotting-paper holder topping his desk. Tuned into subtext, Keir's antennae quivered, suspecting something off kilter here. He hoped that something didn't spell discord. An in-house romance between Richard and Dr Palmer might prove to be even worse than personality clashes. With such an important project at stake, Keir could do without personal issues and the attendant hassle. Inwardly he sighed.

The drug trial commanded high priority. Keir rated it as the most exciting development he'd seen in his research career so far. He rarely admitted it to anyone but, deprived of his young daughter since his marriage failed, his work had assumed an even greater importance than previously. This dependency meant he drove himself hard and expected similar high standards from those around him.

Richard was looking speculatively at him.

'If you vouch for Dr Palmer's commitment, that's good enough for me.' Keir scribbled in his diary. 'If I email you a document, maybe you could forward it for your colleague's attention?'

'Of course,' said Richard. 'I'd like to sit on the sidelines if you'll allow.'

Keir checked his watch. 'That goes without saying. Two of my medical team will be on board and I need to select two or three nurses. Maybe we could set up a preliminary meeting for the end of next week. I'll get my PA to contact yours.'

The two men rose and shook hands.

Waiting for the elevator, Keir experienced a flashback to the woman with the far-seeing grey eyes and translucent skin. How strange it would be if she should now be arriving at the third floor, only to find him waiting to descend. Had she resolved whatever troubled her? What would that full mouth look like when she smiled? He found himself longing to see for himself.

The doors swooshed open to reveal an empty space. Keir stepped into the lift. If he didn't return to the hospital soon, his PA would disown him.

★ ★ ★

Deciding not to ask her mother what brought her to the university, Andrea felt relieved to find her passenger calm and content to be driven home.

'Let me check your seatbelt, Mum,' she said.

Rosemary smiled at Andrea. 'Is Greg due leave soon, darling? I'll need to bake his favourite cake.'

Andrea's throat dried. Hadn't her mother retained any of her careful words? Phrases distilled from anguish, love and pride, chosen to describe how Greg had ended his life as the brave man he'd always been. If only she could deal with her mother as she dealt with her little boy. She'd told Josh he should be very, very proud of his daddy. And yes, of course it was OK to be sad, because even heroes shed tears.

'Mum,' she said, checking her mirrors, 'why don't you bake the cake anyway? You know how Josh loves your lemon drizzle.'

She resolved to book an appointment with the family GP. Since losing Greg she no longer found it easy to pray, but she couldn't resist asking for help — asking someone, somewhere to please make it all go away.

★　★　★

Andrea returned to her desk, concerned at having had to request yet more time off, even if only an hour. She knew she could perform her role to her usual standard, but personal issues loomed. She opened an email from Richard and realised he hadn't lost his enthusiasm over her potential involvement with an upcoming project. She recalled the subject being discussed before she'd learnt her seriously wounded husband was fighting for his life while being airlifted to RAF Brize Norton. Andrea puffed air through her lips. She still felt as though she tightrope-walked between black despair and a kind of bizarre relief because, the worst having happened, it could no longer stalk her.

The professor walked in and stood beside her. 'Is everything all right, Andrea? Did you manage to sort your domestic emergency?'

Andrea guessed he'd be painfully aware everything certainly wasn't all right. She and Greg had been invited for an informal supper with Richard and his wife the previous October, only days before Greg had left for his six-month Afghanistan tour. Despite the age gap between the two couples, they'd spent a relaxed few hours. Now a single mum in the true sense of the word, Andrea valued friends like the prof and his wife Louise.

She shrugged. 'I'm really not sure, Richard. For some unknown reason, my mother turned up at Reception. To my knowledge, she's never done such a thing before.'

He nodded, seemingly unfazed.

'I just had to drive her home,' she said, 'as if I haven't taken enough time off.'

'Andrea. Read my lips. You're accomplishing even more than I'd anticipated. I don't have to tell you to talk to your mother's GP, and you know what? It seems to me Rosemary might be an ideal subject for this pharmaceutical trial. I understand it's been the last thing on your mind since losing Greg. But I urge you to think about it. There's one very positive slant. If she joins in, she'll spend a considerable amount of time over at the hospital.'

'Being pumped with drugs? Locked into a little world of her own?'

Richard raised his eyebrows. 'You make it sound so harsh. Where would the world be without the pharmaceutical industry? Remember, everything stems from nature, Andrea.'

'I know,' she said. 'But in my opinion, science sometimes gets too big for its boots. I believe if alternative medicine can go hand in hand with sophisticated technology, it can only be a good thing.'

'That's why I need to introduce you to Dr Harrison. Apart from being on your wavelength, he's arguably the most dedicated medic I've ever come across. And you know how high I set the bar. I've already told him I want you to join his trial team.'

Did she really have to work with this Dr Shiny Pants? Andrea pretended to scowl. 'You want me and you want my mother on board? Is that wise? Is it even ethical?'

'You leave that to me,' said Richard. 'And by the way, hadn't you better think about finding a suitable carer? That's a must-have, in terms of Rosemary joining in the trial.' His tone softened. 'Not to mention her personal safety and your own peace of mind.'

He was gone, pre-empting protest. He was right and she knew it. She'd pushed this significant problem backstage when it demanded spotlighting. Her mum required more care than Andrea could give, but how would Rosemary react to a stranger strolling into her house?

★ ★ ★

Next day, Andrea received Keir Harrison's findings plus a friendly invitation to call him. As she read, she had to admire the concept of lowering drug levels and boosting the patient's immune system. This so fitted her work ethic, hating as she did the thought of her mother, or anyone's mother, being zombified by medication. Maybe this project really would absorb her. For the first time in weeks, she felt animated and picked up the phone to punch a nine for an outside line.

'I'd like to speak to Dr Keir Harrison, please.'

'Who's calling?' The answering voice sounded protective. Briefly, Andrea closed her eyes. Oh, please, not another PA with a crush on her boss.

'Dr Andrea Palmer, research fellow, University of Hartnett.' Time to pull rank.

'One moment, please.' The voice sounded unimpressed.

Andrea tapped her pen against her teeth. She glanced at the digital time display on her monitor and wondered if Josh was on the climbing frame at that moment. Her thoughts drifted to what her mother might be up to, then she almost dropped her pen as masculine tones, audible melting dark chocolate, sent decidedly unprofessional but pleasurable sensations down her spine.

'Dr Palmer? I'm so sorry to keep you waiting.'

Andrea swallowed. 'That's all right, Dr Harrison. I'm calling to let you know I've read the information you sent and I have to tell you there are questions I'd like answered.'

He chuckled down the phone line. That

kind of sound should come with a health warning.

'What's so funny?' Andrea gripped her pen. Hard.

'Forgive me,' he said. 'I would have expected nothing less. When can we meet?'

★   ★   ★

Andrea delivered Josh to the university crèche next morning and, instead of driving across campus, headed for the hospital. Dr Harrison had a cancelled early appointment and could therefore slot her into his busy schedule. On the way to Hartnett General, she thought again of the near-sleepless night she'd spent. This restlessness had nothing to do with Josh. She couldn't even blame it upon the emotional wounds she doubted would ever heal.

No, the pillow-thumping was purely down to guilt. Could she really hand over her mother as a guinea pig? Keir Harrison had better know his stuff. Otherwise, no way would she let him invade their close-knit personal lives. Ahead lay a huge decision in terms of Rosemary's lifestyle and wellbeing, a decision Andrea would have normally insisted Greg made with her. And that could not be.

Memories often popped into her head

without warning. This time she was propelled back to her wedding. St Valentine's Day that year arrived as if by special delivery from central casting. It was a day stolen from spring, gentle sunshine filtering into the village church through stained glass panels in fruit-gum colours. The heady sweetness of white lilies had drowned the designer perfumes worn by the congregation, causing Greg to sneeze on the verge of saying *I do*. Somehow they avoided collapsing into helpless giggles.

The bridegroom's kiss had sealed the moment. A moment when Andrea felt bound heart, body and soul to Greg. No one could ever snatch away that memory. Apart from the small, vital reminder that was Josh, only by reaching into the treasure chest and clutching at fragments from the past, could she survive the present.

★ ★ ★

When Keir's PA showed Andrea into his office, no way was he prepared to see the woman from the elevator. Today she wore a navy-blue trouser suit and jade-green shirt, unlike the manic button-presser. He recalled admiring her silky chestnut-brown hair, but today she'd scooped it up and coiled it away from her face, not leaving it loose as she had the other day. She held out her hand, hesitating when he didn't immediately grasp it.

Clearly something had happened. He knew at once. That haunted expression he'd rewound countless times alone at night was replaced by something else, something different yet still disturbing. Try resignation mixed with self-preservation.

This potent mix was familiar. Keir recognised a soulmate, and understood how this woman must hurt inside. He suspected she, like him, yearned for the emotional and physical closeness once enjoyed, its loss still mourned. His eyes probably mirrored hers as the final, most poignant reaction kicked in, that of knowing each recognised the other's need. She, like him, couldn't bear to contemplate the agony of loving and losing ever again. Each wore an invisible shield, ironically, only too apparent to the other.

But where were his manners? This was an important first meeting with a professional colleague. He needed to get his act together, and fast.

He shook her hand. 'Dr Palmer, it's good of you to come over so early. I'm Keir Harrison. Please sit down. Coffee's on its way.' He gestured to a green leather couch facing a low table distanced from the polished oak partners' desk.

'Please call me Andrea,' she said. 'It's good to meet you. I've heard a lot about you from Richard.'

She walked over to the couch and sat down, trying to compose herself. Keir Harrison was unmistakeably the man she had encountered at the lift the other day. At that moment she'd been startled to find a part of her, frozen when her darling Greg died, suddenly showing signs of awakening. Rather like a corm lying dormant in the cold, dark earth, only to realise there was still a sun bringing warmth, light and the promise of rebirth.

The consultant radiated confidence. That voice of his must be a crowd-pleaser when he addressed packed conference halls. The man was a powerhouse, just as Greg had been, yet in a totally different way. This realisation that she could experience affinity with — could react physically to — a virtual stranger, unwound her. Because it was too soon, far too soon after the kind of loss she'd suffered. Every nerve in her body screamed the same message, instinct warning her against disloyalty. Despite this reaction, she wondered again whether he'd recognised her. And again asked herself, why on earth should he?

In his turn, Keir struggled to concentrate, trying with all his usually formidable willpower not to see the lovely stranger he'd allowed to drift into his dreams. He strove only to see a competent professional possessing a CV her supervisor Richard pronounced perfect for Keir's purpose. So it was, but did its owner have to be quite so gorgeous?

He glanced at Andrea's hands — slim, with tapering fingers. The almond-shaped nails gleamed with palest pink polish. Artistic hands, he thought as he watched her open her laptop with minimum fuss. No doubt there were numerous questions lurking in the computer's innards. But whatever she threw at him, he'd find satisfactory answers. Suddenly he very much wanted her on his team.

Coping with this onslaught of conflicting emotions, he felt shocked to see the narrow gold band on her wedding finger. Why hadn't he noticed it before? Next to it she wore an engagement ring, a sparkling emerald and diamond starburst. How stupid of him not to consider she might be married. It proved his continuing vulnerability in that the shell constructed so painstakingly had come dangerously close to fracturing. What a fool he'd been. But equally, what a fool Richard Bailey must be if he'd involved himself any way but professionally with a married woman. These mixed responses overwhelmed Keir, unsettling him more than he liked to admit.

Someone tapped at the door. He hastened to open it, only to look blankly at his PA. He took the tray and thanked her.

'Right,' he said, walking towards his visitor. 'Coffee is served. And with chocolate digestives, even. Now, fire away, Dr Palmer. I mean, Andrea.'

2

'Your take on this intrigues me,' she said. 'But checking the volunteers' diets is vital, especially noting any allergies.'

'Absolutely, and I'll personally monitor the shortlist. You have my assurance on that.' He sat back in his chair. If only she'd take a biscuit so he could eat one too. He'd grabbed a banana as he left home, but he relied on breakfast to kick-start him and that morning he'd slept late. Showering and scrambling into one of his 'look at me, I'm a consultant' suits, as Connie used to call them, had taken priority. His former wife had never quite got it. Never really appreciated what lay behind those years of studying and slogging to achieve his all-consuming ambition. It wasn't about munching smoked salmon in the consultants' dining room. He'd wanted to help dispel the demons around dementia.

Now Andrea Palmer sat opposite, her nearness playing havoc with his thoughts, when her expertise to help drive his project to a successful end should take top priority. He also needed to ask her something important, though he sensed the time wasn't quite right yet. But the implications of her answer totally dissolved his reasoning powers. Hopefully, when he could pose the question, they'd be a little more relaxed in one another's company.

Before his stomach could growl its displeasure, Keir picked up the daisy-pattern china plate of biscuits. He'd inherited the crockery from his predecessor, and never had it seemed as twee as it did now. He offered the chocolate digestives to Andrea.

She accepted one, balancing it on her saucer. 'I must say, your suggestions did rather stop me in my tracks,' she said. 'What's the feeling among your colleagues?' She looked him in the eye. 'Scepticism, perhaps? Or don't they dare challenge the great man?' For a moment, as if she'd been caught giggling in church, her face displayed shock at what she'd said.

He couldn't contain his laughter, certain she imagined he might take offence over such a provocative remark. His gut feeling told him she hadn't meant to sound quite so cynical and he struggled to stop himself reaching out and taking her hand to reassure her.

Andrea picked up the cookie without noticing the chocolate melting against her hot cup. She took a bite, causing the gloopy mess to stick to the side of her mouth. Obviously unable to prevent her tongue from seeking out the stickiness, she licked her lips, not noticing the crimson paper napkin Keir's PA had placed within easy reach.

Keir, trying to help, had been about to pass her a serviette when her pointy pink tongue peeped between her full lips. What hope did he have of maintaining a professional relationship with a woman capable of causing his heart and stomach to lurch as if he stood poised at the top of a ski run? What did she just say? Something about scepticism . . . insinuating his colleagues wouldn't dare challenge his theories.

Keir, too, bit into a biscuit. 'Not the easiest of things to eat when you're wearing a business suit,' he mumbled through a crunchy mouthful. Deftly he fielded a falling morsel. 'For your information, Andrea, my most senior colleagues view me as the bad boy in the consultants' dining room.' Damn. Now he'd dropped crumbs between his impeccably trousered thighs. 'Yes,' he said. 'Of course there's a huge appetite for something to take the sting out of the ageing process. Equally, there's a huge determination not to raise false hopes. I should say there's an equally strong wish for this trial, when it commences, to adhere to very high standards.'

She remained silent. They stared at one

another until the tension between them stretched taut as a bud about to burst. His phone broke the silence.

'Please excuse me for taking this,' he said. 'I've asked Lyn to put through only one particular call while you're with me. Hopefully this is it.' He let loose that full-beam smile. 'Help yourself to more coffee.'

Andrea ate the rest of the biscuit and topped up both their cups while Keir concentrated on whatever his caller had to say.

For the sake of her self-esteem, Keir hoped he'd help gloss over Dr Palmer's awkward moment. If the phone call hadn't happened when it did, things might have proved trickier. They were both very much on their best behaviour with one another, but the spark ignited couldn't be ignored. He'd been startled by the electricity zinging between them.

He listened to the verdict he'd awaited. By the time he put down the phone and returned to his seat facing her, Andrea was checking something on her computer screen. He saw her smile as she caught him snaffling the last biscuit, like a guilty schoolboy hoping chocolate counted as one of his five-a-day.

'I'm sorry to keep you waiting,' he said, touching a finger to his lower lip.

24

Her eyes focused upon him brushing away one golden oaten fragment.

'Talk about conversation-stoppers,' he said. 'Andrea, you shall be the first to know. I've just received excellent news.'

So, was he going to tell her? Or was he going to sit there, crunching and keeping her in suspense? He'd somehow stepped out of the timeline. But then he smiled, and he was devastating when he smiled. He was devastating full stop, and she seemed to be turning into an adolescent groupie. It was a miracle she hadn't felt her cheeks glow hot with embarrassment, because frankly she deserved to.

Briefly she closed her eyes. The big man had succeeded in stopping her in her tracks, though this was much more to do with his physical impact than his cunning vitamin cocktails. No way must she give the tiniest hint of this being the case. Andrea desperately yearned to re-establish the cool professional aura she so often relied upon to freewheel her through her days.

'We have lift-off!' He punched the air. 'Funding's been approved, so I can approach the rest of the people I want on the team. You're the first one I've spoken to. Richard suspected you might be seconded in some other direction, and the only way to prevent that was to snap you up while the going was good.'

'I'm flattered,' she said, unable not to respond to his excitement. 'Let's hope everyone else on your list says yes.'

'Thank you, but there's another matter I need to mention.'

She half-expected to hear doubts about her mother's inclusion on the trial, polite rejection cutting short further discussion; but as he spoke rapidly, his words tumbling out, his hand ruffling his velvety crew-cut, for a moment she knew exactly what he'd looked like as a much younger man. And what he had to say caused his eyes to shine with excitement.

'We'll hardly be up and running before I'm due to fly to Canada and speak at a very prestigious conference.' Keir leaned forward, clasping his hands round one long leg looped carelessly over the other. 'I want you . . . I want you to accompany me and present a paper on the possible impact of all this upon the community.'

Just like that. As if he was asking her to scrub up and walk into the theatre with him to observe an operation. Yet to her, it was one of those moments when there was no other cliché to use than 'time stood still'. This was so unexpected — and what a fantastic career opportunity it offered.

A small, insidious voice wheedled its way inside her confetti storm of thoughts: *How can you possibly contemplate flying thousands of miles away from home when you have Josh to consider?*

'You don't have to make an instant decision, Andrea. I appreciate you'll need to talk it over with your ... your immediate family. Lyn will provide details of dates, flights, hotel, etcetera. But she's not Miss Moneypenny. I work her into the ground and expect miracles by the bucketful, but she hasn't tied up every single detail yet. Give her a break and wait until tomorrow before you contact her.'

'How many people are attending this conference?' Andrea wished her heart wouldn't keep behaving as if it played drums in a rock god's band.

'How many? Just me, and hopefully you,' said Keir. 'I thought we could do a joint presentation. Do you have a problem with that?' He paused. 'We'll need to practise together, of course.'

That same cheeky stomach lurch interrupted the thoughts quick-stepping through her mind. She wanted to accompany Keir to Canada, and for more than one reason. But she was desperately torn. No way could she leave Josh with his grandma, even if her mother's neighbour agreed to drive him to and from the crèche and supervise his care. No. Kirsty was the only possible person with whom she'd trust her precious boy, especially as Josh would adore staying with the family for a few days. But Andrea's oldest and dearest friend was pregnant and had her own son and husband to look after. Could she really expect Kirsty to cope, while she flew off to Montreal? Rosemary's vulnerability presented another problem, one still waiting for Andrea to resolve.

If only the conference was in the UK. But it wasn't. It was on another continent for goodness' sake. And much as she longed to take her place at the podium along with a man poised to make waves among his peers, Josh must take precedence over his mother's career.

'You'll be meeting the rest of the team as soon as I can cast my net.' Keir's eyes twinkled. 'We'll need you and Richard here at the hospital for the sessions, if that's in order. And you know I'm coming to the university soon? Delivering a lecture to some of your first-years?'

'Yes,' she said. 'I've been asked to sit in — unless you prefer me not to, of course.'

His eyes crinkled. 'I shall look forward to it, as well as to hearing your decision.'

★ ★ ★

At home that evening, Andrea banished thoughts of her exciting yet scary opportunity until after Josh's bedtime. Maybe then she could speak to her friend and judge her reaction.

'Let's look at some photos of Daddy,' Andrea suggested, patting the space beside her on the couch. She'd taken the family album from the sideboard drawer. Somehow it comforted her more to turn its pages than click on images on her laptop. She'd scanned in every single one of Greg she could find.

Josh joined her. 'Is my daddy dead in the photos?' He began sucking his thumb.

How could her heart keep on beating when it was broken? 'A photograph captures living people at whatever age they are.' Andrea cuddled her son close. 'Look, that's Daddy and Mummy on our wedding day.'

'When I wasn't here.' His tone was matter-of-fact.

'That's right.' She turned over more pages. 'Look, there's your daddy holding you when you were only two days old.' She riffled backwards. 'And here he is when he was a little boy — probably about the same age as you are now.'

Josh's concentration span wasn't great at

the best of times. He peered suspiciously at the first photograph. 'I'm a big boy,' he said. 'That's my daddy with someone's tiny baby.'

Andrea knew he found it difficult to comprehend he was once no taller than his beloved teddy bear. Maybe small nuggets of information were best at this stage. But she so wanted to keep Greg alive in their son's memory.

'Shall we have a cup of tea and a custard cream?' She pushed away dangerous thoughts of brushing biscuit crumbs from Keir's well-honed thighs and mock-punched Josh on the arm.

'Yay! Can I have Daddy's mug?' Josh was a real teapot. Exactly like his father. How poignant she found it, having this marvellous reminder of her husband. How lucky she was.

'Yes, my love, of course you can.'

Andrea switched on the TV so Josh could enjoy the CBeebies bedtime story while she prepared their snack. She'd spoken to their GP after her meeting with Keir, and events would follow their course. Her mother had startled her when she mentioned baking Greg's favourite lemon cake. If Josh became confused by something his gran said, Andrea must get round it as best she could. Talk about a juggling act. The more she thought about it all, the less inclined she felt to approach Kirsty and announce she had the chance to fly to Montreal. It sounded so high-powered. Too much so, if she was entirely honest with herself.

★ ★ ★

Keir sat across the desk from Susie McIntosh. Apart from being a first-rate nurse, she would have made a fantastic hospital almoner in years gone by. Susie's name topped the list of nurses he wanted to have working with him.

'I'm chuffed you should think of me, Keir, especially as these people from the university sound very high-powered. So, which other nurses will be involved? What about Jane Lloyd?'

He laughed. 'I'm seeing Sister Lloyd later this afternoon. You two plus one other are my shortlisted victims. And no more of this high-powered stuff, please. You're a total professional, at the top of your game.'

'Thank you. Dare I ask who the third nurse is?'

'Moira Haynes.'

'Ah.'

He frowned. 'And your point is?' Keir needed a strong, mutually supportive team. His initial concern over Richard's possible

31

closeness to Andrea Palmer still niggled at him.

'No, I, erm, didn't mean anything negative. Not about her work.' Susie fingered the watch pinned to her uniform. 'It's just that Moira's not exactly over the moon about natural remedies. She's very sceptical about people swallowing pills and potions from the health foods shop and anticipating miracles. That's all I meant.'

'Moira's opinions are precisely the reason why I'm inviting her onto the team. Apart from her terrific CV. Something that applies to you and Jane too, of course.'

'Stop buttering me up,' said Susie, eyes twinkling. 'I'd very much like to accept. What you've told me sounds very exciting.'

'Thank you, and welcome aboard.' He rose and held out his hand to shake hers. 'I'm sorry not to offer any refreshments, Susie, but my afternoon's probably going to extend well into the evening. I promise the welcome wagon will be there with bells on when we have our introductory meeting.'

'I hope you're looking after yourself,' she said sternly, looking him up and down, 'though I must say you seem to thrive on hard work. I've known you long enough to realise that.'

'Yes, ma'am.' He escorted her to the door.

'This is my life,' he said simply. 'I'll be in touch soon.'

Once she'd gone, he walked thoughtfully back to his desk. Moira Haynes was a sultry redhead with the kind of eyes in which sensible men should beware of drowning. She definitely wasn't his type, if he had a type. But he wasn't stupid enough to think he never figured as the object of nurses' speculation. Single man. Consultant. Would he be inviting trouble if he asked Moira to join the team? Was that what Susie had really meant when she acted flustered? Should he have probed further? As Susie had pointed out, she and he were friends. But this was rubbish. He needed the cream of the department for this project. Once they came on board, they'd have to put their personal lives behind them and remain focused, as he was so accustomed to doing.

Like a punch in the solar plexus, a guilty feeling knocked him. So how about his feelings regarding Andrea Palmer? But she came highly recommended by her boss, and he'd invited her to meet him without any intention of asking to see her photograph beforehand. Her qualifications spoke for themselves, making her the obvious person to accompany him to the Canadian conference. None of the other team members could compete with her community medicine background. Nor could any of the others be spared from their hospital duties once the trial began. But if Andrea chose to turn down his invitation, how would he feel if he had to invite Richard to fill her place?

Keir's instant and disconcerting reaction contained a monster-sized helping of guilt.

★   ★   ★

Next morning, despite work-related matters nudging her, Andrea dialled Rosemary's number, hoping for a brief chat and maybe a tactful query about eating breakfast. The relentless ring tone told her it might be pointless to go on waiting. She selected a small banana and sprig of seedless grapes from the fruit bowl and placed them in Josh's plastic lunch container before redialling. Maybe her previous call had caught her mother in the bathroom or even outside, topping up the birdseed containers.

'Finish your cornflakes, sweetheart.' Andrea watched Josh push his treasured miniature tank round and round the rim of his bowl. With a pang, she realised Greg would probably have addressed their son as 'mate.'

'Vroom, vroom.' Josh completed another circuit.

Andrea counted to ten. Was she invisible? Probably yes, when competing with a toy Challenger war machine. And still her mother didn't reply. Rosemary never switched on the answer phone, despite Andrea's coaxing. She sighed as she replaced the handset. Well, she'd planned on going round there that morning anyway, as soon as she dropped Josh off.

The little boy recommencing sessions at the university crèche formed part of Andrea's mother-and-son routine. So far, he'd happily latched onto one of the helpers, leaving Andrea relieved at becoming superfluous. Josh seemed to have climbed another rung on the independence ladder and all in the course of a couple of weeks. He'd miss the loving rough-and-tumble relationship enjoyed with his dad, but Andrea had no siblings, and male role models for her son were in short supply. She'd always kept fit, but any commando course she constructed would probably be viewed as a wobbly blancmange.

'Josh, let's see if you can clear your bowl before I finish putting my face on. Pretend you're a big digger like the one we watched on the building site the other day.' She reached for her tube of tinted moisturiser. That and a coat of lip gloss would be all she needed. Yesterday she had applied full eye make-up before leaving the house. Subtle bronze eye shadow and lash-enhancing mascara weren't necessary to boost her CV, but they sure as heck helped boost her confidence. Fortunately, Josh was demolishing his breakfast as if his favourite cereal was about to be banned.

★　★　★

On the way back to her car after dropping off her little boy, Andrea saw the irony of her situation. As Josh grew from babyhood and developed into the strong young man she knew he would, so her own mother regressed. This thought pierced her like a needlepoint while she wove her way through back streets towards the quiet cul-de-sac where her mother lived. Rosemary had moved from her former home near Hartnett and into the bungalow two years before, at a decent interval after Andrea's dad had died.

'It's not fair,' she muttered, turning the corner. First her mother left alone and vulnerable and now here she was, widowed at age 37. She'd always been independent, enjoying her own company and preferring to have one special woman confidante to several. Andrea didn't take after her mum. She was hopeless at girly stuff and would have been the same had she trained as an accountant or air traffic controller instead of an anthropologist. Boy, had those five syllables been a passion-killer back in her dating days.

Andrea parked her car in her mother's driveway and cut the engine. She lingered a few moments, staring ahead, recalling Greg's curiosity about her work the night they first met at a party that clashed with her favourite TV programme. Most of the men she'd dated viewed her as out of their league. Or else they made strange gestures at her as they performed squirm-inducing gorilla impressions. That evening she'd gritted her teeth and put on a little black dress.

'You don't have to pretend to be interested,' she'd said, looking up at the powerfully built man with the kind eyes. 'I'm a doctor. But I don't use a stethoscope these days. I'm hung up on anthropology. There — if I say it quickly, you'll hardly notice. So, tell me what your job is.'

He'd shuffled his feet, mumbling something about being an overgrown squaddie. They both laughed.

'I've never met a major before,' she told him. 'Should I salute?'

'I'd prefer it if we could find somewhere quiet to sit.'

37

She'd caught her breath as the buzz of conversation and gentle jazz music faded, becoming inconsequential. The major was easy to talk to and their meeting heralded the start of something very, very special. Something she missed more and more as each day passed and the memory of which she still clung to, desperately.

The unthinkable had happened and her major had turned into a fallen hero. Andrea was still staring at the bungalow's front door when she blinked hard, realising she could see right inside her mum's hallway. The beige and brown carpet tiles and the telephone table with her son's face smiling from a narrow silver frame stared back at her as if daring her to do something. She wrenched open the car door and hurtled across her mother's front lawn to leap over the neat border of coloured primroses and raucous yellow daffodils.

'Mum?'

No response. Andrea closed the door behind her and hurried to the kitchen. She noticed toast crusts on a plate and an open marmalade jar on the hob. Her mum had changed to the lemon and lime sort. *Focus, Andrea!* The cooker wasn't on but when, cautiously, she held her hand near the kettle, she could feel warmth.

Fear pushed away grief. She called again from the hallway and, hearing nothing, checked the dining area and sitting room. The door to the cloakroom stood wide open, leaving only her mother's room. Maybe she'd gone back to bed.

Andrea called out. 'Mum? Are you in there?'

Still nothing. She went inside. The familiar lily-of-the-valley scent hung in the air and the bed was immaculate, the window opened a half inch. A pair of pink furry slippers was perched on the quilted dressing table stool. She hadn't noticed before, but a photograph of Clint Eastwood looking laconic in Stetson and poncho stood propped before the oval mirror. Ironically, her mum was still girly at 79 years of age.

In the en-suite bathroom the cold tap dribbled, but fortunately the plug wasn't in place. Andrea turned off the water, biting her lip. Wasn't everyone absent-minded some-times? A quick glance showed bland tidiness in the spare bedroom, so she retraced her steps to the kitchen again and unlocked the back door. Even though the bolt had been secured, her mother might have gone out the front way and down the side pathway to feed her feathered friends. But Rosemary was nowhere to be seen.

Now what? Andrea locked the back door and hurried round to the neighbour's house.

Lizzie Dean responded almost at once. 'Hello,' she said. 'I thought maybe it was your mother come to see me.' She touched Andrea's arm. 'What's happened?'

'Mum isn't there, Lizzie. I . . . I'm just beginning to realise how much she's been deteriorating.'

'Come in a minute. Please, please don't beat yourself up. You've had more important matters on your mind. And it's only recently I've begun suspecting things.'

Andrea stepped into the hallway and sniffed the spicy sandalwood headiness. Lizzie must be burning an aromatherapy candle. Calm was definitely not where Andrea was at that moment. 'Suspecting things?' Biting her lip, she waited for the other woman to respond.

Lizzie sighed. 'I think Rosemary's become rather crafty. I've been calling in several times a week to make sure she's OK. She always puts on a good front. But I'm not sure she's eating properly.'

'She seems to have made breakfast today.' Andrea didn't mention where she'd found the marmalade pot.

'OK, that's good. But the other day I asked if she needed anything from the supermarket and she blocked me. Insisted she had more than enough food in the house.' Lizzie looked anxiously at Andrea. 'We were in the kitchen. When the phone rang and she went into the hall to answer it, I sneaked a look inside the fridge. Made my excuses and came back with a few basics.'

Andrea nodded. 'I know what's coming. She probably accepted them and asked how much she owed you.' She gulped. 'Thank you very much. I've let her down, haven't I?'

'Hey, of course you haven't.' Lizzie grabbed a handful of tissues and passed them to Andrea. 'She can't be far away. I saw her in the back garden half an hour ago, refilling her bird feeders. She waved to me. I was about to call round when you arrived.'

'That's so typical of Mum!' Andrea blew her nose. 'Hardly a thing in the fridge, but Joe Robin and Co feasting on five-star banquets. Look, Lizzie, do you think she'd go to the park? My mother's not into calling anywhere else but your place these days, is she?'

'Not that I'm aware of. Sometimes that nice couple opposite invite her in for morning coffee, but they're cruising round the Greek islands just now. Could she not be taking a little walk? She likes to do that, you know.'

'Her front door was wide open when I pulled up. Don't you think that's strange?'

Lizzie sucked in her breath. 'I see. Sorry, Andrea, maybe you should drive towards the park? I'll go knocking on doors. A sunny day like this brings people into their gardens, so someone may have seen Rosemary and asked where she was off to.'

'Thanks, Lizzie. I know you're a friendly lot round here. You do have my mobile number?'

'Yes, of course. I'll ring if there's any news. And — ' She clasped her hands. ' — let's hope we find her soon so she can tick us off for fussing.'

But as Andrea hurried back to lock the front door, she knew her mum would be horrified at the thought of it being left wide open. Doing such a thing was totally out of character. Andrea had no idea whether her mother carried her key on her, but she made the bungalow secure anyway. Her own key would see them back inside once she'd located one missing elderly lady. Somehow she couldn't bear the thought of contacting the police yet. Engine ticking over, Andrea selected what she thought was first gear, but trying to pull away was like wading through thick treacle.

'You muppet,' she scolded herself, hoping nobody had noticed as she quickly selected the correct gear and drove off. It would be such a relief to find her mother putting the world to rights over someone's fence or strolling back towards her bungalow.

She chose the most straightforward route to the pretty park where she knew her mother liked to sit, and managed to manoeuvre her car into a space between the council dog warden's van and a smug Chelsea tractor. Before getting out, she hesitated. Was her mum with a neighbour, after all? Drinking tea somewhere, oblivious to the fact that her only daughter roamed the public highway, frantic with worry?

Andrea banged her fist on the steering wheel, hot tears rolling down her cheeks. Angrily she brushed her hand across her eyes. It was a good job she hadn't bothered to apply eye make-up earlier. She mustn't go to pieces. Not now. Not ever. Especially not after hearing Keir Harrison's good news yesterday, because with Greg gone she had to be the strong one, taking charge of what little family was left to her. But at that moment she wondered how on earth she'd cope.

3

Andrea pulled out her phone and sent a text to Richard Bailey's mobile. At this rate she'd be working all through her lunch hour to make up for lost time. This thought filled her with such shame, such remorse that she should think about her job, about disruption to her day, when her mother could be about to step into the path of a snarling juggernaut. She didn't even know if Rosemary had worn a coat that morning, a dazzling morning marred by a sharp-toothed east wind. Why hadn't she thought to collect a warm jacket from the wardrobe just in case?

Fortunately she'd left a rug on the back seat. She grabbed it and got out of the white Peugeot, locking it and striding towards the park entrance. She'd walk the path leading to a drinks and snacks kiosk beside the ornamental lake. Her mother might be there, maybe buying a sandwich on sell-by date so she could feed beak-sized portions to the waterfowl.

Andrea noticed a council worker raking the earth around the shrubs. She hesitated, almost calling out to ask if he'd seen an elderly woman walking by, but how stupid was that when she didn't even know what her mother wore? She clutched her mobile phone in case Lizzie rang with news.

At first she couldn't believe her luck when she saw the familiar figure strolling towards her. Rosemary noticed Andrea at once and began to wave. Surely, surely, her mother couldn't be too bad if she was capable of recognising her daughter so quickly. Her clothes, including a quilted jacket, even looked as if they were accustomed to being worn together. Maybe things weren't so depressing after all.

'Hello, darling,' Rosemary called cheerfully. 'Isn't it a lovely morning?' She pointed at the rug. 'Are we going to have a picnic? I like picnics.'

'Mum, you worried me. You didn't answer the phone, so I drove round to the bungalow and found the front door wide open.' Andrea took her mother's arm. 'Come on, I'll take you home.'

'My front door, do you mean?' Her mother frowned, head on one side.

'Yes, Mum. Don't worry. I've locked it now. Everything's fine, but we really must have a chat.' She guided the older woman gently but purposefully towards the car. She'd ring Lizzie, but not before Rosemary

45

sat safely belted in the front seat.

As Andrea called up the number, her mother dropped the bombshell. 'It was so nice to see Greg this morning. He looked very handsome in his uniform. You know those shiny round things he wears on his best tunic? They really gleamed in the sunshine.'

★   ★   ★

'So you can see, Richard, why sometimes I think she's fine on her own. Other times I think she should never be left without someone to keep an eye on her. But I don't believe my mother's in need of round-the-clock care. I hope not, anyway.'

Richard steepled his fingertips and sat back in his chunky black leather chair. It always reminded Andrea of the pilot's seat in the old *Thunderbirds* TV show. Face impassive, he didn't interrupt.

'Dr Harrison has told me he's been given the green light,' said Andrea. 'Funding's in place for the drugs trial. If you still think my mother will make a suitable subject, I'm going to recommend to her that she volunteer.'

The prof raised an eyebrow. 'Sure this isn't just a knee-jerk reaction? Your mother gives you a fright. As soon as you find her, she tells you she's just seen your late husband in full dress uniform complete with medals. You're entitled to feel concerned.'

Puzzled, Andrea leaned forward in her chair. 'I thought you were keen on her taking part?'

'I am. Of course I am. But this is your mother, Andrea. You must make a considered decision. And at the risk of being boring, dare I mention contacting her GP?'

'It's OK. I've already rung the surgery. It's easy to convince yourself someone's losing her marbles when she blurts out a comment like Mum did.' She shook her head, her expression thoughtful. 'You know, Lizzie insisted it was highly likely my mother saw Greg in the park. She believes it was proof he watched over us. Especially as Mum said he told her to walk towards the main entrance and find me.' She shrugged. 'As you can imagine, I didn't know quite how to respond. Talk about a conversation-stopper!'

Richard shifted in his seat, not meeting her eyes. 'Yes, well, I think we should concentrate on the practicalities. Your mother's presenting certain signs even though most of the time she seems absolutely fine. Her GP will refer her for an assessment, but have you thought any more about a possible carer?'

Andrea shrugged. 'I suppose I shall have to

47

contact an agency.'

'What about her neighbour? This Lizzie seems to have time on her hands, and her views on the afterlife aren't relevant when it comes to your mother's well-being.' Richard glanced at his computer screen as it warbled a reminder.

'I think my mother can look after her personal needs,' said Andrea. 'Getting dressed sometimes poses a challenge, though not always. The house appears tidy, except that — ' Andrea pictured the tap left running and recalled the glass jar abandoned on the cooker hob. In the kitchen, she'd held her breath until she reassured herself the oven wasn't switched on.

'Let's see what an assessment brings out.' The prof's eyes were kindly. 'From what I've heard, your biggest worry seems to centre on your mother's tendency to wander.'

'Each time it's worked out with no harm done except to my shredded nerves.' Andrea shrugged. 'Maybe there have been other occasions when she's got back OK. Next time, who knows? What if she goes out and forgets the way home? How awful if she's turning into a toddler!'

'You can make sure she's in good hands. You won't be short of expertise to help you put a care package together if that's what you decide.' He smiled at her. 'I know you have a lot on your plate, especially now Keir's offered you this exciting opportunity.'

'It's odd how much easier it is to think straight when you aren't dealing with your own flesh and blood,' said Andrea. She got up. 'Don't mind me. I'm feeling sorry for myself. Thanks for your time, Richard. I'll approach Lizzie Dean and I'll keep you posted.'

★   ★   ★

An appointment was arranged for Rosemary's assessment to be carried out by one of the professionals attached to the GP's surgery. Andrea rang her mum's neighbour to let her know.

'Wednesday at three p.m., you say. Would you like me to be with her?' Lizzie asked. 'So you don't have to take time off work? Or will they need you there?'

'No, I checked with the CPN — sorry, the community psychiatric nurse. He knows how to contact me. Really, it's best he sees Mum without me hovering. Maybe I could ask you to call round beforehand and make sure she remembers she has a visitor coming. If you're sure you don't mind?'

'You can leave it to me. But I do need to

speak to you soon, Andrea, when you can spare a few minutes.'

'Is this something to do with my mother, Lizzie? You can talk to me now if you like.' Andrea crossed her fingers. Was Rosemary concealing some other problem?

Lizzie hesitated. 'It's more about my personal situation. But yes, it does affect Rosemary, in terms of my keeping an eye on her long term. I'm sorry to say, I'm going to have to put my house on the market.'

Andrea gasped. 'But I thought you were quite happy living there!'

'I'm very happy. I know so many people, and there's my little job — I'll miss all the children. And the staff — even though they tease me about never missing a *Corrie* episode.'

Andrea chuckled. 'I can imagine. It all sounds very good.'

'Certainly is.' Lizzie hesitated. 'When we moved into our house, there were three of us living here. I wish I didn't have to make this decision, but the time has come to downsize. The garden's too much for me to manage on my own, and the car gobbles cash. I'm afraid my own feelings don't enter into the scheme of things. It's crunch time, Andrea.'

'Have you said anything to Mum about this?'

'Not yet. She might be upset. On the other hand, she mightn't take it in. Probably best to wait until I know the For Sale sign's going up.'

As she put down the phone, Andrea's spirits plummeted. Lizzie was a terrific neighbour, always friendly and supportive since Andrea's mother had moved in two years before. Lizzie had lived in the close for a decade before being widowed, but she was years younger than Rosemary. As for her job, Andrea knew she worked as a dinner lady at the local primary school. No doubt they'd miss her as much as she'd miss them. But life was like that, all about facing change. Maybe Lizzie would decide to move closer to her married daughter, wherever that might be. Well, that was her decision.

From a selfish point of view, she felt bitterly disappointed by this news. She'd no doubt whatsoever that Lizzie had proved better at dealing with Rosemary than she herself could ever hope to be. That was often the way. But the seed of an idea slowly sprouted, bringing Andrea a tiny ray of hope.

★　★　★

The phone rang around eight thirty that evening. Andrea, on the couch in red pyjamas and slipper socks, jumped at the sound.

'Is this a good time?' Her friend's voice sounded wary.

'Kirsty, I was just thinking about ringing you. Josh is in the land of nod. Otherwise he'd want to say hi.'

'So, how's it all going?'

'Oh, you know. It's often the little things. I found a gold locket the other day, wrapped in tissue paper. It was tucked inside a box full of Greg's old school reports and swimming certificates. Stuff like that. He'd written me a little note and folded it inside the velvet case. The gift was meant for my birthday so I'm going to keep it 'til then and unwrap it again.'

'That's not a little thing, Andrea. That's a hugely wonderful symbol of how much your husband loved you. What a beautiful guy Greg was.' Kirsty gulped. 'Whoops, you've got me reaching for a tissue now!'

'I sometimes wonder whether he knew what was going to happen.' Andrea curled up, tucking her feet beneath her. 'While Josh was playing the other day he found a new miniature tank hidden inside a green plastic hippo he'd forgotten about.'

'I can't answer that one for you, sweetie. It might be something to do with being in a war zone and carrying a kind of acceptance around. It's the real deal, isn't it? Their lives are literally on the line.' Kirsty cleared her throat. 'Now, Luis keeps asking me when Josh can come to stay. I've explained you have a lot on at the moment. That boy can nag worse than I can.'

'You're my oldest friend and I've been neglecting you.'

'I'll forget you said that, honey bun. How's work?'

'Work's fine. Richard should get a knighthood for putting up with me. There are some question marks around Mum. I'll email you about it. We're going to have to make some changes.'

'Move her in with you and Josh, do you mean?' Kirsty sounded concerned.

Andrea sighed. 'I love her to pieces but we're chalk and cheese, as you very well know. I'm looking into ways of keeping her in her own place, but with more care than I can offer.'

'It's quite a while since you mentioned you and Greg had concerns.'

'Yes, on his last leave. I obviously couldn't take extra holiday so he took Mum to do her big shop. She abandoned her trolley while he was looking at DVDs. It was as if she'd forgotten he was with her. Eventually he found her roaming round the car park but she hadn't a clue which car was ours, even though she's been in it dozens of times.'

'I'm sorry you've got all this on your plate,' said Kirsty. 'If only we lived closer.'

'We don't do too badly. 31 miles each way isn't too dreadful, is it? But you mustn't worry. How many weeks are you now?'

Kirsty chuckled. 'Seventeen and counting.'

'Wow. How are you feeling?'

'Amazingly well and utterly determined not to be informed whether this one's a girl or a footballer.'

'Girls play footie too, you know,' said Andrea.

'Hmm,' said Kirsty. 'So were you about to ring just for a chat, or can I help with anything?'

'Kirsty, there is something I need to run past you. It would mean asking you a really big favour. Please don't feel you have to agree. I'll quite understand if it's out of the question.'

'Try me.'

'OK.' Andrea took a deep breath. 'I have the chance to fly to Canada with Dr Shiny Pants and speak at an important conference. Side by side. With him. Keir Harrison, I mean.'

'Surely Dr Harrison can't be all bad if he thinks enough of you to want you along to hold his hand?'

Andrea kept quiet. The image was disturbing.

'When would you go and how long would it be for?'

'It's the last week in May,' said Andrea. 'I'd have to leave on the Tuesday and fly back the following Friday. So three nights in Montreal, but the Heathrow trips and airport formalities either side make the time away longer, of course.'

Kirsty cut short the apologies. 'Of course you must go. We'd love to have Josh stay. And as for him being a bit cranky sometimes, try living with a pregnant woman and a Spanish man who wears his heart on his sleeve. Luis is going to be ecstatic at the prospect of having Josh to play with.'

Andrea felt a rush of relief. 'I just don't know how to thank you.'

Kirsty laughed. 'I'd have been miffed if you'd asked anyone else. Cross, even. Now, hang on a mo . . . yep, sounds like the guys are back from swimming.'

'I'll let you go then. Give Rafael and Luis our love, and I promise to email you dates and flights and contact numbers. Maybe when I bring Josh over, I could come an hour or so before I really need to?'

'Fantastic. Give him a hug from me.'

'I will. Thank you so, so much, Kirsty. Speak soon.'

Andrea put down the phone. Little things

were often what did it, she'd said. Her friend and her architect husband had got on well with Greg. Rafa looked upon Josh as a second son. But no way would she ever again hear Greg bringing Josh back from the leisure centre, gently scolding him for dumping his soggy swimming kit in the middle of the kitchen table. Those days were gone and she'd better face up to it.

★ ★ ★

Keir's gaze focused on the expectant faces. 'Are there any more questions for the moment? No? Well, thanks again for putting up with my less than perfect presentation skills. I'm sorry I'm not as computer-savvy as most of you appear to be.'

A ripple of laughter travelled around the conference room.

'All right, it's time to attack the refreshments. Get to know one another a bit better. We're no longer Hartnett General Hospital and University of Hartnett.' He looked around the room. 'We're . . . erm . . . '

'*The X Factor?*' a bearded, spiky-haired doctor offered.

'Thanks, Marcus, but no thanks, and I wouldn't recommend you giving up the day job.' He paused as people chuckled. 'Any further suggestions can be fielded by my long-suffering PA, and it goes without saying Lyn will be your point of contact if I'm away from the hospital. I'd like you to make known anything unusual in your findings, however trivial, as the trial progresses.'

Andrea was seated next to Richard. 'He's good,' she said as they stood up.

'Yes, he has excellent people skills. That talk impressed all of us, I think. OK, it wasn't *Panorama*, but I prefer good plain facts to smoke and mirrors any day.'

'Your knowledge of popular television shows never fails to impress me, Richard,' said Andrea.

They joined the small group helping themselves to refreshments. Andrea smiled at a petite woman dressed in green scrubs and possessing a fiery halo of curls. 'Hi,' she said. 'Without checking your name badge, I think you're Moira? One of the nurse trio?'

The redhead passed cups and saucers to them. 'That's me,' she said. 'One of the faithful.'

Andrea noticed how Moira's eyes assessed her swiftly before she turned to Richard. He made some quip about the biscuits being more upmarket than the ones they got at the uni.

A man's woman, Andrea thought, watching

Moira focus on the prof as if at that moment she considered him the centre of her world. She filled her coffee cup and moved away from the urn. The nurse who she knew was called Susie and who had a kind face was talking to the spiky-haired doctor. Andrea didn't like to butt in. All of a sudden, a frisson of panic struck her. She put down her cup on a windowsill and stood with her back to the room, intending to find someone to talk to in a moment, once she'd succeeded in painting her professional face back in place.

'It's very stuffy in here, don't you think? Let's try and open a window.'

She didn't need to look around to know who stood beside her. Keir Harrison's physical presence impressed her as much as it had at their first encounter. Would this present a problem over the coming months? The panicky feeling had changed into a feeling of longing for something or someone she couldn't have, or might that be something she shouldn't have? Her emotions were in the blender these days. Nor did it help when Keir reached overhead, the movement sending a drift of aftershave in her direction. Andrea closed her eyes briefly. She hated being battered by synthetic waves of the stuff and Keir used just enough to make her want to move closer. And breathe him in.

His PA, immaculate in a silver-grey trouser suit, brought him coffee. She greeted Andrea, and Keir thanked her as she bustled away.

'Lyn spoils me,' he said. 'I was just about to fetch my own. Scout's honour! I don't just snap my fingers and expect her to pull rabbits from hats. Her theory is that my time's more costly than hers.'

'She seems very efficient,' said Andrea, picking up her own cup and wondering whether his wife's life kept her too busy to cosset him as his PA did.

He pulled out a chair for Andrea and seated himself beside her. 'You were with me when I got the green light to conduct the trial. Now you know what a great mix of skills we have in this team. You included.' He turned his head to look at her.

'Keir, you really shouldn't monopolise Dr Palmer like this.' The red-haired nurse appeared as if by magic, standing as close to Keir as physically possible without actually touching him. She turned her attention to Andrea. 'I forgot to say how much I'm looking forward to working with you, Dr Palmer,' she said.

'Thank you, Moira. Same here. You and I come from different ends of the spectrum, don't we? Let's wait and see if we can't set the sparks flying.'

'If you'll excuse me, ladies, I need a quick word with Richard.' Keir rose and moved away, leaving the two women together.

Andrea needed to subdue a grin. The look of disappointment on Moira Haynes' face said everything. Clearly the nurse harboured a gigantic crush on the consultant. Briefly she wondered what it must be like to be a man capable of commanding such adoration from the opposite sex.

She took pity on the other woman. 'I notice from the blurb we've been given that you worked in Edinburgh before moving down here. I have very fond memories of the place. How has your first year down south gone? And please call me Andrea.'

Across the room, Keir glanced at the two as he waited for Richard Bailey to finish his conversation with one of the other doctors. How different the anthropologist and the nurse were, apart from obvious things like their impressive individual track records and the respect afforded them in their chosen careers. Each was also an attractive woman. But whereas Moira Haynes displayed an open invitation in those Persian-kitten-blue eyes each time she looked at him, Andrea still wore an invisible shield. Yet she was the one he longed to know better. What was more, he didn't only mean in a professional capacity.

This could only lead him into dangerous territory and, to his shame, the kind of thinking he'd previously pinned on Richard Bailey. It was imperative to regard Dr Palmer as a professional colleague. Nor should he wonder, even for one minute, what exactly her feelings were about him.

As soon as Richard became free, Keir saw Moira glance at her watch. From across the room she nodded at him and made her exit. Moira might be a flirt, but her timekeeping could land her a job minding Big Ben.

'Are you in a hurry to get away, Richard? I just need to speak to Andrea,' Keir said. 'Sorry. Didn't mean to be rude.'

'Not a problem. I'm driving her back so I'm ready when she is.'

Keir made his way to where Andrea sat checking her phone. She looked up as he approached.

'So,' he said. 'Do you intend keeping me in suspense?'

For one wild moment she thought he meant their encounter at the lift. Neither of them had mentioned it. Was he going to use the 'I keep thinking I've seen you somewhere before' routine?

Swiftly, she focused. 'You mean the clinical trial? I've given it a lot of thought, Dr Harrison, and my decision is I'd very much like to be involved. Canada included.'

'That's brilliant news, Andrea. But please, call me Keir. It's all about bonding these days, isn't it?' His eyes twinkled.

She nodded. 'I believe Richard's mentioned my mother's situation to you.'

'That's right. I think you've made the right decision there too. But then, I would say that, wouldn't I?' He held her gaze.

Andrea swallowed. How much more intense the blue of his eyes seemed when he wore a forget-me-not coloured tie. She tried in vain to think of something intelligent to say. Why did he possess the power to catapult her back into her tongue-tied teenage days?

⋆　⋆　⋆

Richard's car was a proper one with an engine that purred and room to put your feet without encountering sweetie wrappers, sand, and the odd discarded plastic gun. Little boys and toy guns — big boys and heavy artillery. When Andrea clenched her jaw, it had nothing to do with the prof's driving skills.

'Interesting group of people,' said Richard, waiting at a junction. He glanced sideways at her. 'Forgive me if I'm jumping to conclusions here, but has the nurse with that amazing hair got her eye on Keir Harrison?'

Andrea chuckled. 'You're very naughty, Richard. What an expression to use! Far be it from me to pass comment on my professional colleagues.'

'So I'm just an old gossip? But I'd bet my lunch money I'm right.'

'Your lunch is safe. Of course you're right. What's more, I saw his PA looking daggers when Moira shimmied up to Keir while he dared to speak to me. No prizes for guessing what's going on there either.'

Richard accelerated away from the lights. 'It's difficult being a mere man sometimes. Are you saying both those women are in love with the fellow?'

'No, of course I'm not, though I did wonder about Lyn at first. Now I think it's more about a PA being protective towards her boss. It's obvious how important her family are to her. We had a few words while people were arriving and she told me how nervous she felt about her daughter's music exam today — probably more so than the little girl herself. Sometimes we can all jump to conclusions and be proved wrong.'

Richard cleared his throat. 'Speaking of which, I probably shouldn't say anything to you, Andrea. But we've known one another long enough for me to do so.'

She glanced at his profile. He wasn't smiling.

'Dr Harrison asked me recently about the situation between you and me.'

She frowned. 'What situation? Am I missing something here?'

The professor harrumphed. 'Come on, Andrea. You're not just a colleague. You're also a good friend, and we're easy around one another as old friends are. Keir obviously picked up on that but misread the body language.'

'Spoken like a true people-watcher,' said Andrea.

'I'm very sorry. These are early days for you and far too soon for me to go bulldozing in like this. Forget I said anything, please.'

He turned into the uni car park and drove towards the far end where he had a reserved space. Richard guided the car into his parking bay and cut the engine.

Andrea remained in her seat, twiddling her handbag strap. 'I don't understand what business it is of Keir Harrison's whether you and I are friends or not.'

Richard groaned. 'You don't?' He beat a tattoo on the steering wheel. 'All right, then I'd better spell it out. His reason for quizzing me — and I understand his motive, given the closeness he hopes the team will generate and, of course, this Canadian conference you'll be attending. His reason is that he wondered whether you and I were an item, so to speak.'

Andrea gasped. 'Does the man watch too many TV hospital dramas? Didn't you tell him that you and Louise are godparents to my son? Did you explain how I'm still in bits after the devastating loss of my . . . my . . . '

'I put him right, gently but firmly,' said Richard. 'Told him our working relationship was one hundred percent professional. Yes, outside of work we sometimes socialise, and that includes other family members. But it's not my business to tell Keir Harrison anything about your personal circumstances. Unless of course you instruct me to do so.'

'Thank you.' Andrea felt a rush of relief. She'd overreacted. No way did she want the consultant pussy-footing round her in case he made some gaffe that might upset a recently bereaved wife. It was a bit of a nerve, Keir having made that assumption about her and Richard. But it underlined her suspicion. Dr Harrison was a perfectionist. It proved his aim for his team to be not only squeaky-clean in their workplaces but also in their personal lives. *Pick the bones out of that, Sister Moira Haynes!* She felt a sugar rush of triumph.

'I wish we could offer to look after Josh for

you while you're away, but Louise has plans to take her mother to the coast. You did say late May, didn't you?'

'I did. Thanks, Richard, but my friend is happy to have Josh while I'm away. You remember Kirsty and Rafa? Our boys are good mates.'

'That sounds just the ticket. Much better idea.'

'I have no doubts about Josh having a wonderful time,' said Andrea. As for herself, she still wasn't totally certain as to whether she'd made the right decision about the conference. If Kirsty hadn't been able to help, she'd unhesitatingly have refused the invitation. Now Josh kept asking if it was time for him to pack his case. Andrea was still trying to work out why she'd agreed to fly thousands of miles away from her little boy, even though she knew how many career-enhancing boxes she'd be ticking.

Not for one moment did she imagine Keir Harrison as anything but married, and probably the proud father of two point three high-achieving, shiny-panted children.

4

Keir leaned back in his high-backed office chair and stretched his long arms towards the ceiling.

'Would you like these notes transcribed today?'

He locked his hands behind his head and peered at Lyn. 'Not if it scrambles your schedule. Aren't you finishing early? Rosie's music exam is this afternoon, isn't it?'

'How you remember stuff like that always amazes me, Keir. I could slot these in and probably email them to you before I leave at three.' She hesitated. 'Unless you need that long report first?'

'That can hold till you're ready. So today's notes might be with me sooner than I thought. What would I do without you?'

'My other half says that too.' She grinned. 'In his case, I remind him he could always part-exchange me for two eighteen-year-olds.'

'He's not daft enough to contemplate any such thing. But, if you were headhunted, what would you recommend I did?' Keir looked at her expectantly.

She kept a straight face. 'You could buy a

coffee machine. How about an Italian steam punk job with a sloe-eyed Signorina to manage it? And there's always a voice recognition package. That should do the trick.'

He chuckled. 'I don't think so. I've already got one at home, don't forget. Voice recognition package, I mean,' he added hastily. 'The darned thing insists on turning my dictation into something resembling lumpy mashed potato. It's probably more trouble than it's worth.'

Lyn stood up. 'There's hope for us working women yet, then. I must get on.' She tapped her notebook. 'This stuff's really interesting, by the way.'

'Yes. Yes, it is. Sometimes I'm overwhelmed by the potential we're exploring.'

'Aiming for a knighthood?' She teased him so frequently that he never took offence.

'I wish! I suppose I could always borrow you from your husband to accompany me to Buckingham Palace — even buy you a posh hat for the occasion.'

His PA paused at the door as if about to say something.

An internal call cut short the banter. Realising how sad he'd sounded, even though making a joke, he grabbed the phone with a sense of relief. He'd no wish to discuss the lack of a 'plus one' in his life. His attentive PA might decide to help him find someone.

Lyn left the room, quietly closing the door behind her.

Keir finished his phone call. He'd been awake since five a.m., firstly out jogging round the park then practising his talk while he got ready for his nine-thirty start at Hartnett General. His suspicions about an undercurrent linking Richard Bailey and Andrea Palmer were unfounded. He'd tried to be as diplomatic as possible when sounding out the prof, who'd laughed at him. Laughed out loud and told him much as he found Keir's assumption flattering, he doubted whether Andrea would be equally pleased, given her boss's midriff bulge and flat feet.

'We're none of us perfect, Richard,' Keir had protested.

The prof totally understood Keir's concerns. He'd mentioned how fond he and his wife were of Andrea's family. He seemed to be on the verge of saying something else but their conversation had been interrupted. First Richard and then Lyn. Twice in one day someone had backed off. Well, if these matters were of any importance, the prof and his PA each knew which door he sat behind. Keir was fairly sure Lyn had been about to urge him to resurrect his social life. This he could deal with. She meant well but you'd think she'd know better by now. As for Richard, whatever it was bugging him would doubtless surface, if he meant it to.

At least he hadn't been stupid enough to enquire about Andrea's marital status. Her rings told a story, even if she didn't radiate contentment as he himself had done back in his early days of coupledom. How could someone at the top of his professional game have been so ignorant? How could he have let his own job satisfaction and self-delusion cocoon him from the truth? His failed marriage, if he allowed himself to think about it, still burdened him like a pair of diving boots. His former wife and small daughter were making a new life in Australia with a man who made time for them. He wondered what Andrea's husband did for a living.

* * *

Andrea sat across the table from the psychiatric nurse who'd carried out Rosemary's assessment. 'Well, that's a relief,' she said, clasping her hands beneath her chin.

The tall young man nodded. 'I wouldn't be surprised if loneliness had a lot to do with Rosemary's state of mind.' He watched the corners of Andrea's mouth droop. 'I know you spend as much time with her as possible,' he said gently. 'Don't feel guilty. You have other priorities. So, how about this brilliant idea you began telling me about?'

'I've had a long talk with Lizzie and put forward my idea. It could be beneficial for all of us.'

'And how do you think your neighbour feels about moving in here?'

'At first she was stunned at the idea of letting her house, but she soon began to see it might make sense. She'd been dreading putting her property on the market and moving. We've got a lot to sort out but it'd take a load off my mind and Lizzie obviously would prefer to stay around. She really enjoys her job and she's fit and energetic. One day she says she can see herself moving closer to her daughter. Hopefully not for a long time yet though.'

They exchanged smiles as combined laughter rippled from the sitting room where Rosemary and Lizzie were watching a DVD.

'Keeping your mother in familiar surroundings plus having someone to keep an eye on her and escort her to her hospital sessions sounds ideal. It's looking good. I'll send you a copy of my report.'

'Thank you,' said Andrea. She checked her

watch. 'I must let you get on.'

The nurse grinned. 'I'd like to quiz you about this trial but of course that's not possible. Rosemary's GP couldn't stop talking about the whole concept when I spoke to her last.'

'I know.' Andrea stood up.

He rose with her, reminding her how much he resembled a walking Everest rather than someone in the caring profession.

'This has been really helpful,' she said. 'I feel a lot more positive about Mum's situation now.'

He stuffed his file into a bulging briefcase. 'I've met Dr Harrison once or twice at case conferences. He seems a nice guy as well as being brilliant at what he does.'

As Andrea walked him to the front door, she wondered whether Keir had a dark side. Surely he couldn't be as Teflon-coated as everyone seemed to assume.

★　★　★

'Timed to perfection,' said Keir. 'Thank you, Lyn. I'll check out the hotel website later.'

'The King George has a spa area and pool. If you have any time for leisure, that is,' she added.

'A quiet morning swim will be worth

getting up early for.' He closed the folder she'd handed him.

She shuddered. 'If you say so. Now, when the tickets arrive I'll keep them in the safe until the day before you travel.'

'You know me so well.' He tapped his pen against his teeth. 'How's the guinea pig list coming along?'

'It should be ready for you by this afternoon. I'm waiting on one GP surgery to get back to me.'

Keir nodded. 'I won't keep you, then.' He straightened his tie. 'If you let me have Dr Palmer's itinerary, I may as well hand it to her when I'm over there later.'

'Of course,' said Lyn. 'I'll bring it through now, in case I'm away from my desk when you leave.'

Mission completed, Keir placed the folder in his briefcase. He was due to meet Andrea and the prof in Richard's office that afternoon. He and she would run through their joint presentation, with Richard on the sidelines, having promised not to heckle unless provoked.

This opportunity to be in Andrea's company again gave Keir an extremely non-professional buzz. He had no one to confide in. Neither of his parents was still around and his younger brother worked as a pilot for an overseas airline, which meant they got together very infrequently. The move to Hartnett General after his wife and daughter had emigrated with Keir's replacement had seemed sensible in terms of a fresh start and buying a smaller house. The idea of being the spare part at dinner parties or, even worse, being the available male for every hostess's unmatched friends, had repelled him. Somehow he'd negotiated job interviews, house-selling and purchasing, plus divorce proceedings, and settled into his new life. Occasionally he might ring one of his former colleagues or email a couple of buddies from his old squash club, but still he lacked a confidant.

Keir bit his lip. He and Andrea would be spending hours in each other's company. He didn't want to touch raw nerves; therefore it seemed sensible to keep off the personal stuff. Now he knew about her elderly mother, clearly Andrea's understandable concern for her mum's safety had shown in her expression the day they almost cannoned into each other at the elevator. As she'd agreed to speak with him at the Montreal conference, this must mean she'd arranged for her mother's needs to be dealt with as well as those of her husband and any children she might have. There was no need to probe further.

If only he could focus upon her solely as a colleague. Perhaps he should have invited the prof along after all, instead of this beautiful, enigmatic woman who he longed to know better. But, having suspected Richard's intentions towards Andrea, no way did he have the right to expect her to be anything other than professional in his company. They'd be travelling together and in close proximity for most of the time they weren't tucked up in their rooms. When they weren't talking shop maybe they'd discover something in common other than medicine. But, becoming too close to a married woman while they were each away from their comfort zones would be not only a grave mistake, but could also prove disastrous to his street cred when it came to the clinical trials.

His PA knocked and entered the room. 'I've just received the email I was waiting for,' she said, offering him some printed sheets of paper. 'I've amended my data base — this is the updated version, in case you want to take it with you.'

Keir nodded. 'I can look through and mark the ones I don't think are suitable. If Richard and Andrea can spare the time, I'll run my recommendations by them.'

Lyn's lips twitched.

'What?' He frowned at her.

'Surely it's unlikely they're going to disagree with you? You're the specialist.'

'Andrea's a medic too. She's also the expert on community medicine. She'll make sure we achieve the right balance of patients. I expect her to alert me if I haven't got that right.'

'OK.' Lyn pointed to a yellow post-it note. 'That indicates which one is Dr Palmer's mother. I didn't want to highlight her name on the page in case you were sharing the list with the others.'

'Good thinking.' Keir noted the patient's name and removed the sticky note. 'I gather from the prof that Dr Palmer's sensitive over her mother receiving anything remotely resembling preferential treatment. In fact, it was Richard who originally suggested she might be a suitable candidate.'

'Well, if it was my mum, I'd be crossing my fingers.'

'We'll see,' said Keir.

★　★　★

Andrea riffled through her knicker drawer. Some of this stuff still bore price tickets. She'd indulged in a spree, choosing sensational jewel colours — ruby, amethyst and sapphire, buying matching bra and panties and ignoring her natural urge to choose pristine white or basic black. That was before the worst had happened. Since then, her life had been knocked off course; she'd stuck with practical white, now looking lethargic. She pulled out a matching set in saffron and decided she might as well give it an outing. No one else would see it, after all.

She'd been working at home, preparing her stuff for the meeting where she and Keir would doubtless find areas of agreement and disagreement. Andrea felt strangely calm and wasn't sure whether this was a good thing or not. Snipping the price tag from a pair of silky gold panties, she smiled to herself. Speaking in front of an audience of one — well two, if you counted her co-speaker — was a tad different from facing an audience of hundreds. Some delegates would be on her side and others would not. But even for this practice run, she planned to dress immaculately from the very first layer. And that would be the luxurious body lotion she kept for special occasions. Deep down she knew it was all about confidence.

Andrea reached for a dark chocolate-coloured shirt with a black pinstripe. The slightly butch shirt took on a new dimension over the chic underwear. She'd selected a skirt suit today in a pale shade of khaki which demanded gold jewellery and some kitten heels to enhance the femininity. It was a stylish outfit without being over the top. She just hoped when she collected Josh from crèche later, he wouldn't run to her still bearing the marks of finger-painting. But no way would the staff allow that to happen. Her nerves must be distorting her judgement.

Andrea grabbed the navy-blue tracksuit she'd been wearing earlier and stuffed it into an overnight bag, along with a pair of old sneakers. No reason why she shouldn't change after the presentation. Ever the resourceful mum, she'd be ready for another evening at home then. There'd be many years ahead of this dual role. She could add dutiful daughter to that as well. Thank goodness things were rolling along regarding her mum's situation. Lizzie had matters well in hand and Andrea was grateful the woman had begun transforming her new bedroom, fortunately a decent size, into her own personal space. Rosemary appeared to be totally aware of what was going on. Soon they would know whether she was to join the drug trial or not.

Andrea wondered if Keir realised her mother was one of the hopefuls on the list. All she knew was that Rosemary's GP approved and had assured her she'd be recommending her patient. She riffled in her make-up bag. Maybe today was a bright lipstick day. Would she put her hair up or leave it loose? Up and she'd look the complete career professional. Down and she'd seem to play the femininity card among the grey suits. Oh but it was hard being a woman sometimes. Maybe she was trying too hard. Would anyone care, even?

*　*　*

Keir rode the elevator to the third floor of the university building. Were those two young women ascending with him students, or were they lecturers? Or was it just that he was getting old? They seemed confident, sassy in their eye-catching outfits. He stood staring ahead, holding his briefcase in his right hand. Feeling about one hundred years old.

Richard was waiting to greet him as the lift doors opened. 'I thought we'd use a small meeting room,' he said as they walked along the corridor. 'Impersonal surroundings and all that.' He glanced sideways. 'I keep meaning to ask, do you always dress so smartly for work?'

'People expect to see me wearing a suit,' said Keir. 'Unless I'm in scrubs of course.'

'You and Andrea put me to shame today,'

said the prof, slowing down. 'Here we are.'
He pushed the door fully open. Keir strode in
ahead of him.

Andrea sat at the table, her papers spread
before her. She looked up and smiled. Keir
stopped and stared.

She was wearing her hair loose as she had
that first time they met. He wanted to walk
towards her and take her in his arms . . .
stroke those dark, glossy strands; trail his
fingers in their scented depths. How did he
know her hair would be fragrant? He just did.
Somehow he retained his composure.

'Andrea. Good to see you again.' He
dumped his briefcase at the end of the table
furthest away from her. 'Before I forget, Lyn's
prepared a folder for you. You'll find all the
conference details in it. No, please don't get
up.'

He withdrew the plastic wallet and walked
towards her. She looked stunning. But then,
he wouldn't care if she'd turned up in a pair
of gardening trousers and a sweatshirt,
rivalling the prof for informality. Keir knew a
light-bulb moment when it happened and he
knew he was in for the long run. These
feelings did not in any way relate to the
forthcoming drug trial. But this wasn't the
time to indulge in forbidden fantasies.

'Thank you,' said Andrea. 'As a matter of

interest, how many of these things have you spoken at, Keir?'

'One or two.' He pulled a wry face.

She narrowed her eyes. 'Which probably means one or two dozen? Well, I'll try hard not to let the side down.'

'Don't listen to her, Keir,' said Richard. 'Andrea's a natural speaker. And she's much easier on the eye than you are.'

'I'll forget you said that, Prof,' said Andrea, pretending to look stern. 'How about we make you do some role-play? You can announce us.'

Keir nodded. 'That's an excellent idea, Dr Palmer. I thought I'd give a brief introduction before inviting you to address the delegates.'

Swiftly she moved into her role. 'Maybe I could call for questions afterwards? You two are sure to have questions,' she teased. 'Then I'll hand over to you again, Dr Harrison?'

'Sounds good to me.' Keir moved round to her side of the table.

As the prof began with a brief snapshot of Andrea's career to date, Keir felt a huge sense of relief. His professional persona was well in charge. He looked forward to hearing what Andrea had to say within the time allotted. Richard began on Keir's own biog, then seated himself as far away from the table as possible.

Keir noticed how Andrea's style made her

easy to engage with. Her sentences weren't too long and she didn't fidget, thus not distracting a potential audience. This first run was taking place without the techie stuff, as Richard called it. They'd match the photos, diagrams and colourful charts to their dialogue as soon as everything was prepared. In a couple of weeks' time, they'd be on their way.

As Keir wound up his speech, Richard got to his feet to give the two of them a round of applause. 'Well done,' he said. 'You both sounded not only confident but also passionate about your research. We must get the computerised stuff together as soon as possible. Maybe invite a few faculty members to boost the audience next time?'

Keir looked at his watch. 'Before I leave, could I run through the patient list for the trial? You know, I'd like to get things up and running before we leave for Montreal.'

'I have an appointment at four,' said Richard. 'How about you, Andrea?'

'I'm good. But that looks like a substantial list, Keir.'

'Not everyone on it is suitable. I'd like to explain my reason for turning down a candidate. Tomorrow I'll get the names of the successful patients emailed to you both. Is that OK?'

He saw Andrea glance at Richard and wondered whether to say something about her mother's status. He desperately wanted to put her mind at rest but feared pushing boundaries firmly set in place. There was one small way he could lessen the tension for her, though.

'When I was at school,' he said. 'I hated having a surname beginning with the letter H. Nearly all the other pupils came after me. Laugh at me if you will, but every time I have to complete an alphabetic list, I find myself beginning with the letter Z. So, the first patient I find unsuitable for this purpose is Mrs Zetterman.'

Keir worked steadily through the names. Sometimes the others queried a decision, sometimes not. When he came to the surname Thomas, he noticed Andrea push a strand of hair behind one ear and shift slightly in her seat.

'The next one I have to turn down is John Tebbit.' He paused for a beat. 'Sadly, I think his physical health isn't robust enough to allow him.' He smiled at Andrea. 'Whereas Mrs Rosemary Tarrant fits the criteria to perfection. We scientists can tune into human nature too, Dr Palmer.'

★   ★   ★

Unaware her daughter and a consultant she'd yet to meet were involved in such a momentous decision, Rosemary sat at her kitchen table, munching a crisp apple while she listened to a local radio station.

'I really need a fanfare of trumpets now, listeners. Because tomorrow's the day the mayor declares the new garden open at Hartnett General Hospital,' said the presenter. 'Thanks to a brilliant team of loyal supporters, digging and planting, this garden will provide a haven of colour and scents. There's a special section for the visually impaired and I'm delighted to say one of the Friends of Hartnett General has popped in to tell us a bit more. So if you can't get along there to cheer them on tomorrow, keep listening and you'll hear a bit more about this scheme and how to become involved.'

Rosemary sat back in her chair. She loved gardening. It sounded like they needed people to help. Maybe she should go along now. No time like the present. She abandoned her half-eaten apple, stood up and went to find a carrier bag. She'd take her trowel and gardening gloves from the shed. She could walk through the park and follow the signs to the hospital.

Within minutes, the elderly woman was trotting along the road, passing Lizzie Dean's house without a second glance. Inside, Lizzie was crawling around her loft, moving things to make room for stuff she wanted to store before her new tenants moved in. She glanced at her watch. She'd told Rosemary she'd call round at five o'clock, bringing freshly baked scones for tea. There was plenty of time.

Rosemary walked purposefully through the park. She wore her floppy gardening hat with a silk poppy attached to the brim although the day was dull and a wee bit chilly. No matter. She'd soon warm up when she started work. She arrived at the far gates and approached the pedestrian crossing just as the little green man sign appeared. A couple of minutes later, she saw the hospital looming in the distance.

★ ★ ★

Keir was satisfied with the way the conference preparation had gone. He wasn't quite so pleased with his own feelings about Andrea. Sitting within touching distance of her had been pure hell. When she stood to present her findings, he'd caught a drift of her scent, relishing its fresh, meadow-like fragrance. He hated those powerful brass band perfumes so many women seemed to use. Andrea's scent seemed to suit its wearer's personality.

He groaned as he walked along the corridor towards the rear of the university building where he'd left his car. This kind of thinking was off limits. What kind of a man was he? What would come next? Writing love poems, maybe? He really needed to get a grip.

Keir pushed through the swing doors and strode towards his vehicle, intent on returning to his office and catching up with a bunch of referrals Lyn pointedly kept moving to the top of the pile in his in-tray. The traffic was light for once and soon he was reversing into his personal parking space at the hospital. Occasionally a colleague in a tearing hurry might sneak into it, but luckily not this time.

He grabbed his briefcase, zapped his key and heard the locking system operate. Movement in the newly created garden alongside the car park caught his attention. Keir had been following the steady horticultural progress over many months. Tomorrow the mayor was coming to open it. There'd been emails arriving and eye-catching posters and paper sunflowers pinned to notice boards proclaiming the date, and Keir had been pleased to contribute towards a bench.

He wondered why a woman police officer stood in the middle of the garden. She wasn't alone. A small group of people clustered around her. Keir hesitated. Had he got the date wrong? What was going on? There was nobody there wearing a chain of office, but he noticed an elderly woman who seemed very distressed. His diagnostic antennae tuned. The female police officer took hold of the woman's arm and someone who looked like a security officer stood at her other side. The guy was speaking into whatever sort of communication gadget they used these days.

Before Keir could take a step forward, a police car, lights flashing, turned into the car park and drove straight towards him. The driver parked his distinctive vehicle, blocking Keir in, then snapped his seatbelt loose and jumped out to face him.

'Excuse me, sir. Is this your car?'

Keir nodded. 'It's all right, Officer. I've only just arrived. It looks like I might be of assistance here.'

'Could I ask who you are, please?' The second officer posed the question while his colleague strode straight up the ramp, accessing the new garden.

Keir felt in his pocket and produced his name badge. 'Sorry. Don't really like wearing this thing. I can barely ride in the lift without someone peering at it and asking my advice.'

The policeman nodded. 'I understand, sir. You say you've just arrived. So you don't know anything about what's going on over there?'

'No,' said Keir. 'But seeing an elderly person looking so distressed, I gather something's happened to cause all this attention and nobody knows quite how to handle her. Is that right, Officer?' Could this young constable actually be any older than fourteen?

'That's about it, I reckon,' said the policeman cheerfully. 'After you, Dr Harrison.'

Keir took the nearest walkway, approaching the centre of the garden so he knew the elderly woman would have him in her sights. He walked past lavender bushes and shrubs lovingly planted and about to burgeon. Everything was in pristine order. But at the central circular flowerbed, earth was scattered on the tiles and several bright pink begonias in plastic containers lay higgledy-piggledy as though suddenly abandoned.

The woman officer looked at him with a certain amount of relief. Her colleagues hovered at a distance. After all, they didn't need their riot shields. But Keir ignored everyone except the woman in the pale blue twin set. Under a disreputable-looking hat, her face was streaked with tears and she brandished a shiny red trowel. Keir imagined this might be viewed as a weapon for purposes of preparing a statement. Well, just let them try pulling that one.

'Hello,' he said, looking straight at the woman. 'My name's Keir and I work here. Do you work here, too?'

Her face brightened. 'I'm only trying to help. They said on the radio they needed people to help. So I came at once.'

'This lady removed these plants from the florists across the way,' murmured the WPC. 'Barged into the shop and out again. Then she started digging.'

'Thank you, Officer, I get the picture' He turned back to the woman. 'So, Margaret, why don't we sit down on that bench a minute?'

'My name's not Margaret.' She raised her chin. 'I'm Mrs Rosemary Tarrant.'

Keir's heart did a double flip in his chest as he recognised her surname. So this was where Andrea got those fabulous eyes. 'Right,' he said. 'Well, Mrs Tarrant, I happen to think, with a pretty name like yours, you must know a lot about gardening. Do you have a garden of your own?'

As the WPC walked the perpetrator to the seat, Keir took a ten-pound note from his wallet and handed it to the baby-faced police officer. 'Please give this to the florist with my

89

apologies,' he said. 'Explain this lady is a patient of Dr Harrison from Hartnett General and that I take full responsibility.'

He squatted in front of Rosemary. 'Mrs Tarrant, can you talk me through this planting business? We should get your lovely gift in the ground.' He held out an immaculately manicured hand for the trowel.

'How kind of you to help,' she said, surrendering her weapon of mass destruction. 'I'm not so good at kneeling these days.'

The WPC's jaw dropped as the consultant moved towards the flowerbed and dipped the trowel into the soil. The security man's face was one broad grin. The remaining police officer was on his radio while his partner went off to make peace with the florist.

With the begonias set in place, Keir stood up and rubbed his hands together. 'Now, Mrs Tarrant,' he said. 'How's that? Do you think I've got green fingers?'

'I do. My word, you're lovely and tall. Greg — that's my daughter's husband — he's tall like you. He's an Army major, you know.'

5

Her phone's long ring tone sent Andrea dashing back as she was about to leave her office. It might be something to do with Josh.

'Andrea? It's me . . . Keir.'

'You just caught me. Can this keep till tomorrow?' She kept her tone even, trying to ignore the tingles that had no business tantalising her like they did.

'Actually, it can't,' he said. 'Look, there's nothing to panic about. It's just that your mother's here with me.'

Andrea gripped the side of the desk, trying to absorb the message without drowning in those rich caramel tones. This was serious stuff. 'I'm not panicking,' she said. 'But are you saying she's been admitted to hospital?'

'No, Andrea, I'm not. Your mum's absolutely fine. We're getting on like the proverbial house on fire. Although she has eaten most of my biscuits.' He sounded a tad regretful.

'I just don't understand why she's with you. Will you tell me what's happening? Please!' Andrea's voice expressed her concern.

'It's a horticultural kind of thing. Look, my

91

PA's taken Rosemary to the washroom. Shall I bring her over to the university? Or shall I drive her home? Maybe you should give your mum's neighbour a ring in case she's looking for Rosemary.'

Andrea's thoughts whirled, only to land exactly where they started. 'I — there's Josh to collect. I'll need to ring the crèche and tell them I'm running late.'

'No. Please let me help. Why don't I drive Rosemary home and meet you there after you've collected your son?'

'Your time's valuable, Keir. I feel so embarrassed by this.' Andrea, knowing tears threatened, willed herself to keep calm. He'd think she was some kind of a wimp.

'There's no need to be embarrassed. Your mum's a walking history book. She's going to be a real asset to the trial.' He paused. 'They're coming back. Lyn's given me Rosemary's address and if the neighbour's not in evidence, we'll wait outside in the car and I'll learn more about British prime ministers. One or two of them were really quite naughty, weren't they?'

★ ★ ★

Keir parked outside Rosemary's bungalow to find a sweet-faced middle-aged woman watching from the window of the house next door. The woman came down her path at once and greeted him as he opened the car door.

'Dr Harrison?' She held out her hand. 'I'm Lizzie Dean, Rosemary's neighbour. I just got a call from Andrea. What a relief to know Rosemary's all right.' She stopped and waved at Keir's passenger.

'She's fine, Mrs Dean. It's one of those things. Rosemary has a good perception of traffic and she directed me here. My GPS system didn't get a look-in.'

Lizzie smiled. 'I'm so sorry to put you to all this trouble. What a blessing you happened along when you did.'

'All part of my job,' he said. 'By the way, do you have a key to the bungalow?'

'I have my own key,' called Rosemary, clambering from the front seat. 'Can you stay to tea? We haven't got to Gladstone yet.'

Keir moved round the vehicle to assist her. 'It's very kind of you to invite me but now Lizzie's here, I should get back to my desk. I'll see you soon, Rosemary. I've really enjoyed our discussion.'

As he got back behind the wheel, he wondered if Andrea would expect to find him waiting. After all, he'd agreed to meet her at her mother's place. But with Lizzie to take charge, there remained no reason to hang around. Seeing Andrea with her small son was not what he needed, especially after that clear reminder from his grandmother regarding Josh's father. Andrea's tall husband was obviously very much in the picture, and fantasising about a woman so clearly off limits would in no way help matters.

★ ★ ★

'I have to say, your mother's amazing,' said Lizzie, shaking her head and smiling. 'Nipping off to the hospital garden like that. I reminded her this morning that we had a tea date today. I'm so sorry, Andrea.'

'She does seem to have nine lives. But please don't feel guilty about today's episode. Mum's my responsibility, after all.'

Lizzie looked pensive. 'There was one bonus though. He's a bit of a dish, that consultant, isn't he? Wish he'd stayed for tea. I could have lured him with my sultana scones.'

The two women exchanged glances and burst out laughing.

'Trust my mother to go straight to the top,' said Andrea. 'I still don't know exactly how Dr Harrison happened along, but he seems to have defused an awkward situation. I mean, walking off with those plants like that — she could've ended up in court.'

Lizzie shook her head. 'According to the policeman who rang to make sure she was home safe and sound, Dr Harrison settled the bill and accepted all responsibility for your mother's actions.'

Andrea stiffened. 'I never knew that.' Her heartbeat accelerated into top gear. 'Goodness, she hasn't even begun the trial yet.'

'Speaking of which,' said Lizzie, 'I'm hoping to be able to move in here by the end of next week. There's a lady two doors down from me who says she could do with a bit of company. She's a retired teacher. I told her your mum's a history geek and she said she'd happily come in and spend time with her while I'm doing my school job. I think between the pair of us we can keep an eye on Rosemary.'

'Really? That's such a relief. I was wondering if I should turn down the invitation to go to Canada; but now you've told me this, maybe everything will be all right.'

Lizzie got up and peered round the kitchen door before sitting down again. 'It's OK. Your mum's watching her favourite quiz show. So, what were you saying about Canada?'

'It's to do with Dr Harrison's medical

95

trial,' said Andrea. 'He wants me to accompany him to Montreal to be his co-speaker at an important conference. I've always wanted to visit Canada. My friend Kirsty says she'll happily look after Josh while I'm away.' She drummed her fingertips on the table. 'My mother is more of a problem.'

'But not anymore,' said Lizzie, folding her arms. 'It'll do you good to get away. New experiences and all that. Apart from which, I imagine it won't do your CV any harm.'

Nodding, Andrea smoothed the crocheted centrepiece her mother kept on the kitchen table. She'd worked four, each in tune with a different season. In this one, pale golden primroses gleamed against misty green leaves. 'I'm very grateful to you, Lizzie. It's not easy being single again after you've been with someone in a loving relationship.' She bit her lip. 'What an idiot I am. You know all about that already.'

Lizzie stretched out her hand and grasped Andrea's. 'It's not that time's a great healer, my dear. It's all about moving on and refusing to crumble into a heap. Whether someone's a movie star, an anthropologist or a dinner lady, we all of us share the same problem. You've got your career plus little Josh to keep you focused. You get out there and sock it to 'em.'

Lizzie looked so fierce that laughter kicked into touch the tears Andrea fought to hold back.

'Thank you so much,' she said. 'I never want to forget how lucky I am. Or how important it is to keep our sense of humour — yes?'

Lizzie nodded. 'You bet, Dr Palmer. So, just you say yes to Dr Delectable and seize the moment.'

Andrea couldn't bring herself to confess she'd already found her own nickname for Keir Harrison. Dr Shiny Pants had found yet another admirer now.

★   ★   ★

Keir surveyed the assembled students. Some sat alert, pens poised over notebooks. Others looked as though they wished they were somewhere else. The age range seemed broader than when he'd been a student. One or two of the more mature ones smiled appreciatively when Keir requested they keep any electronic devices switched off.

'Can't stand to hear them tapping at their netbooks or whatever while I'm trying to hold their attention,' he'd told Richard Bailey. 'As for all those bizarre ring tones, words fail me.'

'And I thought I was the old fuddy-duddy,'

the professor had responded.

The talk went well but when Keir asked if there were any questions, there was total silence, apart from the occasional cough or shuffle of papers.

'Nothing?' He looked around expectantly.

A hand shot up. 'My gran's been diagnosed with Alzheimer's. How could she get on a trial like the one you're planning?'

'Good question.' Keir smiled at the young man in the second row. 'But whether Gran lives in Glasgow or Truro, her GP or specialist will be the one to guide and inform. So check out the internet by all means and see what trials are taking place and what they're focussing upon, but remember these are precious family members we're talking about here. The medical history and current circumstances of each patient selected for our trial here at Hartnett have been carefully considered, taking lots of factors into account.'

'Cool. So you don't just look at the stage the disease is at? Other aspects like hearing loss, osteoporosis and whatever, all need taking into account?'

Keir regarded the student with interest. 'You've got it. Now, I can see Dr Palmer tapping her watch at me. I have to let you go.' He looked back at his questioner. 'If I can

98

help with anything related to your course, I'll do my best. That's a promise.'

He smiled as a spatter of applause ran round the room. Tip-up seats thumped back and conversation buzzed as he gathered his notes together. A couple of students approached him and he listened patiently and answered their questions.

As soon as they'd drifted away, Andrea arrived at the front of the room. He snapped his briefcase shut. At least, that had been his intention, but for some reason his fingers felt like sausages and he took two attempts before he succeeded.

'It seemed a shame to stop you,' she said, 'but there's another lecture following yours. Thank you, Dr Harrison. You really held their attention.'

'It's my pleasure, Dr Palmer. Especially with a bright group of students like these seem to be. Are you going back to your office now?'

'I am. You're calling in on the prof?'

He picked up his briefcase. Slowly they began to climb the wide blue-carpeted stairs separating blocks of tip-up seats. 'Yes, though not before checking with you about your mother's situation.' He stopped on the step above hers. 'It's occurred to me you might be wondering if you're doing the right thing.'

She looked up at him. Temporarily, he towered above her even more than he normally did. The sweet curve of her breasts under her crisp white shirt distracted him.

'What exactly do you mean by that?' Her tone was chilly to say the least.

He shrugged. 'She's your mother, Andrea. It's all very well my telling you not to worry. I can tell you I'm sure she'll be fine while you're away but if you don't totally and utterly believe that's the case, then I'd prefer you not to put pressure on yourself by coming to Montreal with me.'

She stepped up beside him, lips slightly parted, cheeks pinker than they'd been before. 'Has Richard said something to you? Is this all about women being torn between career and family, Keir?' She pitched her voice low and mutinous. 'Have you changed your mind about wanting me to be your co-speaker? Because if you have, I suggest you come clean and tell me.'

He moved up and on to the area in front of the swing doors. 'Of course I haven't changed my mind, Andrea. What do you take me for? Nor has the prof said anything. Why would he when you're the best?' He frowned at her, annoyed yet desperate to reassure her. 'Don't you know having you by my side is hugely important when it comes to this conference?'

He dumped his briefcase on the floor as if distancing himself from it and glared down at her.

'Well, you could have fooled me!' She stood, arms folded across her chest, feet slightly apart.

'Look, I truly didn't mean to sound patronising. If I did, then I humbly apologise.'

She stepped up beside him onto the top level. Instead of firing back a comment, she looked at him, her eyes filled with uncertainty. The thought that he'd upset her suddenly slashed through him like a surgical scalpel. He reached out and clasped her by the elbows, pulling her nearer to him, none too gently either. 'Andrea,' he said. 'I . . . '

Because her chin was tilted upwards, their mouths were dangerously close. He found difficulty in moving away even though at any moment, the next lecturer or even a student might burst through the door. Keir was well aware of that. But he couldn't stop himself. He took Andrea in his arms and held her close. He saw surprise flicker across her expression before she closed her eyes and leaned even closer towards him. Somehow those angry folded arms unfolded and found their way around him, holding him close as he'd dreamed of them doing. Somehow he began kissing her, first gently, then hungrily. He kissed her as though he never meant to stop. And what was more, she reciprocated.

It felt so right, even though he knew it was the last thing he should be doing. Her lips felt soft beneath his. So much so that he kept his mouth on hers but moved his hands gently upwards, losing them in her hair, which, he realised with a jolt, was fragrant and silky just as he'd dreamed it would be. He forgot everything in the heat of the moment.

She broke away first. The expression he saw in her eyes was an odd mixture of fear and possibly, he thought, regret. She said nothing but stood smoothing her hair away from her face.

'I'm so sorry,' said Keir, hands back at his sides. 'That was totally out of order. I apologise for my behaviour. You have every right to lodge a complaint about me. I fully understand.' At that moment, all he cared about was Andrea and how offended she might be by such maverick and inappropriate behaviour to a married colleague.

She shook her head but didn't meet his eyes. 'You don't need to apologise. I overreacted.' Hastily, she added, 'To your comment about my concerns over my mother — for that I'm sorry. But it's important you understand my personal life is my own business. If I didn't feel I could offer you one hundred percent co-operation in Montreal, believe me, Keir, I wouldn't have accepted your invitation in the first place.'

Holding out his hand to her, he said, 'Friends then?'

For a moment she looked as if she wanted to say something more to him. But she nodded and shook hands immediately. 'Good colleagues will do, and that's what I hope we'll remain. Now, let's get out of here. I have work to do. As I'm sure you have.'

Andrea strode off, increasing the distance between Keir and herself as she hurried down the corridor. He kept his eyes on her. Watched her ignore the lift disgorging a chattering group. Saw her begin climbing the staircase. She didn't check to see whether he followed her or not.

* * *

Once on the third floor, Andrea shot into the women's washroom, fortunately unoccupied, to stand at the basin, hands gripping the edge of the vanity unit, glaring at herself in the large mirror so thoughtfully provided for people who'd just been comprehensively kissed when they shouldn't have been. Even more significantly, for people who'd kissed the other person back when they shouldn't have. Because Keir unlocked feelings in her she'd never thought to experience again. Ever.

Andrea tucked her hair behind her ears, ignoring the thought of how Keir's fingers had touched it so tenderly only minutes earlier. His face, the skin retaining a hint of whatever shamelessly expensive aftershave or cologne he'd used, had touched her face. She stroked her cheeks, then smelt the tips of her fingers. Lovingly. Tenderly.

'No way,' she snapped, jabbing at the tap, flinching as cold water gushed into the basin. She splashed her face, then reached for a paper towel and blotted it dry.

How the heck had that happened? Of course she knew how it had happened — she'd riled him, rattled his cage more furiously than he'd rattled hers. Now her fantasy over how it might feel to be kissed by Keir Harrison had been fulfilled. Fine. Perhaps now the head of steam had exploded, the pair of them would be able to settle down together as friends or colleagues or anything else not remotely linked to lovers. She hadn't expected him to kiss her. Nor had she expected to enjoy it quite so much. Maybe he considered himself to be a ladies' man. Now, why hadn't she thought of that before? It might be the kind of expression her mother would use about the leading man in one of those black and white films she adored, but Keir certainly had the CV to fit the role. Think Moira the red-haired nurse. Even Lizzie Dean, who admittedly would have had to be really precocious in order to be his mother, had described him as Dr Delectable. There must be many other females worshipping at his well-shod feet, without including his long-suffering wife.

But Dr Keir Harrison truly didn't come across as God's gift to women, despite his immaculate suits and charming manner. He didn't do smarmy. And there was genuine hurt in his eyes after she'd snarled at him like an angry dragon. It was clear to her now, having calmed down, that he had her best interests at heart. Whatever the temptation, she must not allow herself to relive that kiss. To do so would only forge a chink in her defences, and for all sorts of reasons that mustn't be allowed to happen.

With the word 'kiss' echoing round her head, Andrea screwed the paper towel into a ball and hurled it into the waste bin. If only she could dispose of her guilty feelings with similar ease.

★ ★ ★

Keir arrived at his office with a certain amount of relief. He'd watched Andrea disappear up the staircase without a backward glance and had opted not to use the elevator but to wait a suitable interval before climbing the stairs to the third floor. He'd no intention of developing the equivalent of a pilot's paunch and often found using the stairs quicker than waiting for a lift to lumber into position. He tried not to think what might have happened had the two of them been locked in a lift together. Something very disturbing threatened to erode his self-control.

On arrival at Richard's office, the prof plied him with strong coffee, which Keir accepted with gratitude, almost scalding his tongue on the steaming liquid. But every other sentence of their discussion seemed to begin with 'Andrea says this' or 'Does Andrea think that?' Although it was all perfectly valid and reasonable, Keir didn't need her name in his ears when it already whispered at him inside his head at all times of day and night, just as the memory of her fragrance stirred his senses in a dangerous way.

When he returned to his office he found Lyn had left his opened mail and phone messages on his desk together with a lurid pink post-it note saying she'd gone to lunch and would be back at one o'clock. That gave him time to regroup. The fact that he'd kissed a colleague so impulsively weighed upon his mind, still worrying him. The fact that he'd enjoyed it so much, heightened by the way the recipient hadn't leapt away in horror, and had even seemed to kiss him back, was another matter entirely.

He should head for the dining room and eat something to soak up all that caffeine while he talked medical politics or whatever was on that day's menu along with the hot food. But for just a few minutes, would it be so very wicked if he just relived that moment again?

Even the prof's high-octane coffee couldn't wash away the taste of Andrea's mouth. Her light, sweet scent still lingered in his nostrils, but no way could he let his guard down like that again. He'd lost his own wife to another man and suffered the fallout. He didn't intend stealing someone else's spouse, no matter how delightful and witty and dedicated and attractive he found her. Loving her wasn't an option. His forbidden feelings couldn't be declared.

She'd made the decision to travel to Canada with him. He hadn't exaggerated when he told her how much he valued her as a colleague. But it was going to take every

ounce of his willpower to keep his relationship with Dr Andrea Palmer on a strictly
professional footing.

Keir groaned and put his head in his
hands.

★　★　★

On the morning of departure, Andrea ferried
Josh to Kirsty's house soon after breakfast.
She watched her son disappear inside the
spacecraft formerly known as Kirsty's kitchen
table. Faded curtains secured by hefty
cookbooks concealed the scrubbed pine
surface, a small side opening allowing chinks
of daylight so the two brave astronauts could
operate their equipment and command a
crew consisting of three portly teddy-bears, a
worried-looking Tigger and a smiling felt
penguin.

Kirsty winked at her. 'I'm instructed to
deliver milk and flapjacks to the flight deck at
eleven o'clock. Sure I can't tempt you before
you go?'

Andrea shook her head. 'I'll be fine, thanks.
I'd stay longer, but maybe I should fix a
sandwich after I get home. Dr Harrison's
picking me up, so I don't have to leave my car
at Heathrow. After all, we're booked on the
same flights.'

'Sensible thing to do then — and while I think of it, I don't want you rushing over here to collect Josh as soon as you arrive home again. You'll still be jet-lagged, don't forget.'

'OK, Mum,' said Andrea. 'Let's see how things go. If the flight's delayed, we might get back too late for that anyway. I'm very comfortable about leaving him with you, Kirsty. You know that.'

'And with Lizzie in charge of your other chick, all you have to do is look drop-dead gorgeous while you dazzle a lecture hall packed with delegates.' She shuddered. 'I'd rather cook a casserole for two hundred than stand in front of that lot and give a talk. Rather you than me, kiddo.'

'Yes, well I don't know about the drop-dead gorgeous bit, but Keir and I have put together a pretty comprehensive package to stun them with. That's the plan, anyway.'

Kirsty glanced at the kitchen clock and looked enquiringly at Andrea. 'Should you make a discreet retreat now? So you can drive back in leisurely manner.'

Andrea nodded and rose from her seat beside the dark blue kitchen range. 'Mum calling Josh . . . Mum calling Josh.'

No response. She said it again. Two helmeted heads appeared in the gap.

'Haven't you taken off yet, Mummy?' Josh

clutched a plastic ray gun to his chest.

Andrea stooped to her son's level and sneaked a kiss. 'I'm going now. Goodbye, you two brave astronauts. See you soon. I won't forget to bring you both something back from Canada.'

'Yay,' said Josh. 'Bye, Mum.'

The heads of the two boys disappeared back into their imaginary world.

★ ★ ★

Andrea completed the drive to Hartnett with a strange sense of disengagement. For the first time ever, since Josh's birth, she had no childcare responsibilities. Nor did she need to worry about her mother. The trial had begun a few days before, without Rosemary showing any sign of recognition towards Keir. Andrea had accompanied her mother and Lizzie for this first session and knew the memory lapse was entirely in line with her mum's condition. She tried not to wonder whether Rosemary might in time forget Josh or even her own daughter.

The house seemed abnormally quiet when she let herself in and she had to force herself not to tiptoe like an intruder. Her luggage stood in the hallway and she already wore cotton trousers and layers to adjust to temperature changes. She wasn't sure now if she even wanted to fix herself a sandwich. Maybe she'd sit quietly and listen to the kitchen radio until she heard Keir's car pull up. She didn't need to check all the windows were closed and locked again. When the telephone rang suddenly, she gasped. What if her mother had succeeded in wandering off and Lizzie had just noticed? The poor woman couldn't fasten Rosemary into a highchair like you could a toddler. Or could Josh already be needing reassurance, so Kirsty was on the end of the line?

Worst of all was the thought of Keir being proved right when he'd wondered whether she was entirely calm about her mother's care. It might even be the man himself ringing. What if he was snarled up in traffic? If they missed check-in, it wasn't like there'd be another plane along in ten minutes.

Andrea didn't recognise the caller on the display but snatched at the phone to stop its irritating ring. 'Hello,' she said, not disclosing her name or confirming her number. She held her breath, but to her relief this proved to be a cold call and she responded as politely as possible. People were only trying to earn a living.

She walked into the kitchen, feeling less tense and telling herself to stop being so paranoid. This was the beginning of a brief but exciting phase in her career, including the chance to sample Canadian culture, something she'd always fancied doing. No way would she risk her credibility or peace of mind by allowing what amounted to a silly schoolgirl crush to overwhelm her.

And then she heard the sound of a car engine, and suddenly and incredibly happiness engulfed her.

★ ★ ★

The lounge for business-class ticket-holders was dotted with people tapping away on laptops, reading, snacking or chatting quietly with their fellow passengers. Keir placed two bottles of sparkling mineral water on the low table between them and seated himself opposite Andrea. 'Chicken salad?'

'Thank you,' she said, taking the sandwich. 'This is a great way to begin a trip, though I have to say I wasn't anticipating travelling in such style.'

He made a wry face. 'Quite honestly, it's all about my legs.'

She paused, sandwich halfway to her mouth. 'Your, erm . . . legs?'

'Leg room, that is.' Straight-faced, he removed the plastic seal from his bottled water. 'Curling myself into my regulation 18 inches or whatever it is these days, is all very well for a quick hop to Glasgow.'

'Such exaggeration.'

'OK,' said Keir. 'Seven hours in an aeroplane with limited room to stretch is a nightmare once experienced and not to be repeated. Even with my flight socks on.'

'I feel a bit guilty. My legs are shorter than yours. I could've travelled in economy.' Her eyes danced as she bit into her snack.

'They're not that much shorter,' he said, hastily looking anywhere but at those legs. 'And you shouldn't ever feel guilty about travelling in comfort. It's performance-enhancing anyway. Much quieter if you need to get some work done, and the food's better quality, therefore better for our systems.'

'OK,' she laughed. 'You don't have to justify anything to me. I'm lapping this up, but do we have to work all the way to Montreal?'

'Yes. You can ride on the flight deck and see that George doesn't misbehave.'

Puzzled, she thought for a moment, remembered he must mean the autopilot, then stuck her tongue out at him, relieved at his light-hearted mood. Big-brotherly was good. She could handle that very well.

He ripped open a packet of gourmet potato

crisps and offered them to her. 'You might even find a movie you haven't seen before. Truthfully, Andrea, I'd recommend using this flight as a buffer between working at home and all the stuff we'll be doing over there. Believe me when I say I shan't be opening my briefcase unless it's to take out my John Grisham paperback.'

'I'm looking forward to the conference now. Strange really, considering its importance.'

'Well, that's good,' he said, munching crisps. 'Sorry. Now you know why I rarely eat these things. They're addictive. Would you like me to fetch you a packet?'

'Don't they feed us on board?'

'You bet. This is just to keep me going. Nothing will prevent me from devouring my three courses plus maybe a glass or two of bubbly to toast our future together.' He cleared his throat. 'Our professional prospects are at stake here. We set our stall out right and there'll be a lot of medical people fixing their beady eyes on us. Our online presence will be vital in terms of progress being charted and making everything totally transparent, as the buzz-word boys like to say these days.'

She nodded. It seemed rather overwhelming and she hoped she didn't let him down.

High-powered she was not, but if he thought she could help his cause then she'd do her best to live up to expectation.

He gestured towards the newspapers arranged nearby. 'Mind if I catch up with what's happening in the world? To my shame, I rarely read a daily paper these days.'

'I know the feeling. Please go ahead.' Andrea selected her own choice and disappeared behind its pages. Was he trying as hard as she was not to dwell on the fireworks that had exploded between them that morning in the lecture hall?

Keir's hearty appetite so reminded her how Greg's used to be. Despite, or because of those broad shoulders, impressive height and powerful limbs, men like this could eat for Britain and somehow burn off all the calories — calories that would gleefully settle around Andrea's hips and remain there, an awful reminder of past dalliances with jam doughnuts and chocolate bars. Since the life-changing events of last December, she'd slimmed down considerably and relished the thought of being waited upon as the plane soared above the clouds — seven hours of being, as Keir had pointed out, in limbo between her everyday world and the heady prospect of the unknown continent awaiting her. Food she hadn't prepared herself, plus a glass or two of champagne, sounded tempting. Maybe she'd totally block out current affairs and put her headphones on to enjoy a sneaky peep at some electronic candy, while Keir read his book.

So far they'd succeeded in relaxing into each other's company. Being with Keir wasn't like putting on a pair of velvet slippers. No way. Perhaps after three days together, they'd achieve the right mix of comradeship to see them through whatever it was that flared so dangerously a matter of days ago.

But Andrea gave her full attention to the safe haven of the newspaper books' section. She rarely read anything these days that wasn't one of Josh's bedtime stories or a work-related article. Maybe this trip would be a chance to reassess her habits. Sprawling, zonked out in front of a television programme she barely remembered next morning, couldn't be good. Soaking up every possible new experience that came her way might encourage her to lose some of her more slapdash habits.

She glanced up from her paper at precisely the same moment as Keir did. Their eyes met and he gave her a slow, lazy smile that made her tummy lurch and sent zinging sensations coursing through her body. Ooh no . . . surely she shouldn't still be experiencing these feelings. She'd thought it was kind of a rebound thing, fixating on an attractive man once the initial, devastating grief over losing Greg blurred into another, more manageable, yet still sensitive emotional state. She'd thought that impulsive kiss after her hissy fit might snuff out whatever it was smouldering between them. Evidently, in her case this didn't seem to be so. Thank goodness he gave no signs of being uncomfortable in her company.

6

Keir amused himself watching his companion settle into her personal space. They were only half an hour into the flight and already he decided she'd checked out every available seat angle and facility.

'My own remote control? Wow. That's something to savour.'

He hadn't commented. Maybe this was one of the things husband and wife didn't agree on. Maybe Mr Palmer was a control freak. That would be tall Mr Palmer, the military man whose wife seemed to tread a fine line between tension and relaxation. Hurriedly he'd stopped himself thinking along those lines. It wasn't his business. Except, if Andrea really was putting up with bad stuff at home and under stress, whether physically or emotionally, Keir would find it difficult to back off. His hackles agreed with him.

The flight attendant handed them each a menu.

'Are you good at making decisions?' Keir studied the choices.

'Not where food's concerned,' said Andrea. 'I'm never sure whether to go for something I really enjoy but rarely make, like these crab cakes.' She paused. 'Or, to try something new.'

'It's the kind of choice to revel in, don't you think?'

'Absolutely — what possible impact can it have on the scheme of things?' Her tone was light but when he glanced across, her eyes revealed sadness.

They sipped their drinks and when the cabin attendant returned, found they'd made identical choices for their starters though neither commented upon this.

'I could become used to this way of life,' said Andrea.

'I've never before seen anyone look so comfortable in an aeroplane seat,' he said. 'Believe me, the novelty will wear off. I did a lot of commuting between New York and London some years ago. It wasn't too much fun.'

'I suppose not,' she said. 'But that's what comes of having a high-powered job. Risks and inconvenience are greater than the norm. Hopefully, salary and various perks should outweigh the negatives, or at least counter-balance them.'

He hesitated. There was still a barrier of self-imposed politeness between them. He wanted to talk to her, properly talk to her. Tell her how, as his career progressed, his personal life had begun a downward spiral he didn't notice increasing until it was too late to reverse it. He wasn't looking for sympathy. All he wanted was to talk to someone who also seemed not to have made quite the correct life choices. Unless he was totally misreading the situation, in which case maybe he should shut up and see how things went in Montreal. This desire to unburden his thoughts was off-putting in that it was so powerful.

Their starters arrived and Andrea picked up her fork. 'This is weird,' she said.

He leaned towards her. 'Do you want to send it back? Try something else?'

'I didn't mean the crab cakes.' She took a bite. 'They're delicious. No, I meant sitting here with you, out of touch with reality.'

'I'm sorry if I have that effect,' he said ruefully.

'What I'm trying to say is, I feel anything I talk to you about is going to be stuff I wouldn't dream of saying if we were at the hospital or the university.'

His throat tightened. He wasn't the only one in that kind of mood. 'You don't have to say anything about your personal circumstances, unless you really want to.' Purposely he didn't remind her she'd made it plain her personal life was her own business. Maybe the small quantity of champagne she'd drunk was loosening her tongue more than she realised.

'I do want to explain something. It's no secret among my colleagues and at first I didn't see any point in telling you. Believe me, Keir, I'm not looking for sympathy. But it's possible you're forming perceptions of me that aren't totally accurate.'

He chased a salad leaf around his plate. 'I'm good at keeping secrets. I think you already know that, don't you?'

She watched him pick up the obstinate bit of greenery with his fingers and pop it into his mouth. 'It's very comforting to hear it anyway. I feel you should know more about me, now our working relationship is stepping up a gear, so to speak. And my mother's participation in the trial and certain things she might or might not accurately disclose are another factor in my decision.'

Their plates were whisked away and their glasses topped up almost without them noticing. In the lull between starter and main course, Andrea drank some water. Keir waited and wondered. He truly hadn't a clue what she might be going to say, but he'd no intention of interrupting her and spoiling the moment.

'Richard told me you'd enquired about our relationship,' she said at last. 'That is, my personal relationship with him.'

Keir replaced his glass in its neat holder. The remaining liquid barely shimmered, so placid was the big Boeing's progress over the ocean. 'I see,' he said slowly. 'You must have thought that very impertinent of me. I can only say I'm sorry if you found it intrusive, but I did have my reasons.'

'I'm sure. This is why I'm telling you things I think you should know. Because sometimes I overreact.'

He waited for her to mention their kiss and when she didn't, was unable to decide whether to be disappointed or relieved.

'I know how it's all part of the bereavement process. I've written a paper on it yet here I am, questioning my own behavioural patterns. How odd is that?'

He'd heard similar comments. 'Watching a parent's faculties diminish is, of course, a form of bereavement. We mourn the person that was, even though the person in question is still very much alive.'

She nodded and drank a little more white wine. 'You know, I was trying to push away Rosemary's slight, shall we say, eccentricities. But last December, something happened which changed my life so much that for a while I almost hated my own mother.'

'Your lamb medallions, madame.' The

steward beamed at Andrea as he placed her meal before her. The sight of the couscous and deliciously crispy-edged roasted vegetables tickled her taste buds. She waited while Keir's medium-rare beefsteak arrived complete with baby new potatoes and fresh asparagus gleaming with butter.

'Maybe I should postpone what I'm about to say until we've eaten,' said Andrea once they were alone again.

'Whatever you feel is best. I'm not planning on going anywhere.'

★ ★ ★

The food provided something to focus upon as she let her back-story unfold. Their meals proved to be equally delicious and neither she nor Keir suffered any loss of appetite throughout her explanation and his questions. Each refused more alcohol when it was offered. Each looked sheepishly at the other when the steward arrived again, offering temptation in the shape of delicious desserts.

'I will if you will,' she said. 'It has to be tiramisu for me, please.'

Keir laughed. 'How could I possibly let you eat alone?'

The steward smiled as he took an order for strawberry and almond tart.

Over cups of dark, smoky coffee, Keir thanked Andrea, not without diffidence, for telling him about her late husband.

'I don't want to cause you any more pain,' he said, 'but I want to tell you how brave you are. When I think of my crass attitude, demanding if you were sure you wanted to go ahead with this trip, I could kick myself, or worse. No wonder you thought I was some kind of chauvinist.'

'This project's massively important to you. Quite simply, I need to move on with my life. It's important to keep the happy memories of course.'

He nodded agreement. 'Sounds like you're making sure your son retains his dad's memory. What a lovely guy Greg must have been. I like the thought of his leaving surprise gifts for you both like that.'

'Lucky girl, wasn't I? Finding happiness with him, I mean. Not only was he a great husband but a terrific dad too. Some people don't ever find out how much that can mean to a woman.'

For a moment she regretted her remark as she saw a spasm cross Keir's features. He had his own emotional baggage but already she'd talked a lot, maybe too much, though the sense of unburdening left her feeling calm, if a little sleepy.

'I need you to know I don't expect you to feel sorry for me, Keir,' she said. 'That was my main reason for not disclosing I was widowed in the first place. I'm sorry to offload all that on you but I felt it was the right time. Now, maybe I'll close my eyes for a while.' She reached for the soft pillow so thoughtfully provided by the airline.

'I'm honoured you felt ready to confide in me,' he said. 'Enjoy your nap, Andrea. I think I'll listen to some music.'

Andrea snuggled into her seat. Yes, it was bliss to have so much space. And she'd decided it was far better for Keir to know her single status and all it represented. He'd admitted taking note of her rings and presuming she must be married. More than that he hadn't said, doubtless feeling there'd been enough confidences disclosed for one flight. She hadn't wanted to remind him of the kiss they'd shared. Surely two adults could put such an incident behind them. At that moment it felt very comforting, very right, to have his silent presence beside her. Hopefully she'd made it clear she needed no special treatment.

She was conscious of him checking the aircraft position on the small screen in front of him. They must be well over halfway there by now. It was so relaxing lying back, being transported to another continent. And the lovely thing was, because of the time zones, if they landed on schedule, she'd be able to ring Kirsty and say hi to Josh. Andrea floated in a dreamy, white wine-tinged haze.

★   ★   ★

With formalities completed at Trudeau Airport, Keir loaded their luggage into the boot of the rental car. He watched Andrea walk back towards him, her whole persona radiating joy. With a pang he reminded himself this must be because she'd spoken to her son, not because she was about to set off for Montreal in his company.

'All well?' He held open the passenger door.

'Brilliant, thanks.' She tossed her hair back from her face. 'Josh was so excited about it being half-term so he and Luis have so much extra playing time, he couldn't have cared less about his mother being on Canadian soil. I could hardly get a word in.'

She settled into the passenger seat and by the time he seated himself, she'd strapped herself in and was opening a travel guide.

'You'll only end up wishing you had more time to visit places,' he warned as he checked out the controls.

'Oh, I know I'm here to work. But with you driving, it's a chance for me to look for landmarks.'

'Don't expect too much too soon,' he warned. 'Anyway, I suspect you've already toured the hotel website.' He swung the car into the exit lane.

'But of course! I'm intrigued by the sound of that underground city.'

'You'll probably find everything you want without needing to step outside of the hotel,' he said.

'Including the indoor pool, state-of-the-art steam room and hotel complex? Not to mention the choice of eating places.' She paused, eyeing the silver grille and scarlet bonnet of an oncoming vehicle. 'Josh would adore all these trucks. They're so different from the ones at home. And he'd love driving on the other side of the road.'

'Something I need to concentrate on doing,' said Keir.

'You seem very much at ease, if I may say so. Shut me up if I talk too much.'

'I enjoy driving. And talking. Montreal's one of my favourite cities. We . . . I went skiing at a resort called Mont Tremblant some years ago. It's not a huge distance from here.' He overtook a slow-moving van. 'It's somewhere I'd like to revisit but, well, saying you'll go back is very different from actually doing so.'

'Maybe you'll make it one day.'

'Maybe,' he said.

Andrea gave him a quick sideways glance, taking in the taut line of his jaw.

'I did take a look at the conference facilities,' she said.

'Impressive, aren't they? I haven't stayed at the King George before but it looks as though we'll be very comfortable.'

'I'll say! Those beds look fabulous.'

He coughed.

Andrea buried her nose in her guidebook. 'Anyway,' she said. 'Comfortable is not the word I'd use in the same sentence as standing up and addressing row upon row of critical medics and academics.'

'You do it all the time. Anyway, I thought you said you were looking forward to this conference.' He glanced quickly at her and this time she met his gaze.

'Just keep your eyes on the road, Dr Harrison. For your information, I'm very excited about being here. But addressing two hundred savvy delegates is a bit different from speaking to a lecture room full of students, some of whom are sometimes more concentrated on catching up with sleep than psychology. Though, of course, you didn't hear that from me.'

'You think this'll be any different?'

They both laughed.

She closed her guidebook. 'I'm happy to soak up all the experiences. And I'll try my best not to let you down.' She bit her lip as she realised she'd let slip her fear.

'Of that, I have no doubt whatsoever,' he said softly.

Andrea blinked rapidly, turning her head to watch the suburbs dissolving into the city. The atmosphere between the two of them differed now from that of the seven-hour flight so recently accomplished. There was a subtle charge, almost tangible in its intensity, though no way did either of them attempt to touch any portion of the other one's body throughout the car trip. It was almost as if the confession she'd made high above the Atlantic had taken a while to settle into their consciousness. At this point, he knew much more about her than she knew about him. Until that state of affairs changed, she was the open book. He was the mystery man.

'Not far now.' Keir slowed to approach a set of changing traffic lights.

'Everything's so high and so big. It looks like you have to pack a rucksack just to cross one of these roads,' said Andrea.

'Fortunately they allow plenty of time for

pedestrians. Folks in general are very considerate. So, don't worry. I'll look after you.'

His words hung in the air between them. He must surely have meant them as a joke. But Andrea's own reaction shocked her. With anyone else, say Richard Bailey or Kirsty's husband, she'd have made some kind of quip about being a big girl now. Might have joked about them having to catch her first! But the tone of Keir's voice hadn't lent itself to light-heartedness and the unexpected glow spreading through her body owed nothing to the temperature of the vehicle in which they travelled.

Andrea had intimated to Keir her disclosure of the traumatic events around losing her husband seemed appropriate at a time when her professional relationship with her colleague seemed set to move up a gear. But this was something else. It was something exciting and she felt nothing she could do now would affect it. If she had to analyse Keir's attitude, she could think of only one way of describing it. And that was tenderness.

★ ★ ★

Keir found a parking space without trouble. Their hotel towered above them like the tiers of a giant frosted wedding cake. As he cut the engine, Andrea reached for her shoulder bag and stuffed the guidebook inside.

'I have to keep reminding myself most Canadians haven't eaten their evening meal yet,' she said. 'How are we supposed to stay awake till bedtime?'

He opened his door. 'You'll be surprised. Adrenaline has a lot to do with it. It's the other side you need to worry about. Returning to UK time will be more testing.'

'Now he tells me,' she muttered, getting out and stretching. 'That only took half an hour. We still have time for tea.'

'No problem in the lounge,' he said. 'But don't go looking for a kettle and teabags once you're in your room.'

'Really? In a hotel of this standard?'

He filed a personal snapshot of her affronted expression. 'You're in Canada, ma'am. Coffee is the norm. And I don't mean instant. You'll find first-class coffee-making facilities and I guarantee you'll enjoy the experience.' He reached to open the boot.

She looked unconvinced. 'I suppose we are in the French-speaking area,' she said grudgingly. 'Anyway, I need to freshen up. I feel as though I've slept in this outfit.'

'Probably because you did. Seriously, you look fine. Let's take our luggage and check in.

Then we should discuss what time we'll meet with Pierre and his wife.'

'And they are?' Dutifully she trundled her wheelie case beside him as they headed for the hotel entrance.

'My apologies, Andrea. I meant to email you. Obviously you needn't join us if you prefer not to, but I've known Pierre a long time and he's very supportive of the research we've been doing. I just need to ring him and confirm what time we can meet for dinner.'

'I'm not particularly keen on dining alone. But you're old friends. Maybe they won't appreciate a stranger joining you,' said Andrea.

'Lisa will be delighted to have you there. She's a GP if you want to talk shop, but she's also very knowledgeable about Quebec and all its history.'

'Now, that's more like it.'

'Absolutely. Why don't we ask them to meet us in the Bistro bar at, say, seven o'clock? That should allow us plenty of time to unpack, shower, whatever. Unless you can't wait to be rid of me, we could even order tea for two after we check in.' He found himself holding his breath.

'I think I can bear your company for a while longer,' she said. 'It'll be worth it for a pot of tea.'

The remark was entirely non-flirtatious and

Keir wouldn't expect it to be otherwise. But the confidences shared on the flight were taunting him. If they enjoyed each other's company not only during the conference hours but in leisure moments too, would it be in order to invite Andrea out socially once back in the UK? Or would she misconstrue his intentions and wonder if he perceived her as fair game for any advances, now he knew the real story behind the rings she still wore so proudly?

Ignoring the revolving panels of the main entrance, the hotel commissionaire held open a smaller door for them and beckoned to a uniformed bellboy. 'Welcome to the King George, Doctors. I hope your stay with us will be a happy one.'

★　★　★

Lisa's blonde outdoor girl looks contrasted with her husband's unruly dark hair and rather saturnine features. Over drinks they chatted about the hotel and the conference, with the other three skilfully avoiding reminiscences and issues about which Andrea possessed no knowledge. She felt at home with them and happily discussed Josh while Lisa chatted about her twin girls. Warming to her, Andrea found it perfectly natural to explain her single state.

Lisa took the information on board with a grave nod of the head. 'Actually, Keir told Pierre over the phone earlier. I hope you don't mind. I imagine he didn't want either of us to say something inappropriate.'

'It's not quite so raw now,' said Andrea. 'But I only just told Keir on the flight over.'

'Is that right? I thought you two had known each other for a long time.'

'Not at all. We've been thrown together as colleagues on this project, that's all. I know nothing about his personal life and I don't expect him to confide in me if that's his wish. It's just that I felt the time was right to tell him I've been widowed. It's still not something I find easy to speak about, as you can imagine.'

'And the people you do tell probably find it difficult to know what to say?'

'They do.' Andrea picked up her water glass.

'For what it's worth, I admire you for coming to Canada. I don't imagine it was an easy decision. But when your son's older, I think he'll be full of admiration for his brave mama!'

'Do you think?' Andrea chuckled. 'At the moment, he's more interested in what I'm going to bring him back. Except that makes

Josh sound as if he's spoilt rotten. Believe me, I'm trying my hardest not to let that happen.'

'A little spoiling never hurt anyone now and then. You seem far too sensible to go over the top, if I may say so.'

'I hope you're right.' Andrea looked up as a waiter appeared, carrying enormous red leather tasselled menus.

'Good,' said Lisa. 'We can finish our drinks while we choose our meals.'

Once they'd moved into the restaurant and settled themselves at their window table, Lisa asked whether Andrea would have any opportunity to see something of the city.

Andrea looked across at Keir. 'It won't be possible tomorrow, but hopefully the next day after lunch?'

He nodded. 'You should go for it. Most of the conference is packed into tomorrow and we're expected to attend the evening dinner of course. But after lunch on the last day, you could spend a few hours away from the grindstone.'

'I'd like to take a tour of the city — maybe see a bit of the underground area. I'm sure I'd love the Biodome but I think that's impossible this time.'

'You enjoy wildlife? So, you must come back soon and explore properly,' said Pierre.

'Of course,' said Lisa. 'You'd be welcome

to stay with us. We have a little flat for guests so you could come and go as you wished. And if you wanted more company — '

'You could borrow the devilish duo!' Pierre interrupted.

'Take no notice of him, Andrea,' said Lisa. 'The girls are very sociable and only a year older than *le petit* Josh.'

Andrea felt her cheeks heat. She wasn't sure whether Keir would approve of her becoming involved with his friends. But she didn't want to sound ungrateful. 'That's very kind. Please don't think I'm not interested. Coming back to Montreal and staying with you sounds a wonderful idea. But there's a lot of stuff to be settled yet, my mother's participation in the trial being one of them.' She smiled at Lisa.

'Of course,' said Pierre. 'The invitation's there. When you decide you'd like to travel, just get in touch. Keir has all our contact numbers.'

The two men began talking again, Pierre speaking in French and teasing Keir when he stumbled over his response. It was all done in a relaxed, joking manner. But Andrea noticed that Keir seemed to be avoiding meeting her eyes. Something didn't seem right. But now wasn't the time to dwell on whatever bothered him.

The rest of the meal passed pleasantly and when the coffee stage arrived, Andrea decided to leave the others to it.

'If you'll forgive me,' she said, 'I won't join you for coffee. Suddenly I feel the need to fall into that luxurious bed.'

Pierre rose as she did. He pulled out her chair before Keir too got to his feet. 'It's been a total pleasure to meet you, Andrea,' he said.

Lisa, too, stood up and moved forward to give Andrea a hug. 'I'm sure I'll hear how you and Keir get on tomorrow. If we don't meet again this time, I shall see you and Josh when you come to visit.'

'I hope so. Thanks again, Lisa. It's been lovely to meet you both too. See you tomorrow on the firing line, Pierre.'

'I'll walk you to the lift,' said Keir. This time he met her gaze.

'There's really no need,' she said. 'I'll meet you for breakfast, shall I?'

He escorted her through the restaurant before answering. 'Is eight o'clock all right?'

'Perfect,' she said. 'Thank you for a lovely evening, Keir. I've enjoyed your company. And your friends are delightful people.'

He watched her cross the lobby to the elevators. She'd coped brilliantly with everything so far. He could only imagine how sad she must feel, especially being in the company of happy couples when her relationship had ended in such a tragic manner. Yes, of course he appreciated her confiding details of her past to him. But, for all his experience of dealing with people, his own feelings for her were so strong, so intense, that he knew he teetered dangerously close to declaring them. And that, he told himself as he went to join his friends in the residents' lounge, would be a huge mistake.

★ ★ ★

Andrea paused, reached for her water glass and sipped. Certainly as far as she could tell, no one out there was fidgeting, and that she found impressive. The next part of her talk might cause her audience to look down at their notes or even close their eyes. She'd been a little uncertain whether to travel this path but when she talked it through with Keir, he'd wholeheartedly agreed.

'They'll respect the fact that you've done the long slog and worked as a GP. As for your academic qualifications, why not just tell them how many badges you earned when you were a Girl Guide?' Andrea had mock-punched him at that point.

'Some of them will have checked out your profile on the internet,' he continued more seriously. 'But if you appeal to them as a working mum trying to juggle career, young family and your own elderly mum who's struggling with difficulties that won't go away, they'll really sit up and listen. You're a real-live case history, here to tell them how much you want to help your mother retain the remaining independence she has. Go for it.'

So here Andrea was to do just that. She didn't dress up her problems with wishy-washy statements. She didn't whinge about her lot. She introduced herself as a young widow, something which, unknown to her as she gazed out at the tiered rows of professionals, caused a spasm to cross Keir's countenance, plainly visible to anyone who might have been watching.

'The situation kind of crept up on me,' she told her audience candidly. 'For sure, male or female, we all know what it's like to be busy. Often family has to take a back seat. But once I realised my mother's safety was on the line, I didn't take much persuading to put her name forward as a candidate to join Dr Harrison's trial.'

A hand shot up. 'Dr Palmer, does this mean you have absolute confidence in this com-bined drugs and diet programme? Pardon me for asking, but if you're one hundred percent certain this procedure could interrupt, possibly prevent your mother's deterioration, well then you've definitely sold the idea to me.'

There were murmurs of agreement among the listeners. Andrea saw some were leaning forward, waiting eagerly for her response. She experienced a brief moment of panic, realising how vital her contribution could be.

'I'm pleased you did pose this question,' she told them. 'Because I can assure you, my mother's welfare is very important to me. No way would I have contemplated her joining the patients being treated at Hartnett if I didn't have absolute trust in Dr Harrison's revolutionary idea. And even if my mother hadn't proved suitably fit in her general health, I should still have agreed to join Keir's team. That's how much confidence I have in his findings.'

She turned towards Keir, seated behind her on the platform. 'I'd like to hand back to you here, Dr Harrison,' she said. 'I'm sure there'll be more questions for you.'

He rose and was at her side in two paces. Lightly he placed an arm around her shoulders. The affectionate gesture was a heart-stopping one and Andrea felt momentarily as if she'd stepped out of real life.

'I think we'd all like you to stay just where you are, Dr Palmer,' he said. 'I doubt the conference is going to let you go without knowing how your mother has reacted to her first couple of sessions.'

Andrea felt a glow which she wasn't sure was caused by the supportive words or by the casual but comforting pressure of his arm. When he removed it, she felt a twinge of regret. But the consultant was a showman. He was presenting the pair of them as a strong team and she happily played along.

The questions kept coming. She answered honestly. She answered as a daughter, not a doctor. Then to her relief, Keir glanced at the brass-rimmed old clock on the wall. 'That's it for today, ladies and gentlemen. Thank you for your attention and for your very astute questions. Refreshments await you next door, after which there's a talk by a member of the drug company research team. Unmissable, in my opinion.'

Andrea sank back in her chair. 'Phew,' she said. 'I thought they'd never stop. Talk about a grilling! You were superb.'

'It's a mutual admiration society, as far as I'm concerned. You swayed them in our favour if I'm not mistaken. Among them, they probably possess more street cred than the Royal College of Surgeons.'

'Thank you for inviting me to Montreal,' she said suddenly. 'I'm so pleased I came. I really mean that, Keir.'

He cleared his throat and turned to face her. For a moment she wondered if he was about to put his arms around her. But he busied himself gathering his notes into their folder, and hurriedly she followed suit.

'I'd better show my face out there,' he said. 'There were several people I recognised in the audience — time to go and talk shop.'

She stood up. 'I want to hear the next speaker, so I'll grab a quick cuppa and see you in a while then.'

It seemed to her he couldn't move away fast enough — which meant, of course, she'd been right in thinking that little show of comradeship and even affection had been intended as a crowd-pleaser. The thought acted like a douse of cold water on her high spirits.

Andrea followed Keir out of the conference hall, wondering why she felt such a pang of regret. Hadn't she already advised him that as far as she was concerned, their relationship was simply one of colleagues and friends?

★　★　★

She barely got a glimpse of him throughout the rest of the day. During the refreshment break, delegates kept coming up and greeting her as if she was a part of their lives. Business cards were pressed into her hand and questions posed about her academic research and as to whether she missed the hurly-burly of a practising GP's life. More than one confessed to their feelings over dealing with the care of an elderly parent. The same thing happened as she left the final morning session. She tried her best to answer everything truthfully before heading for the washroom.

On her return she glanced around and noticed Keir deep in conversation with a striking woman who wore her shiny jet-black hair in a swinging bob. Andrea saw Keir's companion place one hand upon his jacket sleeve and deliberately kept her distance. No way did she want to interrupt. She joined the queue for the buffet and began helping herself to a tempting seafood salad just as Pierre appeared at the opposite side of the table, balancing a well-loaded tray.

'Dr Andrea Palmer, may I steal you away from all this? Before your fan club realises?'

She chuckled. 'I'd love your company over lunch, Pierre. Keir knows so many more people than I do. Not that I've noticed anyone being unfriendly,' she added hastily. A quick glance over her shoulder showed her Keir now in conversation with a couple of men. There was no sign of the elegant woman.

'Unfriendly? I should hope not, indeed,' said Pierre. 'I'm sure any one of these folk would trample me into the deep pile carpet for the pleasure of eating lunch with you. But I got here first.' He grinned at her. 'I've laid claim to that table for two over there.' He pointed to his jacket draped over one of the chairs. 'Come and join me when you're ready.' He moved away, carefully clutching his tray of goodies.

Andrea chose from the tempting array of food, heaping salad beside a slice of quiche but then being tempted by a golden-crusted cherry pie. She hesitated and ladled a generous dollop of cream on top. She'd been rushing around burning up calories for months now. Suddenly she was hungry, properly hungry, and not in the least fazed by the generous Canadian portions.

'Please don't get up,' she said as she approached Pierre's table. 'Aha — I'm glad to see you've chosen a dessert too. I shan't feel quite so much like Miss Piggy.'

He heaved an elaborate sigh. 'Mark my words, dinner tonight will be clear soup and fresh fruit. My lovely Lisa is only too aware of my bad habits when I'm away from home.' His eyes twinkled.

'So how did Keir and I come across?' Andrea sipped her apricot juice.

'You don't need me to tell you that,' he teased. 'You know very well you two have been a major hit. You are, of course, much more beautiful than he is.'

She waved her fork at him. 'The other speakers have been excellent, in my opinion.'

'Yes and I'm all for having several short sessions. I'm looking forward to this afternoon too.'

'Goodness, don't tell me you're prepared to put up with me again?' She pretended mock horror.

'I might just manage it,' he said. 'I already read your paper on how different cultures view the ageing process. But the real reason I wanted to spend time with you in private was to ask if Lisa and I have managed to put our collective feet in it.'

'I'm sorry?'

'I'm talking about last night at dinner, when we invited you and your son to come and stay with us.' He speared a chunk of spicy chicken and munched. 'Hey, great food again . . . anyway, I noticed Keir was looking kind of uptight last night. Forgive me if I'm speaking out of turn, but that made me wonder if you and he were an item. Or if he has hopes you might be, so felt miffed not to

145

be included in our invitation. Not that he said anything about it,' he added. 'He has an open invitation anyway. Hell, but I'm making a complete mess of this. Lisa will kill me.'

'Keir and me an item? No way,' she said. 'I may be single, but I'm not about to have a fling with a married man. Even if I was seriously on the lookout for male company, which I'm not, it's far too soon after being widowed.'

Pierre put down his fork and reached for his water glass. 'Andrea, I'm sure I don't have to tell you how sorry I am to hear of your loss. Nor do I mean to offend you. Lisa and I genuinely enjoyed your company last night and we'd love to see more of you and to meet young Josh, of course.' He pursed his lips. 'Now, how exactly can I put this? Um, just how, I wonder, did you get the idea that Keir's a married man?'

She stared at him. 'Well he must be, surely?'

'Once upon a time, yes,' said Pierre. 'But he very definitely went through a painful divorce. His former wife and their daughter live in Australia now.'

Andrea frowned. 'When Lisa and I were talking last night, she told me Keir had mentioned my being widowed. But she didn't say anything about his being single.'

'She probably thought you already knew. Maybe Keir doesn't like talking about it. All I can say is Connie definitely remarried. But if Keir has taken a new wife, he's certainly not told me about her.'

7

The hotel bar that evening seethed with delegates booked into the King George and determined to enjoy their leisure after a full day. Andrea would have been happy to order room service and sample Canadian TV programmes in the comfort of her luxurious bed, but Keir wanted her to network. She'd hardly exchanged a word with him since their joint session that morning and was totally unprepared for the jolt of pleasure exploding in her midriff as she stood in the doorway of the sumptuous Versailles Bar and saw him turn around to meet her gaze.

Those words so vehemently spoken to Pierre at lunchtime returned to haunt her. What nonsense to think she could contemplate dating another man when she still clung to the memory of Greg, whom she'd loved so much. How hypocritical would that be, if she should ignore what she knew to be right and allow her stupid, faithless heart to rule her head? Anyway, why had he not told her he was no longer married?

Telling herself to behave like a mature woman instead of a besotted teenager, she composed her features as Keir approached.

'Here you are,' he said, gently cupping her elbow. 'I'd like to introduce you to a couple of people who haven't yet had a chance to speak to you. And let me get you a drink. White wine OK?'

Andrea nodded, her gaze taking in the elegant décor; the secluded corner tables had surely been designed with assignations in mind. Lush sapphire-blue drapes made an excellent backdrop for the striped emerald and cream of the seat cushions. She let herself be drawn into conversation with yet another pair of charming doctors, concentrating on answering their questions as best she could. One, who reminded her of a younger Hugh Grant and who was based in Toronto, made no secret of his scepticism concerning Keir's theory. He seemed determined to wear down her resistance but Andrea, equally determined to convince him, upped her game, counter-arguing and eventually leaving the Toronto medic searching for words.

'Game, set and match to Dr Palmer, I think,' Keir said. 'Tom, I take on board your concerns but all I can say is, let's see what results the trial produces, OK? Just now, I could use some dinner. Shall we go through?'

Andrea had already checked the seating plan outside the restaurant. The various speakers were each allocated places at different tables. She turned to her adversary. 'You and I are placed next to each other, Tom. What say we call a truce?'

'Sounds good to me,' he said, smiling back. 'How are you on ice hockey stats?'

Andrea laughed out loud. 'Rubbish, as well you know. You talk ice hockey and I'll talk tennis.' As she walked away from the bar, chatting with Toronto Tom, as she'd privately named him because of his place of work, she knew Keir's eyes were focused on her. But his slightly proprietorial attitude was probably all to do with their joint conference presentation. It would be good to spend time not talking shop, especially with someone she'd only just met and with whom she knew enjoyed a spirited discussion.

Andrea looked forward to her dinner and hopefully to a not-too-late night. She'd managed to make a quick call to Kirsty during the afternoon break and everything was fine. She'd smiled to herself as Josh excitedly told her what he'd been doing, without letting her get a word in. Obviously a boring grownup function didn't rate against an ongoing spaceship voyage with tentacle-waving monsters attacking from every direction. Her mind remained very much at rest because Kirsty was also first point of contact for Lizzie Dean while Andrea was out of the country. Her friend had reported no problems back home in Hartnett either.

Andrea's unpredictable emotions were unwelcome gatecrashers. But that was something only she could deal with. The fleeting rushes of joy when she caught Keir's eye and felt the flare of intimate connection weren't experiences for confiding. Maybe, just maybe, she'd let it all out to Kirsty once she was back home again. Hopefully her friend would comfort her by saying such an attraction was perfectly understandable. After years of marriage to a lovely guy like Greg, maybe she subconsciously sought a masculine shoulder to cry on? Especially as she now knew Keir was, according to his friend Pierre, unattached. Who was she kidding? The buzz between them had begun well before she'd found out Keir was single.

She tuned into Toronto Tom's explanation of the Canadian passion for ice hockey, trying hard to listen and ask intelligent questions. It wasn't easy, given all she knew of the sport involved a mass of ice and a small ball, but it seemed so much safer an option than allowing personal feelings to overwhelm her and send her spiralling back into a dangerous dream world.

★　★　★

Next morning, Keir challenged himself to swim lengths in the hotel pool, part of the beautiful spa complex his PA had sighed over. One side of the pool opened onto a terrace and sunken garden, sunshine lighting the azure tiles. Light classical music floated from concealed speakers. It was still horribly early by his home standards, yet he swam in company with two other guests, until he became aware of a fourth person jumping into the crystal-clear water. When he reached his target number of lengths he stopped and lay back in the shallows, toes anchoring him to the poolside.

The female swimmer, hair tucked into white bathing cap, possessed a mean backstroke, Keir noted. She ploughed down the pool towards him as if her life depended on it. Would she stop or would she execute a classy turnaround and set off again?

'Hey,' he said good-naturedly as she arrived at the end of the neighbouring lane. 'I like your style.'

'Good morning,' said Andrea, touching base with her feet. 'No way could I keep up with you. Five lengths is my limit today.'

'But that's great. Does your little boy swim?'

'Yes,' she said shortly. 'I must get back upstairs. See you at breakfast, Keir.'

She waded towards the steps and climbed out of the pool, picking up her towel from a lounger. If she gave him a backward glance, he didn't know. He was desperately trying to avoid looking up at her. She wore a sleek red swimsuit which clung in all the right places, and it would have been unprofessional of him to treat Dr Palmer as anything more than a colleague. But how he'd longed to pull that unflattering rubber helmet off her head and release those kitten-purr soft strands of hair.

You're going gaga, Harrison, he raged. *Will you never learn?* It was so ironic, after the mistakes he'd made in his first marriage. Now, not only older but hopefully a little wiser too, here he was, discovering that the first woman since his divorce he felt an affinity with was out of his reach. Once the trial concluded, they probably wouldn't see much of each other as their careers progressed. Maybe that would be a good thing. But while still here in Montreal, with no meet-and-greet dinner on the agenda once the conference closed after lunch, he was determined to do his utmost to show her a few features of the city he loved.

Keir hauled himself from the water and reached for his robe and flip-flops. As he rode the lift to his floor he wondered whether, if he asked Andrea to join him later, he could convince her of his wish to be her colleague and, hopefully, friend. Sometimes he felt this could be achievable; while at other times, all he wanted to do was take her in his arms and show her love could still be hers. Even though he knew she still hurt after the loss of a man he could never dream to emulate, surely she would let him into her heart if he insisted there were no strings attached to his motives? A pearl of pool water rolled like a tear down his cheek.

★   ★   ★

Andrea took yet another picture of a cute black squirrel.

'Didn't you capture that little guy just now?' Keir teased.

'Yes, but he wasn't tucking into his lunch then,' she said.

'I hate to drag you away, but we should take the Metro if you want to fit in a couple of hours at the Biodome.'

She stuffed her camera into her shoulder bag. 'I know it can only be a flying visit, but Josh will be much more interested in hearing about the animals than learning about architecture and maritime history.'

Keir led the way back to the entrance. 'And you can catch up with some shopping later.'

'I can't believe the conference is over and we're heading back tomorrow. Everything seems to have happened so quickly.'

'I don't want to talk shop, Andrea. But you've been a tremendous support to me. I do mean that. It's not just professional schmoozing.'

She avoided his gaze. 'Thank you.'

'The snag is, there'll be a lot of people watching out for us now. They'll be waiting for us to post good results. They'll be ready to praise and ready to commiserate.'

'No pressure then!' She pouted.

He took hold of her elbow. 'Enough already. Let's cross here then hop on the Metro.'

The light pressure of his fingers upon her arm felt comforting. It was precisely this sort of considerate gesture from a man that, after years of being partnered, she missed so much. She tried to ignore the tingles flying down her spine when Keir's fingers touched her body; knew she mustn't read anything into his courteousness. He'd be exactly the same with any woman he escorted, of that she was certain.

* * *

'I'm quite happy to go shopping on my own,' she said later when they arrived back at the hotel. 'Even I can't get lost if I just have to use the subway to descend to the depths. Besides, you'd be bored out of your skull.'

'Well, if you're sure,' he said. 'I'm going to check at the desk for messages, then go for another swim. In case I'm not up early enough tomorrow.' He checked his watch. 'If you'd rather eat on your own this evening, please say, but there's a great place I know within easy walking distance. I shall go there anyway, but it'd be more enjoyable if you came too.'

She hesitated. This was the last evening in Montreal and tomorrow the hours would count down as they travelled to the airport to catch their London flight. It might be the last chance she got to eat in a classy restaurant for a very long while. Why visit a fast-food outlet in a solitary state, or shut herself away in her room with a tray and the TV for company, when she could dine with an attractive male companion?

He was waiting for her answer, his expression slightly anxious. The powerful consultant, poised on the brink of a momentous breakthrough in medical science, stood waiting to see if she'd join him for dinner. In the words of her friend Kirsty, wasn't it a no-brainer?

'I'd like that,' she said. 'I'll do my retail

therapy for a couple of hours, then get changed and meet you down here in the foyer?'

She hadn't noticed before how his smile could light up his face, take away the little worry lines and melt the tension from his jaw. At that moment Andrea almost raised her hand to touch his cheek, but somehow resisted the powerful attraction sizzling between them. To stay out of trouble she forced herself to turn away, completely forgetting her manners.

'Hey,' he called after her. 'We haven't fixed a time. Is 6.30 too early?'

'It's fine,' she replied, feeling warmth flood her cheeks.

'Enjoy the shops,' he said.

She had a feeling he remained there, watching her walk away from him, but she forced herself not to look back; concentrated on keeping her thoughts fixed on the new dress she'd promised herself as a reward for not collapsing like an unset jelly when she made her presentation. Even one glance over her shoulder would surely be interpreted by Keir as flirtation?

★ ★ ★

Before she descended, Andrea sent black squirrel photos to Kirsty's phone and texted a

157

message saying everything was fine. Now that she was wandering through a retail wonderland with so much choice, she found difficulty knowing where to plunge in. The brightly lit mall offered everything from chunky woollens and fur-trimmed leather gilets to slinky dresses in rainbow shades and little jackets too wicked to ignore.

She wandered into a boutique which looked like her kind of store. A pretty girl smiled a welcome and said, 'Let me know if you need any help.'

Andrea stopped and smiled at the assistant. 'That's a lovely Scottish accent. Dare I ask what brought you here?'

The young woman nodded. 'I fell in love with the city when I came out on holiday with my parents a while back. I just had to return. Which part of the UK is it you're from?'

'The west country,' said Andrea. 'I live in a town called Hartnett. It's not far from Stonehenge. Most people seem to have heard of the standing stones.' She turned towards a rack of summer clothing. 'I'd better get on.'

The friendly assistant gestured to a display at the side of the shop. 'You'll find plenty more in your size over there. Are you into maxi dresses?'

'Maybe,' said Andrea. 'I think I'll know

what I want when I see it. Does that sound stupid?'

'Certainly not, but I'd love to see you wearing this sea-green number.' She walked over to the rack and picked out the dress, holding it so its skirt draped over her other arm.

'Oh wow,' said Andrea. 'That is so beautiful.'

'You suit the colour and it's reasonably priced too,' said the assistant. 'You can tell I'm a Scot, can't you?'

Laughing, Andrea picked up an ice-blue short frock, skirt cut to float when the wearer moved. 'I'll try just these two on. Otherwise knowing me, I'll be floundering with too much choice.'

Once in the changing room, she slipped into the maxi dress first. It looked good, she decided. And it would cover legs that didn't see the sun much these days. Accustomed to practical, certainly not eye-catching, clothes for work, and jeans and T-shirts for leisure, her soul suddenly craved soft fabrics and flattering shades.

The short frock appealed to her even more once she was wearing it. She did a little twirl and saw the skirt spin around her knees and settle again. Regardless of her pale limbs, it suited her.

Andrea wriggled out of the dress and

checked its price tag, then found the store's label on the first garment and nodded. How could she resist? Mission accomplished, and with gifts bought earlier for Josh, her mum, and for Kirsty and clan, she could relax and enjoy the remainder of her brief visit to Montreal.

'Are you going somewhere exciting tonight?' The assistant deftly folded the purchases and slid them into a gold carrier bag.

'Out for dinner with a friend. I don't know the name of the restaurant we're going to.'

'Promise me you'll wear one of your new dresses. Go out there and wow him!'

Feeling about sixteen again, Andrea paid for her purchases, thanked the Scottish girl and retraced her footsteps. Wowing the man was the last thing on her mind. Subduing a dangerous tendency towards letting Keir under her radar must be her top priority. But it was lovely to feel like an independent woman again and not a harassed breadwinner, daughter and mum. She'd definitely wear one of her new dresses.

★ ★ ★

While Andrea shopped, Keir strolled in the park across the road from their hotel in the company of an attractive woman.

'Thanks for seeing me at such short notice, Dr Harrison,' she said.

'Not at all, and please do call me Keir. I, um, had a window between appointments and besides, your request intrigued me. Especially as we'd enjoyed a short conversation earlier.'

His companion stopped, gesturing to a nearby bench. 'Shall we sit a while? It's a joy to escape from the hospital on such a lovely afternoon.'

He followed her to the wrought-iron seat. Rhonda Pierce wasn't the kind of person one argued with. A tall brunette, her glossy bobbed hair swung either side of a narrow, pale face. Long-lashed hazel eyes surveyed the world from beneath a feathery fringe, its simplicity doubtless down to a breathtakingly expensive hairdressing bill. She wore a lime-green linen shift dress, with a buttercup-yellow cashmere sweater slung casually across her shoulders. Rhonda Pierce resembled a fashion model. She was in fact chief geriatric consultant at a prestigious Montreal teaching hospital.

'I didn't mention this earlier because I didn't want to risk anyone hearing what I had to say,' she said. 'We're both busy people and I shan't detain you long, but I wanted the opportunity to drop a snippet of information

161

your way, Keir. The rest is up to you.'

He turned to face her.

'I'd appreciate it if you'd keep this matter close to your chest,' she said. 'I don't want it becoming common knowledge until I'm ready to spill the beans.'

'This sounds very cloak-and-dagger,' he said.

She didn't laugh.

'All right,' he said. 'I guarantee absolute confidentiality. Have no fear. But you really are ratcheting up the mystery, aren't you?'

'My husband calls me the drama queen. I'm sorry, Keir. What I want to say is that Professor Patrick Pierce, he who put these rings on my finger, has been offered a fantastic job opportunity over on the west coast.' She crossed one slender tanned leg over the other. 'Poor guy was dreading telling me. He knows how much I love my work here at the Montfort.'

'Well, congratulations on your husband's new job. But, am I missing something here? With respect, Patrick works in a different area from me and of course from you. Why are you telling me this?' Keir was genuinely puzzled, given the secrecy surrounding his meeting with Rhonda.

Her face creased into a happy smile. 'Obstetrics is kind of dissimilar to what you and I are involved with, that's for sure. But I'm thrilled for him and also very proud of my guy. No way am I going to let him pass up on this opportunity, and no way do I want us taking turns to fly east or west in order to grab a few hours together at weekends. That's why I shall be handing in my notice in a few weeks' time. Even Patrick doesn't know that yet.'

'Wow. Right,' said Keir, still not understanding. 'Well, of course I wish you all the best too, Rhonda. Believe me, I know better than most how distance can affect a relationship.'

'Would you be interested in applying for my job, Keir?'

He sat up straight, placed one hand on each knee and closed his eyes briefly before turning to her. 'Are you serious?'

'Cross my heart and hope to die.' Her eyes danced. 'I've headed the department for quite a while now. The board will probably snap my hand off if I tell them I've asked you to email me your résumé. You're hot property at the moment, Doc.'

'I don't know about that,' he said. 'I have an excellent team around me, including Dr Palmer. Did you meet Andrea, by any chance?'

'I didn't get to talk to her, but that

presentation of hers was impressive. Anyway, please don't change the subject.'

'I never expected anything like this. I wondered if maybe you wanted a bit more information about the trial.' He was floundering.

'Nope, everything came over loud and clear. I'll be following progress on your blog. It's such an interesting concept. So tell me, Keir — will you at least think about what I've just said?'

'I hadn't planned on leaving my post at Hartnett General for a good while yet, if ever in fact. I certainly couldn't desert the trial.'

'Keir, of course you couldn't. Nor do I have any intention of leaving my department wallowing in my wake. My contract requires I give three months' notice. Patrick won't take up his new role in Vancouver until September. That's the best part of four months unless there's something very wrong with my math.'

He sat back and folded his arms. 'OK. Thanks for being so frank with me. As I said, this has come as a surprise. I'm obviously flattered.'

'Oh come on,' she said. 'Don't be coy. The world's your oyster now. Hard work plus your gutsy idea deserves recognition.'

'I promise to give great thought to your

suggestion. How's that for starters?'

'So long as you do, I guess I'll have to be satisfied with that.' She glanced at her wafer-thin gold watch. 'Hey, I have to go now, but let me give you one of my cards. Don't you dare lose it.'

'I expect you'd track me down,' he said, taking out his wallet. He handed her his own card and tucked hers safely away. 'Can I walk you anywhere, Rhonda? Put you in a taxi?'

'I love you Brits. You're so polite,' she said, standing up. 'But no thanks. I have my car parked nearby.' She held out her hand as he, too, got to his feet. 'You stay and sit a while. Or go back to the King George and mull things over with a dry martini. I'll just disappear down that path.'

'If you're sure,' he said. 'And thanks again for thinking of me.'

'It was great talking to you,' said Rhonda. 'The thinking's down to you now.'

Keir stood, watching her stride purposely down the walkway. He took a deep breath. No way had he expected such a proposition. And, sworn to secrecy, no way could he talk the matter over with anyone, including Andrea. He too glanced at his watch and set off in the direction of the hotel. A dip in the pool tempted him more than a dry martini. He'd push himself, concentrating on nothing but stretching his body to the limits as he swam through that Olympic-sized tub of water.

★ ★ ★

'What a lovely old building,' said Andrea later as Keir stopped outside a restaurant. They'd left the busy thoroughfare and turned down a side road. A striped black and white awning sheltered the forecourt where several small tables stood sheltered by foliage.

'It's still warm enough to sit outside. What do you think? Order something to drink out here and move inside to eat?'

The restaurant door stood open. As they hovered, a waiter approached.

'I rang earlier to reserve a table,' said Keir. 'I'm Keir Harrison.'

The waiter nodded. 'I remember you. May I say it's a pleasure to see you again, Doctor Harrison? Might I suggest an aperitif here first, perhaps?' He moved a corner chair out for Andrea. 'I hope you enjoy your first visit here, madame.'

'It's Nicholas, isn't it?' Keir used the French way of pronouncing the name. 'The beard had me fooled.'

'*Oui, c'est moi*,' said the young man. 'It is still me, for sure.' He placed menus before

166

them. 'Would you like time to decide what you wish to drink?'

'Andrea?' Keir looked enquiringly at her.

'A glass of white wine for me, please.'

'Perhaps you'd like a dash of melon cordial with your wine?' The waiter's pen hovered over his notepad. 'It's very popular with our customers.'

Keir looked at Andrea, then smiled up at Nicholas. 'Madame seems to approve, so yes please, and a glass of house red for me.'

The waiter hurried inside. Keir leaned back in his chair. 'I keep forgetting to tell you how much I like that dress. Did you buy it today by any chance?'

Andrea almost told him he didn't have to pay her compliments but thought better of it. 'I did. I'm glad it meets with your approval,' she said, keeping her tone light. How dreadful if he thought she'd bought it especially for their dinner date. Not that it was a date, of course.

He looked slightly uncomfortable, as if he had something on his mind. *Oh, no, she* thought. *Please don't let him think he has to take me to bed tonight.* That would shatter the friendly atmosphere formed over the last days. She'd have to turn him down and then he'd be miffed, probably . . . definitely . . . and how would they survive the flight back with that enormous elephant in the cabin?

To her relief, the friendly Nicholas arrived with their drinks plus a basket of miniature bread rolls.

Keir proposed a toast. 'Here's to the successful conclusion of our trial.'

'I'll certainly drink to that,' she said, holding her glass up to his.

He waited for her to taste her wine. 'But I want to toast you next, Andrea. You've contributed so much already, both back at the hospital and here at this conference. You've given me total support and — oh, heck — I just want to say thank you for being here with me.'

Her heart seemed determined to do that clunkety-clunk thing which probably only a medic could accept for what it was without panicking as to its cause. She knew what was happening of course. The attraction sparking between them wasn't going to go away any time soon. One sip of wine couldn't be blamed for the way she felt. She needed to shift her legs under the table, try to put a stop to the buzz between her thighs. The soft fabric of her sea-green dress caressed her limbs as she changed position. Without a doubt, she wanted Keir Harrison. Even before his friend Pierre revealed Keir was legally single and therefore available, she'd wanted him. So what price her attempts to obey what her conscience dictated?

* * *

'It's just as well I'll be back on the straight and narrow soon,' said Keir as they were dining. 'I don't know how anyone could resist these tiny potato wedge things.'

He picked one up. She watched his fingers, then looked into his eyes, mesmerised as he moved the delicacy to her mouth. She opened her lips before her brain engaged in time for her to protest. This was another of those intimate gestures couples enjoyed and which she missed these days. It sent an immediate and intimate message.

'Lovely,' she said, trying to sound brisk. 'I can taste the coriander. Enjoy them and remember all those calories you've burned in the swimming pool.' Maybe he was waiting to sample her sweet potato mousse, but she daren't allow herself to follow his example.

Fortunately they didn't have to eat in silence. Subtle guitar music set at just the right sound level kissed the atmosphere. Skilful lighting transformed the old building's thick stone walls into soft, dusky rose. Pewter sconces held pale pink candles, their flames flaring pools of light. A small lamp burned on the table between Keir and Andrea although it was barely twilight. Andrea gazed at the macho suit of armour standing in one corner, its enigmatic visor seeming to look back at her, adding a touch of mystery to the surroundings.

'Andrea,' said Keir, interrupting her thoughts. 'I need to say something to you.'

'I thought we weren't going to talk shop,' she said, spearing a last slice of sundried tomato.

'We're not. This is personal.' He drank a little more red wine.

Her heart did that thumping thing again. Her meal finished, she put down her knife and fork. Whatever he wanted to say, his face showed his determination to go ahead with it.

Nicholas materialised beside her. 'Finished, madame?'

'Yes, thank you,' she said in French.

The waiter beamed as he removed their plates. Within a beat, he placed a dessert menu in front of each of them.

'Let's be very decadent and eat dessert,' said Keir. 'You're right. We should enjoy our last evening in Montreal without feelings of guilt.'

This time she met his gaze. She moved her hands so they were clasped loosely in front of her on the table and not too many inches from his. She waited for him to look away. It wasn't going to happen.

'We'll take a few minutes, Nicholas,' said Keir, still holding her gaze.

As the waiter moved away she felt Keir close one of his hands over hers. His thumb stroked her fingers and moved to her palm where it rested before lightly pressing its centre. Longing blazed inside her. How could she sit there like that, allowing her carefully constructed defences to disintegrate? How could she sit there, enjoying his touch and wanting it to continue?

Gently she withdrew her hands and picked up her menu. 'We should choose our very decadent desserts,' she said, not allowing herself to meet his gaze.

He broke the silence, but not until he'd taken a few moments. 'Andrea?'

'You first,' she said.

'OK. I'm going for the miniature crêpe with ice cream and raspberry coulis and a rain check on the guilt.'

She chuckled. 'For me, it has to be pear and ginger ice cream. Chocolate sauce, please, and no self-reproach on the side.'

Their drinks arrived and Keir ordered the puddings, requesting Nicholas to give them a fifteen-minute respite between courses.

Andrea picked up her fresh glass and sipped the cool, fragrant liquid. Why shouldn't she stay relaxed after such a tough workout? She was enjoying herself and maybe she'd read too much into Keir's body language. He'd been under more pressure than she had, as the consultant fronting the UK trial.

'Andrea, do you recall our bumping into one another that day when I was coming to see Richard? Remember? We met at the lift, though neither of us has mentioned it.'

Immediately she pictured the scene. 'It didn't seem important,' she said. Except for being the most significant wake-up call to the love-starved woman hiding away inside that she'd ever experienced.

'I disagree,' he said. 'Your face — your whole demeanour attracted me right from that unimportant moment, as you call it. I didn't notice your wedding and engagement rings at that point. Shall we say that when you turned up in my office and I recognised you and later noticed the rings, it was a defining moment. I had to tell myself to back off.'

'You'd no way of knowing your assumption wasn't correct.' Andrea's fingers pleated her starched pink linen napkin.

'Yes, thanks to your very poignant explanation on the flight over.' His hand moved towards hers, slowing their movements, calming her, beguiling her with his touch. This time she didn't pull back.

'You were very frank with me on the flight over,' he continued. 'I didn't think it was the right time to explain my own situation. It would have seemed too corny.'

'Keir, before you say another word, I don't know where this going but I want you to know you don't have to tell me anything that might prove painful. We haven't known each other very long. I decided to tell you about my immediate past because I thought it needed saying.'

'Was this down to me drawing the wrong conclusion about your friendship with Richard?'

'Partly,' she said, her gaze focused on the hand still covering hers.

'I can't apologise enough for that. It was entirely stupid and thoughtless. I admit to having had feelings of, well, unease, for all sorts of reasons. And of course, you'd arrived at the wrong conclusion about me,' he said softly. 'I know that because Pierre has told me you were convinced I was married.'

'You've been discussing me with your friends?' She pulled both hands back sharply.

'Of course not,' said Keir, shaking his head. 'It's only that Pierre gave me a ticking-off before he left the hotel — accused me of being a buttoned-up Englishman among other things. I'm sorry I didn't tell you about my divorce. Most people around me know. It just didn't occur to me to say anything.' He sat back again. 'But now we both know we're two single people.'

Wistfulness tinged her smile. 'Single maybe, but still attached.'

'We all have baggage, Andrea.'

'How I feel is probably too complicated to explain.'

'I didn't mean to sound insensitive. Please don't think I don't respect your feelings. It's just — '

Nicholas arrived with their desserts. The scrumptious puddings weren't intended to induce serious conversation and Keir and Andrea ate in silence.

'Good?'

'Much more than good, thank you.' She picked up her glass. 'We probably need to get back.'

'No coffee?'

She hesitated. 'Are you having coffee?'

'I could be persuaded if it means more time alone with you.'

She managed to keep the conversation in still waters, questioning him about Pierre and Lisa and how long he'd known them, wanting to hear about his first trip to Canada. They fell silent when the cups stood empty. Keir called for the bill.

They walked into the cool Canadian evening.

'Aren't you cold?' He glanced at her flimsy dress.

'I'm fine,' she said, wondering how she'd been so stupid as to forget a wrap.

He took off his suit jacket and draped it around her shoulders. She felt the warmth of his body transfer to hers and caught a whiff of his aftershave as he leaned in. Her longing to be kissed transcended her resolve. The quiet street in which they stood remained free of passers-by.

'You know how much I'm attracted to you, don't you?' He watched her face.

'I . . . '

'That first day when we barged into each other at the elevator, I couldn't get you out of my mind afterwards; couldn't stop wondering what caused that hurt, frightened expression in your eyes. I wanted to scoop you up and take you somewhere calm and safe. Do I have to spell it out to you, Andrea? That feeling hasn't gone away. I tried to fight it because I thought you were married.' He took her in his arms. 'I love you. You don't have to say a word. Just let me hold you, please.' The last word was a whisper.

He wrapped his arms around her, beneath his sober grey jacket. She closed her eyes and tilted her face towards his. At that moment she forgot everything else in the world — where they were, who she was, their professional status — nothing could stop that moment of joy.

This kiss didn't flare as their first had. It began cautiously, gently, tentatively. Andrea uttered a little involuntary purr, the kind a woman makes when she sinks into a warm scented tub or snuggles between freshly laundered sheets. Keir pulled her even more tightly to him, binding them together as if he couldn't get close enough. His lips were more insistent now, demanding a response, which she gave readily.

At last they released their hold on one another. 'Let's go back,' he said, gently pushing her arms inside sleeves that dangled, concealing her fingertips. He took her hand. 'Don't think too hard, darling. Please don't worry about a thing.'

She walked beside him, temporarily inhabiting the masculine guise of his crisply tailored pinstripe suit jacket. They walked purposefully but he didn't try to hurry her along. It was as if each accepted their destination and trusted the other to remain focused.

Inside the hotel foyer, Keir still held on to her hand. They headed towards the lifts and he pressed the call button. She watched the floor numbers flash in descending order — five, four, three, two, ground and lower ground where they waited. The car stopped and two people stepped out. Keir placed his hand lightly on her back and they entered. He pressed the button for the sixth floor.

The gates slid across and she felt him kiss the top of her head, a butterfly touch before he squeezed her hand.

She nestled against him, trusting, anticipating. It was as if she'd shrugged on a fluffy cloud of longing the moment he draped his sensible jacket over her shoulders. When the lift eased to a halt at their floor, they got out and she removed her hand from his to find her key card in her handbag. Still he said nothing.

They walked down the carpeted corridor to Number 622. His room was located on the same floor but a few doors further along. Andrea hesitated, then operated the card key system. She stared as the green light shone. How symbolic was that? He pushed open the door for her and waited for her to enter. She didn't hesitate to step inside before holding out her hand to him.

8

Lizzie Dean awoke to an unusual alarm call, a tuneful vocal of a number she recognised as a Perry Como hit, probably from the fifties and definitely a tad too enthusiastic for the time of day. She squinted at her clock and uttered a good-humoured *Okay* as she realised it was six a.m.

'Rosemary,' she called on her way down the hallway. 'What are you doing up so early?'

'I'm making Andrea's lunch. She's going on a school trip today.'

When Lizzie reached the kitchen she realised the reason for the activity. Last night there'd been a documentary about academic excursions on television. Afterwards, Lizzie had reminisced about her first time away from home and also her first attempt at skiing. She'd enjoyed Austria but not by her own clumsy attempts on the snowy slopes. Rosemary had listened and laughed without once mentioning her daughter.

Rosemary proudly held out the sandwiches she'd made. 'Look,' she said. 'I wonder if that'll be enough.'

'I think that'll do fine, Rosemary. Why

don't you sit down now while I make some tea?'

'Lovely. It's so kind of you to spend time with me. Can you stay for a while?'

'Yes, my dear. I can stay all day if you like. I don't have to go to work today. It's Sunday.'

Rosemary sank down on one of the kitchen chairs. 'We could have our lunch outside.' Her face radiated happiness.

Lizzie patted the elderly woman's shoulder. 'Whatever you wish, my dear. I could drive you to the garden centre after breakfast if you like. You were after a few more bedding plants, weren't you?'

Rosemary nodded at her carer and started humming 'Magic Moments' again, her frail body swaying in time to the tune.

While she waited for the tea to brew, Lizzie picked up the unbuttered slices of bread and placed them beside the toaster. She wondered where exactly Rosemary thought her daughter was at this moment. Did she imagine her to be still in bed, just down the corridor? Doubtless Andrea would be safely tucked up in her Montreal hotel room. Lizzie calculated it must be a quarter past one over there and Andrea's flight back to Heathrow left at 10.00 a.m. local time. She'd need every single moment of her beauty sleep.

* * *

Andrea looked out at the ground rushing past the aircraft. She felt the smack in her back as the powerful engines thrust them from the runway, the big bird reaching for the clouds, lifting them up and away from Canadian soil. The rush of emotion she felt startled her. How silly was that? Images of indigenous wild life, quirky frog memorabilia in the gift shops and flirtatious French-speaking waiters drifted in her mind's eye. She pictured the conference audience clapping as one after she thanked them for listening, her eyes widening in disbelief at the warmth of their response.

She had an open invitation to go back one day and stay with Keir's friends. Josh would adore such an adventure and she'd no doubt whatsoever that Pierre and Lisa would be perfect hosts and ensure they enjoyed their holiday.

She smiled, picturing her little boy's face. Andrea longed to see him again, and her mother, of course. It would be interesting to learn how Rosemary had fared in her absence. Had mother even noticed daughter wasn't around? Knowing Lizzie, there'd have been plenty to occupy Rosemary's gently wandering mind. The woman was an absolute jewel and Andrea knew Mrs Dean was far more skilled at caring for her mother than she herself was. She wondered how her mum's hospital appointments had gone.

And then there was Keir, sitting in silence beside her. When the next trial session took place on Tuesday, she and he would both be there. Back where they belonged. Already the last few days were taking on a dreamlike quality. It had been an amazing experience, every bit of which she'd enjoyed. Was she kidding? Her cheeks grew hot at the thought of the passion the two of them had shared, but she reminded herself it belonged to the past now. Like the sightseeing together and the scrumptious meal eaten in those last precious leisure hours. Real life beckoned.

Beside her, Keir rustled the pages of the *Montreal Gazette* as he focused on the newsprint. Maybe he, too, had filed their night of passion away under 'Completed Business.' Maybe she wouldn't need to worry about excuses and explanations. He probably took his pleasure whenever the opportunity arose, whereas she had ached to be held in his arms, longing for a few hours of oblivion, responding to the needs of her body without neighbours tweaking curtains or colleagues looking the other way as she approached.

But was she being one hundred per cent truthful? She recognised herself as a woman who didn't give herself lightly. Keir had murmured words of love, but didn't men do that in order to get what they wanted? In her case that short, significant phrase had trembled on her lips, daring her to utter it. She hadn't found the courage to do such a momentous thing. In the end, guilt inhibited her thinking, despite having found the kind of empathy she'd missed. Once again wearing her cloak of rationality, it was too soon for another love affair — far too soon after a marriage that, sadly, proved to have been a synopsis not a saga.

'Coffee, Dr Palmer?' The smiling cabin attendant broke Andrea's reverie.

Keir glanced up too. 'And for me, please,' he said.

The stewardess filled two cups. 'Enjoy,' she said as she moved away. 'I'll be back to take your luncheon orders. You can ring if you need anything before that.'

Was it Andrea's imagination, or had the woman's glance lingered a little too long upon Keir? She watched the svelte figure move down the cabin — hair seal-sleek, make-up immaculate, her long legs lightly tanned. Was she or wasn't she wearing tights? The flight attendant made Andrea feel like a pile of crumpled laundry, and after only twenty minutes in the air.

'So,' said Keir, 'is it OK for me to have my turn now?'

'Your turn?' Andrea turned to face him. 'Have I missed something?'

His lips twitched. 'I'm offering to do what men hate doing, Andrea. Unburdening my soul is a very rare occurrence.'

Oh, no. This shouldn't be happening. Their return flight was something entirely different from the outward-bound Montreal trip. A few days ago they'd been colleagues, fast becoming friends. Telling Keir about Greg had seemed the natural thing to do. Having stepped over the boundary and become lovers, she feared learning too much about him. Surely he knew how the script went? What was going on here? Her mouth dried and still he looked expectantly at her.

It was easier to say nothing. Easier to give a swift nod.

'If I still look married, I can't think why that should be,' he said. 'And I want you to know my failed marriage was mainly down to my own stupidity. Connie and I met through friends. We were each invited to their wedding and weirdly, were seated next to one another at the lunch, wedding breakfast or whatever these things are called.' He hesitated. 'There was an instant attraction. We established neither of us was really attached to our respective plus-ones. My then-girlfriend and I were fast realising we were going nowhere. Connie's escort was a cousin of hers dragged along when her boyfriend decided he didn't do weddings. Even as a guest.'

'Somehow I'd assumed you'd met your former wife at work.'

'No, and with hindsight, it was my work that drove us apart.' He folded his arms. 'That sounds like a convenient excuse but at the time, it seemed like the right thing to do. Work hard, work harder and turn round and do it all again next day, I mean.' He grunted. 'She got pregnant very quickly. I still don't know how that happened!'

'You don't? Did you miss the lecture on reproduction while you were at med school?'

'Sounds unbelievable, doesn't it? Seriously — I'd thought we would wait a few years before starting a family. My daughter's arrival somehow made me even more determined to climb the ladder. Eventually we moved to a house with attitude, but I didn't want to take the kind of holidays Connie coveted. It was all part of a package, in her book. Bigger and better.' He sighed. 'I don't think she was ever unfaithful to me. I just think when she and Naomi went on holiday and I stayed at home, it rang alarm bells. Made her receptive to another man's advances.'

He had a daughter and he didn't live with her. Andrea turned to face him. 'You didn't sit down together and try and work out a compromise?'

He shook his head. 'It sounds pathetic but no, we didn't. Fate had arranged for a single father to be on holiday with his two sons and staying at the same hotel. Connie returned and told me she'd decided to move away.' His flippant tone didn't match his grim expression. 'How about that for speed?'

'I'm sorry,' said Andrea. 'I can only imagine how you must have felt. I don't honestly know what to say.'

'There's nothing to say, Andrea. I'm not looking for sympathy. I obviously wasn't husband material. Now I regret not being around to see my daughter grow up, but I've no one to blame but myself.'

'It's usually six of one and half a dozen of the other, surely?' said Andrea softly. 'When a marriage falls apart, I mean.'

'I don't think it was ever really a marriage.' He sounded wistful. 'There was a huge physical attraction in the early days. Not a lot more than that, except for our daughter of course. I'm sure I don't need to spell it out.'

No, he didn't. Andrea realised with a pang, dismaying in its intensity, that he was spelling out his intention never to make another mistake like that one. But what was she thinking about? That meant good news for her, didn't it? They could each draw a line under the conference and everything that went with it. Of course Keir Harrison was every hostess's dream — unattached eye candy. It was the stuff of Jane Austen. It was manna for a society where people changed partners and where, even with so many women competing in the workplace and achieving success in their own right, that magical state of coupledom still beckoned like a traditional end of the rainbow image. Everyone wanted to believe in the happy-ever-after even if they knew it didn't always happen.

She realised Keir was watching her, his expression tender — loving, even. Her longing to be touched by him, kissed by him, held by him, overwhelmed her, disturbing her beyond belief. This just had to be a rebound thing — after Greg's death she'd been hit by shock. Anger followed numbness and grief — anger at the sheer waste of life. While realising the futility of doing so, she'd fretted and fumed over her widowed state and about Josh's loss. She kept the tears mainly to herself, grinding her way through the days and weeks and months until, now having a break from domestic responsibilities, she'd behaved like someone let loose from a nunnery. Love should not and could not be brought into the equation.

'Andrea,' said Keir, 'please. I didn't mean what I think you imagine I mean. I'm sorry that came out wrong. I didn't mean to sound bitter and twisted. What happened between us wasn't just a one-night stand. Not as far as I'm concerned, anyway.' He reached for her hand and wrapped both his around it. 'I don't care if anyone's watching.'

She felt him squeeze her fingers. 'I want you to know you've become a very important part of my life,' he said.

She gazed at the tiny screen monitoring the aircraft's steady progress eastwards. That spelt reality and she needed to stop him before he said too much. 'Please, Keir, could we just step back to where we were? Colleagues and friends, like we agreed, remember?' She neglected to remind him that would be like they agreed after their first sizzling kiss in the Hartnett lecture hall.

He removed his hands as if she'd scalded them. 'Are you going to tell me you regret what happened in Montreal?'

She bit her lip, still focusing on the tiny blip denoting their aircraft travelling through the skies but not seeing it.

'Look at me, Andrea,' he said. 'Look at me

and tell me what happened was all about lust.'

'Well, what else could it have been?' She steeled herself to turn her head and look at him. The pain she felt when she read the anguish in his eyes was too much to bear.

'Keir, I can't handle an affair. I have . . . you know precisely what demands I have on my time. There's no place in my life for intimate suppers and nights in hotels and all that stuff. Surely you must see that?'

'Do you not credit me with any common sense?' His calm tone contrasted the white knuckles betraying how hard his fists were clenched. 'I want to help you,' he said. 'How does that fit with your idea of a passionate affair?'

He didn't wait for an answer.

'Do you have any idea how fantastic it was watching you taking those photographs, talking to those animals, giggling at those jokey frog things in the gift shop? I've seen the fun side of Andrea Palmer and I want to help her hang on to it when she's back on home territory again. Don't use your work and your family as a barrier to shut me out, please. I care about you. I love you, Andrea. I've never been more certain of anything in my life.' Emotion tore holes in his voice.

'Excuse me.' Andrea rose abruptly and

moved towards the washroom. She needed time to compose herself. If the tears had their wicked way and she let him comfort her, the resolve to manage her own life would surely crumble. She needed to stay strong. He needed to remember just what a difficult road she followed. Hiding the pain of knowing she'd rejected him challenged her self-control. Her only hope was to tell herself he suffered from hurt pride rather than a broken heart.

When she slipped back into her seat, Keir sat staring at the cloudscape. She'd insisted they take turns to sit beside the window. Neither of them spoke until cabin service broke the awkward silence with drinks and food doubtless delicious, but the memory of which faded faster than Cinderella's sequins at midnight.

After their attentive stewardess cleared everything away, Keir placed his hand on Andrea's arm. 'I shan't pester you, but I beg you to reconsider this decision of yours. I can't force you to let me into your life. All I want to say is that our parents fade away and our children grow up and leave the nest. That's the scheme of things. Please don't throw away this chance of happiness without giving it serious thought. Please believe me when I tell you I've never felt like this before.

Whatever demons pursue you, I've got patience enough to help banish them.'

★   ★   ★

The late-night car journey down the M4 then on to Hartnett via Keir's imaginative but quiet route was accomplished with the help of the radio, driver and passenger each eagerly grabbing at the chance to lose themselves in someone else's life, someone else's dilemmas and decisions.

'I hope you don't suffer too much from jet lag.' Parked at her gate, Keir hauled her luggage from his boot.

She followed him as he carried her case up the pathway and waited for her to unlock the front door. He deposited the case inside her porch as if it weighed grams not kilos.

'Thank you,' she said. 'Thanks for everything. It's been great.'

They stood looking at one another until he stooped and picked up a small pile of mail from the doormat, handing it over with a quizzical look.

'You already know how much I've valued your professionalism over the course of the conference. I imagine you don't want me to remind you of anything else.'

She looked down at a gaudy flyer for a local

take-away food outlet. She could throw her mail back on the floor, put her arms around this man and feel him pull her close. He could stay the night. Kirsty didn't expect her until the following morning. It would be so, so easy. But that could not, must not be an option. Such an easy fix could only lead to heartbreak, and that was something to be avoided at all costs. Hadn't they both had enough of that to last a lifetime?

'Can I offer you something to drink?' She forced brightness into her voice.

His jaw tightened, the little lines showing his struggle to keep his self-control, his eyes betraying his hurt. 'No thanks,' he said. 'I'll let you get on. I hope Josh enjoys his gifts.' Keir's long legs took him down the path and through the gate in moments.

Andrea, hurting inside, almost called out to him, but he got back behind the wheel without a backward glance. Well, what did she expect? Changing her mind would only bring another set of problems, despite what he'd said.

She closed the door, locked it and attached the safety chain, only to lean against the wooden panels, allowing the tears she'd held off for most of the day to overwhelm her. She sank down on her knees and rocked back and forth. Wondering. Wishing. Regretting.

Next morning at breakfast time, Andrea pulled into Kirsty and Rafa's driveway. Almost immediately, the front door opened and Kirsty was hugging her friend hardly before she was out of the car.

'Hello, you.' Kirsty stood back and frowned. 'Andrea, what is it?'

'Oh dear, that bad is it? I'm obviously showing my jet lag.' Andrea hugged her arms around herself. 'I haven't had an amazing amount of sleep since I saw you last.' Horrified, she wondered if Kirsty would pick up on this.

'Hope it was all worth it,' said Kirsty.

'It was quite an experience,' said Andrea.

'I suppose you can always go to bed when Josh does tonight. Catch up a bit.'

They walked through the open front door and Kirsty closed it behind them. 'Come into the kitchen. The guys are outside and there's a treasure hunt going on but it seems complicated to me.' She pulled a face. 'Must be a man thing,' she said, putting on a deep voice.

Andrea laughed. 'How's it been? I know you kept me posted but I imagine there might've been a few blips.' She followed Kirsty through the hallway.

'Bedtime the first evening was a bit iffy.

Josh kept asking where you'd be sleeping, then how long it would take for you to get back if he needed you. There were a few tears, possibly because I mentioned Canada. I guess it dawned on him that he couldn't just have you back in a twinkling. Rafa was great though. He totally changed the mood — brought in a beautiful book of stories he'd bought without saying anything and tucked both boys either side of him while he read aloud.' Kirsty reached inside the fridge and took out a jug. 'I must admit I stayed to listen too.' She pulled out a tray of ice cubes.

'That doesn't surprise me,' said Andrea. 'Your husband could make an instruction manual sound like poetry with a voice like he has. It must be something to do with his accent.'

'I know. Anyway, both boys were mesmerised. When the story ended, Rafa lifted Luis into his own bed then we tucked them both in. I don't think either of those two little guys was far off the land of nod.'

'And the rest of the time?'

'Sweetie, it was fine. An occasional little spat but that's what happens between siblings. And our two boys are rather like brothers, don't you think?'

'They're really good mates, probably more so than some brothers are.'

'I hope,' said Kirsty, 'after the babe arrives and we've got over the first few crazy weeks, Josh will come and stay again.'

'Kirsty, you can do without the extra work. I wouldn't dream of imposing on you.'

'Rafa will be due paternity leave. And I'd like Josh to be part of it all. I hope he'll be another big brother for the baby.'

Andrea turned away to hide the tears she felt welling up.

'Oh, honey, I'm so sorry. I didn't mean to upset you.' Kirsty put her arm round her friend's shoulders. 'You're so brave. You must be exhausted after the last few days, standing up in front of all those people, missing Josh and thinking about your mum as well, knowing you. You need to let go sometimes. It's less trouble when Josh is here, believe me. They play so well together. He's a calming influence on Luis.'

Andrea fumbled for a tissue. 'I wish I didn't keep doing this. It was the thought of my son growing up without a dad or a sibling, I suppose. We're lucky to have all of you in our lives.'

'You're being human, is all. Now, go and bathe your eyes while I get a tray ready to take outside. We'll pretend the chocolate cake's homemade like the lemonade and we'll sit under the big umbrella.'

'If you'd found time to bake a gooey cake as well as make lemonade I'd hate you forevermore! I'll collect my goody bag from the car before I show my face though.'

'Sure you won't stay over?'

'Certain, thanks. I think it's best if I get Josh back to our routine. I'm sure he'd love to stay another night but I should take him round to visit Mum and Lizzie.' She smiled ruefully. 'I probably do need to get to bed early. You and I've been known to sit up till the small hours once or twice . . . '

'I doubt you'd achieve that the way I am these days. I'm not often vertical after nine o'clock. We'll have a girly evening some other time. Fix for you both to come for the weekend like we planned before the conference came up?'

'I'd like that. You're the only person I feel I can bore with personal stuff.'

Andrea missed the enquiring look her friend shot her as she headed for the front door. She longed to confide in Kirsty, but the huge step forward she'd taken with Keir followed by her decision to keep him at arm's length had left its mark. Some things were just too sensitive to discuss with anyone, let alone one's very best friend.

★　★　★

Keir faced a barrage of emails and phone messages as he settled behind his desk on Monday morning.

Lyn appeared. 'You look absolutely drained, Keir. What did they do to you over there?'

'Thanks for the vote of confidence, Lyn. They were brilliant over there. I . . . I just take a while to readjust to time differences these days.' He shrugged his shoulders. 'Getting older I suppose.'

'I doubt that. But I gather the conference took off, according to the comments I read online yesterday. I've emailed you the hashtag so you can look at Twitter.'

'Beyond the course of duty,' he teased. 'You know I hate that kind of stuff. I do try to keep up but it's great of you to remind me. I'm sure you've better things to do with your time.'

'I manage. Multi-tasking, you know?'

'I don't,' he said. 'Nor do I want to. I like things to happen in an orderly manner.' He shut his mind to the fact that somehow he ran out of clean shirts now and then.

Lyn pointed to the folder in front of him. 'That's a run-down of what's been happening in your absence but there's nothing desperate. A few requests to give talks, of course.'

He picked up a pen and rolled it between his fingers. 'I really need to speak to the trial team once I've dictated my notes from the conference. Could you contact Andrea?' The corners of his mouth drooped for a moment. 'Could you get in touch with Dr Palmer please? See if you can fix an hour or so for us to debrief everyone? Try and make it before or after the next clinic session, if possible. If you email the team, please tell them it's not vital they attend. It's just keeping them in the loop as regards the mood of the conference, feedback we received and so on.'

'Brilliant idea,' said Lyn. 'Otherwise, it's business as usual?'

But Keir, already reading his messages, hardly noticed his PA leaving. He took a sip of his coffee and realised it was as high-octane as she'd warned. Good. He needed all the help he could get, whether from his PA or from his old friend caffeine, just to face the day. Face the bleakness of the future, because that was how it seemed just then. All he wanted to do was jump in his car and drive round to the university. He fantasised about bursting into Andrea's office and taking her in his arms. He longed to nestle his face in her hair, breathing in her perfume and holding her close, assuring her he'd never, ever, let her go again.

Those days in Montreal seemed unreal now. His confidence, his pride and his belief in what he'd strived to achieve — how come it seemed so shallow? He'd missed out on happiness big-time by messing up his marriage. Now, having found someone with whom he believed he could forge a relationship, find joy even, it seemed still denied to him. What had propelled Andrea into his arms? He couldn't believe it had just been about sex. The connection between them wasn't something that switched on and off. She knew that as well as he did, of that he was certain.

Of course she still needed to mourn her late husband. He respected that. He'd no intention of trying to compete with a ghost. No way would he even try to replace Greg in the lives of Andrea and her son. But he wanted her to move on . . . move on with him. And he longed to meet her little boy. Josh was a part of his mother and a living reminder of a man Keir felt sure he'd have enjoyed getting to know. He had the weirdest of feelings about this, almost able to imagine the late Major Greg Palmer saluting him in approval. But how the heck could he tell Andrea that? It seemed like soap opera stuff, even though he hadn't watched one of the things in years.

Keir leaned back in his chair, feeling an immense weariness wash over him. He was being blocked out. He'd have to say something to Andrea when they next met. He'd have to find some way of being alone with her. Maybe, if he could actually put his arms around her and hold her, it would hit home that the two of them belonged together. That this was something much deeper than a tumble on a king-sized luxury bed. What they had went far deeper than any casual sex Keir had ever experienced, not that the list could by any means be called extensive.

Andrea had reawakened something in him he'd never thought to feel again and he wasn't willing to abandon it without a fight. Dr Palmer had better realise that. Maybe she missed those little but vital romantic touches that helped weave a foundation for happiness. He knew that much, just hadn't had the wits to put it into practice very often. Well, he'd see about that. No longer did he have to fight for recognition and reward. He'd never become complacent, but he knew he could afford to take his foot off the pedal occasionally. The trial still required a lot of his attention but he mustn't let this chance of true happiness pass him by, for both their sakes. The mission began now.

He buzzed for Lyn.

'You're still awake, then?'

He grinned and addressed the intercom.

'You bet. When you get a moment, could you let me have the number of that florist opposite the hospital, please?'

He leaned back in his chair and stretched both arms in the air. He wouldn't rush Andrea. But he'd show her how much he cared. How much she was in his thoughts. He'd been a tad abrupt with her since she dropped that bombshell on the flight back. Probably he'd come across as morose. He mustn't be selfish and expect her to react just as he wanted her to. Who could analyse a woman's emotions? Maybe, just maybe, he'd be able to convince her how his feelings for her went far deeper than those associated with being a colleague and friend. How he hoped Andrea would come to realise they had something pretty good going for them.

Suddenly he remembered the meeting he'd had with Rhonda Pierce in the park near the King George Hotel. He felt for his inside jacket pocket and took out her business card, holding it between finger and thumb. He'd no wish to leave his position at Hartnett General. But what if Andrea firmly refused to contemplate giving their relationship a proper chance? What then?

Thoughtfully, Keir opened the top drawer of his desk and dropped the piece of pasteboard inside. Rhonda would doubtless be in touch if he didn't email that CV of his to her. It could hold for the time being. This needed his full consideration and just at the moment he teetered on the brink of something life-changing. He hesitated. Maybe he'd keep Rhonda's details in his inside jacket pocket after all. He'd take it home and file it away. Just in case.

9

Richard Bailey arrived in Andrea's office doorway next morning, trying to pretend he wasn't clutching a cellophane-wrapped bouquet of perfect yellow rosebuds. 'Ahem,' he said.

'Richard, I'm sorry I missed you earlier.' She glanced up from her computer screen. 'Gorgeous flowers! Have I forgotten Louise's birthday or something?'

'No, indeed.' He held out the roses. 'Fortunately my wife isn't receiving bouquets from George Clooney, because these are for you. You won't even need to find a vase. See this goldfish bowl thing?'

She looked unconvinced 'You're saying these are for me?'

'Hey, don't shoot the messenger. I happened to walk by the desk as the receptionist was about to ring you. The local florist delivered them, apparently.'

'Goodness,' she said. 'Thanks for bringing them, but who on earth would send me flowers?'

'Maybe if you read the card?'

She placed her hands either side of her head. 'I think I'm still on Canadian time.'

'Speaking of which, I gather you and Keir are going to reveal to us everything you've been getting up to in Montreal.'

Andrea stared at him, a slow blush colouring her cheeks. 'Um, oh yes, of course. Sorry. Keir's PA got in touch yesterday. We agreed to do it tomorrow morning, before the patients arrive. The debriefing, I mean.' She looked down at her bouquet and tweaked the cellophane.

'Of course,' he said without batting an eyelid. 'How did things go while you were away? On the home front, that is.'

She raised her head again. 'Good, thanks. Josh had an amazing time, just a few first-night wobbles. As for my mother, I doubt she noticed I was gone.'

'But that's excellent, isn't it? Did she recognise you when you walked in?'

'She did,' said Andrea.

'Great stuff. Now, I must get to my desk and make a few calls.'

Andrea turned the beautiful arrangement around and found the tiny silver envelope stapled to the cellophane. Her heartbeat accelerated in a disgraceful manner. There was no reason she should receive such an extravagant gift.

Just to say thank you for everything . . . Keir

She could hardly complain about the message's wording. It was an entirely appropriate way for one colleague to address another. But the very fact he'd omitted to send love, or even mention their forthcoming meeting, couldn't hide what lay behind the brief bread-and-butter sentence. He'd made his wishes very clear to her on the flight home as regards their future relationship. She'd rejected him. Upset him. This wasn't merely a bunch of flowers. This signified a plea.

Taking the scissors from her desk drawer, she pierced the wrapping, releasing the fresh rose fragrance. It seemed as significant as a kiss. Why couldn't she unlock herself as easily? If only she could have met Keir further down the line, maybe a year or two from now. She ached for him but still felt convinced she'd made the right decision. To allow him into her personal life could bring nothing but anguish. Again she told herself her longing for him must be a simple case of rebound.

★ ★ ★

Keir looked up from his notes as someone walked through the clinic reception room door.

'Hello, Moira,' he said. 'I thought maybe I was being stood up.'

She dumped her bag on the table and walked over to him. 'As if. It's great to have you back again.'

He wished she wouldn't invade his space quite so blatantly, but it seemed churlish to step away. He was already positioned in front of the window. Doubtless some men would envy him, up close and personal with a woman whose figure was shapely and whose hair shone like new pennies. Keir had never been given to flirt excessively but the invitation in Moira's eyes was clear and present. It would be so easy to accept. But there was only one woman he wanted. The fact that she didn't seem to want him was something he intended dealing with. A dalliance with Moira, even with no strings attached, was not the way to further his case with the gorgeous yet troubled Dr Palmer.

Moira lifted one carefully manicured hand and leaned even closer. Close enough for him to catch a drift of sultry perfume. Whatever scent she used, it must be quite something. If he closed his eyes he'd never guess he stood next to a busy ward sister.

Her long fingers plucked at his jacket lapel. 'Just a stray thread,' she murmured.

'Good morning,' said a voice.

Keir could have wished the redhead to the other ends of the earth. Andrea stood just inside the doorway, briefcase in hand, smile seemingly painted on her lips. She walked over to one of the smaller tables and pulled out a chair before he could dodge round Moira and reach her.

'Andrea,' said the nurse. 'I do believe you're looking a little peaky. I hope Dr Harrison didn't work you too hard while you were in Montreal.' Her eyes gleamed. Her voice purred.

'We certainly didn't get much time away from the conference,' said Andrea, looking the nurse in the eye. 'There were lots of hands to shake — lots of talking, plenty of questions.'

'Well, I look forward to hearing all about it,' said Moira, moving away from Keir and patting her hair as two other team members arrived.

To the consultant's relief, Richard Bailey walked into the room and hurried straight over. 'Good to see you back safe and sound, Keir. Maybe we could grab a few minutes afterwards.' He looked at the others. 'Good morning, everyone. I'm going to sit down so these two can get started.'

Keir moved towards Andrea's table and put his notes down beside hers. 'OK if I perch here with you?'

'By all means,' she said, slipping a pale grey

envelope into his folder as though adding some information he needed. 'It's a note from a patient's carer,' she said.

Keir was conscious of watching eyes. 'Thank you,' he said. 'Now, Dr Palmer, why don't you describe how you saw off the dissenting doctor, otherwise known as Toronto Tom?' There was a ripple of laughter. He nodded at the rest of the team. 'That was no mean feat, I can assure you.'

He didn't find it easy, sitting beside her but apart from her. As she picked up on his lead, she kept her hands clasped on the table before her. From time to time he glanced sideways, admiring her profile. Her hair was drawn away from her face today, knotted loosely at the nape of her neck. She wore a navy-blue linen dress, enhancing her slim figure. They'd become so close, so quickly, in Montreal. Now she blanked him unless it was work-related. Surely she could trust him not to go blundering into her house and upsetting her son? That was the last thing he'd do.

He turned his attention back to what she was saying. Then came his turn to give the flavour of the conference to his colleagues. Yes, some of the questions had been tough. He thought they'd acquitted themselves well. Dr Palmer had anyway, he'd said self-deprecatingly.

The prof wanted to know the names of some of the attendees possessing a community medicine background. Andrea provided the answer. Moira asked a couple of questions about the general standard of Canadian care of the elderly. Andrea answered that one too.

At the end, Richard Bailey got to Keir first. Those needing to be ready to greet the first patients went next door to begin work. Keir noticed Andrea hesitating as he listened to what Richard had to say. He caught her eye and she nodded before leaving the room.

As soon as he was able, Keir hurried into the room where the trial patients were seen. No sign of Andrea. His attention moved to Moira, who was dealing with one of the trial participants. She was listening to what the woman had to say, nodding her head, smiling and cracking a joke. She was a terrific nurse and he knew he'd made the right choice by inviting her to join his team.

But now, she glanced up and saw him watching her. Swiftly he looked the other way. Inevitably one of the patients called out to him. Keir gave the elderly man his full attention.

As he moved away again, intent on returning to his office, Moira called to him. 'Leaving already, Dr Harrison?'

'You're all doing fine without me looking

over your shoulders,' he answered pleasantly.

Walking away, he knew she still watched him. Keir didn't turn around.

★ ★ ★

His PA had messages. Lots of them. There were a couple of referrals needing his urgent attention but as soon as he could, he slit open the envelope handed to him by Andrea. It was, as he'd suspected, a note written by her. She'd sent a polite expression of gratitude for the beautiful flowers, unexpected but nonetheless welcome, she said. He stared at the neatly written paragraph. She'd ended by sending *Best regards,* and signing her name below. That was it. No regrets. No apologies. No hope.

Was he supposed to back off totally? After the joy they'd experienced in each other's arms, Keir felt saddened by the polite words on the page. But why should he have expected anything different? Andrea had obviously drawn a line under the Montreal trip and clearly she expected him to do the same.

He worked until six p.m. Lyn had left an hour earlier. He wondered what he'd do with himself that evening, wished he could think of something to douse the restlessness within him. No way did he want to hit the whiskey bottle. That wasn't his style. Maybe he should take himself off for a walk.

He was almost at his car, still lost in his own dreary world, when he heard someone call his name. It was a female voice.

He turned around, his heartbeat overreacting to the sound. How stupid of it. Of course it wasn't Andrea calling him. She'd be at home with her son by now. If only he could be there with them.

The approaching woman arrived in a wave of freshly applied perfume. 'Hello again,' said Moira Haynes. 'I hate to be a nuisance, Keir, but could I ask a really big favour?'

'What's the matter, Moira?'

She was practically purring. She'd also perfected the iconic Princess Di upward glance. How long did it take to get that right?

She bit her lip. 'It's my car. That little blue one over there.' She pointed. 'I can't get the wretched thing started.'

'Forgive me, but are you sure you haven't run out of petrol?'

'Perlease! Believe me, the tank's half full.'

He shrugged. 'Cars aren't my forte, I'm afraid. Do you belong to one of the motoring organisations?'

She shook her head. 'Never got around to it, but I've already rung my garage and said

I've left the key under the seat for them. I just need a lift home now. You happened to come along and I thought maybe . . . '

'Not a problem,' he said, pointing his key at his BMW.

'Are you sure I'm not delaying you?' She did the upward glance thing again.

'Positive, except you'll have to give me directions. I don't have a clue where you live.'

'Well, at least we can put that right, can't we?' She placed one small hand on his arm and slid into the passenger seat as he held open the door.

He slung his briefcase on the back seat before settling himself behind the wheel. 'Good session today, I hope.' He avoided looking at her.

'Excellent,' she said, fastening her seatbelt. 'I'm so thrilled you wanted me on board.'

'Yes, well I had my reasons for selecting the team I did,' he said, turning the ignition key. 'It's not all about skills. It's about experience, judgement and intuition. It's the ability to engage with a person and gain their confidence.'

'I'm flattered,' she said.

He opened his mouth to protest he'd been referring to all the team but she beat him to it. 'It must have been a fantastic experience, going to Canada to the conference,' she said.

'I really envied Dr Palmer.'

'By the same token, there was an important reason for selecting her to accompany me. With respect, Moira, you don't have her qualifications.' Was he sounding petulant? Hastily, he tried to put matters right. 'Of course, if I'd needed to take a senior nurse with me, you, Susie and Jane would all have been in the running.'

She didn't answer. But as he turned to check the space behind, he caught the triumphant expression on her face. He had a feeling he'd been set up but he was in no mood for mind games.

'Which lane do I take at the lights?' Keir drove through the exit gates in second gear and entered the one-way system.

'The right-hand one, then it's straight on until you reach the big roundabout. I'll direct you from there. It doesn't usually take more than ten minutes.'

Neither of them spoke a word until Moira pointed out the exit lane he needed. Traffic was light and he drove straight on until she directed him towards a small estate of new-ish houses, each with a bite-sized front garden.

'That's Westbury Close. I'm right at the end. You can park in my space of course.'

He slowed down. 'That's OK. I'll just drop

you off and turn around.'

'Oh, but surely you'll come in for a drink, Keir? Unless you have somewhere else to be?' Those catlike eyes dared him.

He was about to say he'd work to do. But how sad that made him sound. Moira was by no means his preferred choice of company, but she probably got lonely too. He had a suspicion she'd been in a long-term relationship and its conclusion prompted the relocation to Hartnett. What harm could it do to be sociable and spend half an hour in her company? Without any further thought as to the signal he might be sending, he parked his car in the space she indicated.

★ ★ ★

Josh was in a grumpy mood. He chased his fish fingers round the plate. 'Can I have more ketchup, please?' He sneaked a hopeful look at his mother.

'Why don't you use what's on your plate first?' Andrea nursed a mug of tea.

Josh put down his fork and folded his arms.

'What's the matter, little mate?'

His lower lip jutted. 'I wish my daddy was here. You're no good at football.'

Ouch. 'I know, sweetheart. But when you start at the proper school there'll be loads of chances to play with other little boys and there'll be teachers and daddies to help you.'

'I'm a big boy. Uncle Rafa's ace at football.'

'Well, we'll be going to see them again soon, so you can have some more coaching.' She reached for the ketchup bottle and brandished it like a trophy. 'Do you want to eat up those peas and make room for a bit more tomato sauce? If you're keen on football, Uncle Rafa will want to know if you've been eating enough to help you grow big and strong.'

It did the trick. Josh even looked more cheerful. Andrea knew there would have been plenty of times when his dad wouldn't have been around to do all the father-and-son things the little boy could possibly wish for. But this would have been compensated for when Greg came home on leave. And, if fate hadn't decreed otherwise, she'd probably have been sitting opposite her husband at this moment, maybe switching off temporarily while the two males discussed whether the back lawn was big enough to erect one of those practice nets like Luis and his father had. It still seemed cruel, having happiness denied so close to the end of Greg's final tour.

She pushed the thought away. 'Brilliant, Josh. That's the way to build muscles. Would you like a pudding now?'

Life went on. She needed to remember she was a fortunate woman to have a son and to have such excellent care in place for her mother. Her mind drifted to Keir as she watched Josh select a carton of strawberry-flavoured yoghurt. She wondered how often the consultant managed to spend time with his daughter. Did they have regular contact? Maybe he had the technology in place at home so he spoke to her via Skype each weekend. She knew so little about his private life, and why would she? It had been a mistake to draw closer to him. She knew that now. Because how on earth could they expect to put back the clock, having overstepped that boundary? She could have wept. Instead she listened to Josh gabbling about a playground game. Her hands remained laced round her mug of rapidly cooling tea.

★　★　★

Moira came back into her pretty sitting room, wine bottle in hand, and wearing, Keir noticed with a flash of alarm, what appeared to be a black cling film top with tight white jeans.

'Sorry to keep you,' she said. 'I like to freshen up after work. Won't you change your mind and stay for supper, Keir? It's no trouble to whip up an omelette. I have to eat anyway and it's not often I have company these days. Let me top up your glass.'

He felt guilty, acutely aware he should have dropped her off and run. Fraternising socially with his team on a one-to-one basis didn't fit with his personal code, and suddenly he regretted having come inside her house. No way should he risk setting himself up for a compromising situation with the nurse some of his colleagues referred to in private as 'the honey trap'. He guessed they exaggerated but he didn't want to find out. Worst of all was his awareness of a sophisticated woman on her own ground and doubtless revelling in his discomfiture. Keir wasn't used to playing games, couldn't be bothered to flirt and felt out of his depth and just a tad irritated. He could do without this.

'I'm fine, really, Moira,' he said. 'I should be getting off anyway.'

She pouted. 'We don't often have the chance to talk in private and really get to know one another. Why not relax and have some more wine? I certainly intend to.'

He shook his head. 'You're the perfect hostess but I'm driving, don't forget.'

She leaned forward, holding his gaze. 'Why not relax? Take a taxi home later . . . if you must. We could enjoy each other's company tonight. Two single people. No strings, Keir. I don't cling. Nor will I ever kiss and tell.'

They gazed at one another. This was a quiet cul-de-sac, he thought. No one would know or care what he got up to. How strange life was. A few weeks ago, he might even have been tempted. He didn't particularly enjoy all those evenings on his own, nor did he appreciate being invited along to dinner parties as a convenient spare male to balance the numbers. He found making small talk torturous and he never knew half the names of the celebrities whom almost everyone but him seemed to have intimate knowledge of these days.

Moira sat back again and sipped her wine. 'Talk to me, Keir. Am I out of order here? Can I ask if you and Andrea Palmer are becoming an item?'

He sat up straight. 'Sorry?'

'I don't have to spell it out, surely? I do have some knowledge of body language, you know. It's quite obvious something's going on between you two. I especially noticed it this morning. You were seated side by side but you were both incredibly careful not to make contact with one another. If you're trying to hide something, it's actually not working.' Her smile was sly.

'Moira, I really don't know what you're talking about. Dr Palmer and I are close colleagues, nothing more. It's not been all that long since she was widowed, you know. And she has family responsibilities. Lots of plates to keep spinning.'

'Poor Andrea, yes, I am aware of her predicament. And I can understand how, kind and generous as you are, you can well do without the hassle.' She put down her glass and sat forward in her chair. 'You need someone uncomplicated to unwind with — someone who doesn't have a son to find a replacement father for. You and I are kindred spirits, Keir. Why not give me a chance? We could be very, very good for each other.' Her voice dropped to a purr.

He'd taken only two sips of wine from the half-glass she insisted on pouring for him. Now he replaced it carefully on the art deco coaster and got to his feet. 'Moira, I don't want to be rude but I really do have to go. I have some calls to make. You're a very attractive woman but I respect your professionalism too much to jeopardise it.' He paused but she made no response. 'To be honest, I don't think I'm the right man for you.'

She stood up too and came towards him, lacing her arms around his waist and snuggling against him.

'Enough!' He pulled away from her. 'Can't you get it into your head, Moira? I'm not interested.'

Her smile was no longer beguiling. 'You fool,' she snapped. 'Men don't turn me down, Keir. You've just made a very bad mistake.'

'No, Moira, I think it's you who's made the mistake. I don't involve myself with my colleagues. I'm sorry. Perhaps I should have made that clear before I came into your home.'

'Yes, maybe you should, Dr Harrison.'

He knew she found a certain pleasure in his discomfiture. He also knew he could be on rocky ground. Would she decide he must pay the penalty for doing what he'd considered to be a good turn? This was nothing like that impulsive, urgent kiss between Andrea and himself. This was far more dangerous, but for a different reason.

'I think I'd better leave,' he said. 'Let's go back to square one.' Even to his ears the remark sounded incriminating.

She pursed her lips. 'OK, fine. Whatever you say, Keir, but when you get back to that empty house of yours, just take a few minutes to think what you might be missing.' This time her smile was teasing, seductive and very, very knowing.

They walked into the hallway and suddenly she moved in on him again. Her mouth found his lips and she kissed him with a great deal of determination. But the memory of holding Andrea in his arms was too recent for him to co-operate. Keir froze. His arms remained at his sides and after a few moments she broke away and wrenched his jacket from the hallstand.

'OK, have it your own way,' she said. 'Good night, Mr Iceman. It was worth a try, I suppose. Thanks again for the lift.'

'I'm glad I could help,' he said, slinging his coat over one shoulder. 'I'm sorry, Moira. It's not that I find you unattractive, please believe me.'

'Goodbye, Keir,' she said and opened the door. 'Our paths will keep crossing. Some things you just shouldn't fight. You wait and see if I'm not right.'

★   ★   ★

Keir drove off, knowing he was too rattled to travel far. He left the close where Moira lived and on his way back into town, he pulled into a supermarket car park and drove to the far end. It was a relief to park and cut the engine. He leaned back against the headrest and closed his eyes. The woman was lethal. And obviously jealous of Andrea, which was absolute rubbish because Moira had a lot going for her too. Without the kind of responsibilities Andrea shouldered, Moira could have a great life.

He grinned as it occurred to him that was probably what she aimed to achieve. Though why she'd picked on him was a mystery. He didn't exactly have a reputation for being a party animal. But he enjoyed the company of an intelligent woman who was on his wavelength as much as he enjoyed discussions with not only his colleagues, but also the tradesmen he needed to employ from time to time. Keir had neither the expertise nor the time for DIY and had a great deal of respect for people who could hang wallpaper and paint ceilings without changing their hair colour.

He shook his head. Poor Moira. Obviously, when she approached him in the car park, he should have had the wit to tell her he was on his way to an important appointment before calling a cab for her on his mobile. The whole incident had been a total embarrassment for both of them. He'd obviously hurt her pride, but she'd made the overture. Just because he was single didn't mean he was constantly on the prowl. That criticism of body language and personal stuff about Andrea had been embarrassingly awful and he could only think Moira had temporarily lost control of her senses.

But hadn't he noticed her sideways glances rather a lot over the last few months? Ever since she'd taken up nursing at Hartnett and entered his orbit, in fact. Of course she'd done her homework and knew he was single and lived alone. His peers teased him about his so-called eligibility, but he believed he came over as uptight. He'd been entirely truthful with Moira though. He had no wish to be anything but Sister Haynes's colleague.

At once he thought of Andrea, who possessed equally strong opinions about her relationship with him. That situation differed entirely. She and he each recognised the erotic tension each of them created when around each other. He still felt unsettled, still wished he could talk to someone. He wished that someone could be Andrea. But unfortunately the only woman eager for his company was someone who made him feel he was being eyed up by a predator. The only woman whose company he longed for was one who'd made it painfully clear she wanted to be nothing more than his colleague and friend. Talk about sending in the clowns.

Keir glanced at his car clock. It was only ten past seven. He dug into his pocket for his phone and searched names beginning with the letter P. It was worth trying. He listened as the ringing tone began.

★ ★ ★

Andrea flung herself across the lawn, totally missing the white ball whizzing annoyingly through the air and way beyond her reach.

'Yay,' yelled Josh. 'I've won! I've won!'

'Yep. You're a star,' said his mother.

'Another go each?' Josh asked hopefully.

'All right, but then we need to get you in the bath.'

She'd just managed to kick the ball past Josh but with him still having scored twice the number of goals she had, when she heard her phone ringing.

'Bother,' she said. 'Josh, can you pick up your toys, please? I'll just see who that is.'

She ran in through the patio doors and picked up her mobile from the coffee table. 'Hello?'

'Is this a good time, Andrea?'

She gulped. Closed her eyes. Wished he could fly down the phone line to her. Correction — she longed for him to fly down the phone line to her. 'Um, it depends. Josh is just about to jump in the bath.'

There was a pause. 'I'm sorry. I didn't

mean to disrupt your evening.'

That rich, dark voice of his sounded so subdued. Suddenly she very much wanted him to disrupt her evening. She couldn't help herself, in spite of her pronouncements. Something must be wrong for him to ring her like this. He wasn't stupid. And nor was she made of stone, for goodness sake. 'Would you like me to ring you back, Keir?'

Again she noticed that hesitation.

'I was really hoping you'd let me call round and talk to you. But if you don't feel that's appropriate, I shall understand.'

'Right. Well, um, it sounds as though it's something you'd rather deal with as soon as possible?' He sounded anguished. She knew a lot about that state of mind.

'It is,' he said. 'It's an important matter and not something I want to deal with during working hours.'

'Where are you now?'

'In my car.'

She suppressed a chuckle. 'I meant how far away from here?'

'Ah, I see. Probably I'm about four miles from your house.'

'Why don't you come round after Josh is in bed? Give me an hour and I'll be sorted.'

'What if the doorbell wakes him when I arrive?'

224

'Josh can sleep for Britain,' she said. 'See you in a bit.'

Keir kept on staring at the phone in his hand. She'd agreed to see him. He put the phone away, suddenly remembering he was parked in a supermarket car park with an hour to spare. This was a golden opportunity to give his store cupboard a treat, if only he could remember what he'd run out of. If only he could stop hoping and dreaming.

10

'Sweet dreams, little one.' Andrea hugged Josh and left him listening to one of his favourite CDs. Already his eyelids fluttered but he shot her a smile, so heartrendingly like his dad's. Greg's son had inherited his long, dark eyelashes. It was odd how a small detail like a fleeting expression on Josh's face could unleash an unexpected deluge of love.

She sighed and went into her own room to change from T-shirt and shorts into a loose pink cotton top and black leggings. She pushed her feet into purple suede loafers and stood before her mirror to pull her hair from its scrunchie and brush out the tangles so hard for soccer players to avoid during a game.

When she walked downstairs, Josh already slept. She switched off his music and pulled his door halfway closed, arriving downstairs just as she heard the sound of a car pull up outside.

When she opened the front door, Keir, carrier bag hooked over one wrist, was paying off a taxi, which seemed very odd given he'd said he was ringing from the car when he called earlier. Instead of his well-cut suit, he wore a polo shirt and a pair of chinos, still managing to look smart.

As soon as he began walking up the path towards her, Andrea knew she was a hopeless case. It was pointless trying to pretend otherwise and she couldn't even greet him properly because of the flood of emotion engulfing her. She'd better get used to keeping these feelings of hers in rein.

'Hey,' he said. 'Are you all right? Andrea?'

She pulled herself together as best she could. 'I'm fine. Just a bit whacked after today. We had a game of football, then bath time — typical day really.'

'I'm sorry. It can take a while to get over jet lag too.' His eyes couldn't hide his concern. 'You should have told me to get lost. I didn't mean to make your day even more difficult.'

If only she could admit the truth. How much she cared yet couldn't commit. But still she held back. 'I'm sorry,' she said. 'I didn't mean to moan. Let's go into the kitchen and find something to drink.'

He thrust his hand into the carrier bag. 'I brought a bottle of wine and a few beers, just in case. They're still cold from the chill cabinet. I, um, did some shopping after I rang you, then realised I needed to drive home and put stuff in my fridge.'

That explained the taxi. 'I see,' she said. 'Well, that's very kind of you. First those fabulous roses, and now wine.' As soon as the words left her mouth she knew he'd probably think she sounded like a suspicious wife.

He shook his head and followed her into the kitchen. 'It's not a charm offensive,' he said. 'I didn't want to barge in empty-handed. Anyway, you've already thanked me for the flowers. You didn't need to write me a letter though.'

That dreadful, polite little note! She felt warmth rush to her cheeks. She knew this was one of the things Greg had loved about her — her ability to blush and turn his heart over. What was happening here? Whatever Keir needed to say, she must keep things on a strictly professional basis. It would have been better if they had met somewhere neutral like a coffee shop or even the park. But she had to admit that here, in her own home, it felt good to have adult company. Even though she wondered what could be important enough for Keir to see her away from the hospital or the university. Maybe it was to do with her mother's condition.

She remembered her manners. 'I'm afraid that was a very stilted little note,' she said, reaching for two glasses. 'I didn't want to send mixed messages.'

'I think I've got the message, thank you. It's whether I can change your mind about it that's the important thing. I can't go on like this, Andrea. And I need to be absolutely sure where I stand before making any decision about the future.'

It was the sincerity in Keir's voice, the voice capable of stealing her reason and dismantling her defences. His words caused Andrea's heartbeat to forget to behave as all well-behaved female hearts should. She took a packet of salted nuts from a cupboard and reached for something to empty them into. Her hand trembled as it closed around a small jug. Hastily, she replaced the jug with a bowl and hoped he hadn't noticed her flustered state.

'Let's go into the sitting room,' she said.

★   ★   ★

Keir waited for her to settle into one of the two leather armchairs either side of the hearth. He hesitated for a couple of beats, then sat down on the settee. It seemed to be the tactful thing to do.

'How did Josh enjoy his football game?' Keir's eyes focused upon a colourful framed photograph on the pine sideboard. It was undoubtedly the small boy and his dad, sporting identical grins. Greg seemed to radiate health and energy and Keir felt a pang of compassion for the fatherless family. How could he possibly persuade this lovely woman to let him into her life when she still fought grief?

'Enjoy is an understatement,' she said, sipping her Chardonnay. 'By the way, have you eaten?'

He felt a twinge of embarrassment. 'Um, no, but I had a decent lunch.'

'I'm going to need a sandwich soon so you're very welcome to join me.'

He forgot tact. He forgot to reason. 'I want to share more than a sandwich with you, Andrea.'

She put down her glass, her expression serious. 'We've already gone through this, Keir. I invited you here this evening because I assumed there must be something of importance you needed to say to me, away from the hospital.'

'You're not wrong about that. What I have to say is hugely important.'

'Then you have my full attention.'

There was that brittle, bright smile again. He ached to go over to her, gently draw her to her feet and hold her close. He forced himself to remain where he was but leaned forward, hands clasped.

'First of all, contrary to what people, including you, may think, I don't play the field or whatever today's equivalent of that may be. In other words, what happened between us in Montreal didn't happen as some kind of fling.' His voice dropped to a huskier tone. 'I happen to have fallen very deeply in love with you. And, at the risk of embarrassing you, I don't think you invited me to your room just for a bit of fun. I think . . . I hope you might be experiencing the kind of sensations I am. Forever kind of sensations.'

The last few words slipped out before he could stop them. He noticed she was looking down at her rings, twisting them round and round her finger.

'No way do I want to rush you,' he said, dropping the words like pebbles into a silent pool. 'No way do I have any intention of trying to replace Greg.' He watched the delicate line of her throat as she swallowed hard. 'That would be impossible.' His voice was gentler now, less urgent. 'Darling Andrea, I just want a chance to help you heal. I want to be around for you and I don't mean just take you out for dinner when you can find a babysitter. I'd like to get to know you properly and when I say you, I mean you and your family. Because . . . because I can't bear to have you in my life merely as a colleague. Not when there's so much more I want to be.'

She remained silent, eyes downcast.

'I know we haven't known each other very long.' He took a deep breath before continuing. 'But already we've shared a lot of experiences. You know how passionate I am about my career. I think you share that passion. You did a brilliant job at the conference. We maintained an entirely professional front and we can be the same now. We don't have to broadcast the fact that we're anything but colleagues until we, and I specifically mean you, are ready to do so.'

She looked up, eyes glittering with unshed tears. 'We hadn't spent the night together when we had to speak in front of all those people. Do you have any idea how hard it is for me to keep my emotions in check now? Do you not realise how much our private time in Montreal meant to me? This isn't all about you, Keir.'

'Do you think I don't understand because I'm a man? As it happens, yes I do know, because I'm struggling to do the very same thing, especially at this moment. For goodness' sake, if you'd just let me put my arms around you, wouldn't we both know the Montreal thing wasn't just born of the moment? Without a doubt, we both know it very obviously was not.' He picked up his glass and took a huge swallow. The liquid went down the wrong way, making him splutter and cough as he fumbled for a handkerchief.

Andrea got up and stood behind the settee to provide a couple of thumps on the back.

When he'd recovered himself he stood up too. 'What an idiot. I'm sorry about that. Thank you, darling.'

Her face crumpled and he rushed round the couch to stand at her side, taking her hands in his. 'What is it, Andrea? Whatever it is, let me make it better. Please!'

Once his arms were around her, he didn't care if he was trespassing on her privacy. All he cared about was trying to take the hurt away. It wasn't going to happen like lightning, but he so wanted to bring joy into her life.

Their mouths met in a tender kiss. He didn't try to take it any further but held her, breathing in her fragrance and closing his eyes, hands gently stroking her back and shoulders, lightly massaging her neck under the silky curtain of hair she wore loose that evening. *I've come home*, he thought.

To his dismay, she broke away from him and sat down. 'You're a very kind man, Keir,' she said. 'That's what makes this so dreadfully hard.'

He shook his head impatiently. 'I know it's difficult for you. That's why I want to help you. Can you not understand that?'

'Yes I can, but we're going round in circles.' She sounded more assertive and this time her gaze didn't waver. 'I'm not trying to deny I'm attracted to you. I think we both knew that when I tried to dash past you that first day at the lift. If I pull away from you, it's because it's for the best, Keir, not because I want to.'

He marched over to the window and stood with his back to it, arms folded across his chest. 'I'm sorry but that's absolute rubbish,' he snapped. 'Pushing me away when you admit you're not exactly desperate to escape from me.' His stern expression relaxed. 'It would be funny if only I didn't care so much.'

'I know, and it's because I care about you so much that I don't intend to burden you with me, my family and my personal baggage.'

'So that's it? Your decision stands. Do I have any say in this whatsoever?'

But she wasn't attending. She rose and walked over to the half-open door, cocking an ear. Then she turned back. 'It's OK. Josh must've cried out in his sleep. That still happens sometimes.'

Keir nodded. 'Poor little man, I'd love to meet him some time.'

'That's a big part of my concerns.' She walked closer to him but stood slightly out of reach. 'If I let you into my life, which is what the selfish part of me longs to do, then if something goes wrong between you and me, what's going to happen to Josh and, to a lesser extent, my mother?'

'Hell's bells, Andrea. I may not have been the perfect husband but I was motivated by the right reasons, or so I believe. I'm older, hopefully wiser, and more patient nowadays. I wouldn't turn up with a sack full of toys for Josh. I wouldn't expect you to let me stay over at night. I'd use my common sense and hope your little boy would come to love and trust me in time.' He spread his arms as if demonstrating their ability to encircle her and her family.

He still didn't try to approach her. 'I want to make a commitment,' he said. 'If only you'll let me. And what's all this about you being selfish? That's just downright crazy.'

Moira Haynes's hurtful words rang in his ears. She couldn't have been more wrong about Andrea casting around for a replacement dad, but he wasn't going to correct her. It was none of her business.

'I shall say it again. No way would I try to

235

take the place of Josh's father.' His voice was gentle. 'As for your mother, Rosemary seems to be enjoying a quality of life many people her age would love to achieve. That's without the possibility of improvement once the drug and vitamin combo really kicks in. You have to take the credit for that — you and Lizzie Dean if you like. Gold stars all round, Andrea. You're selfish? I don't think so.'

He spread his hands, his expression apologetic. 'Sorry to keep lecturing you, but I think there's another reason for this decision of yours. I don't think it's your emotions causing this barrier. You say it's too early for you to be with someone else, but the way you responded to me at the hotel told me the truth. Forgive me for saying this, but you told me Greg hadn't been home on leave for months when he lost his life. You felt cheated — resentful because he was so close to the end of his tour. That's understandable, but my guess is you'd been kind of mourning him, albeit subconsciously, before you received the terrible news.'

He feared he'd overdone things, but she looked at him now with a kind of recognition unseen before.

'It was always part of the package,' she said. 'Military wives live with a kind of half-expectancy of the worst scenario.' Her voice faltered. Then she whispered, 'I love him so much. That's not going to change, Keir.'

Keir felt the sting of his own tears. He stepped forward and placed his hands gently upon Andrea's shoulders. She didn't try to resist him.

'I know that, sweetheart. That love will always surround you. I don't have to spell it out, but I'm darned sure Greg wouldn't have wanted you to be on your own for the rest of your life. Not a caring, warm, fun-loving woman like you are. I'll tell you what I think, Andrea. I think you're afraid to let things go any further because you don't trust me. It's my past history, isn't it?'

'That's such nonsense, Keir.' She still didn't try to distance herself from him. In fact his feeling was that she'd moved just a tad closer. He breathed in the drift of light floral perfume but knew she must be the one to make the next move.

'Then prove it, darling,' he said. 'Let me love you. Let me into your life. It's where I want to be and you know it. I promise I shan't let you down. Don't fight me, please.'

For moments she stood there, like someone poised on the edge of a diving board, finding the courage to jump into a very deep pool. 'You're very persuasive, Dr Harrison.'

He caught his breath, noticing the glint of humour in her eyes. 'You're very beautiful, Dr Palmer,' he said, 'and very, very precious to me.' Still he waited. Still he didn't attempt to kiss her.

He could hardly believe it when she moved closer and wrapped her arms around him. Their lips met and her fingers stroked his ears, his cheeks and the nape of his neck before curling themselves in his hair. Their very special kiss deepened into a giddy kind of sweetness so they were both breathless when at last they broke apart. At once he hugged her to him again and rocked her gently in his arms, murmuring incoherent loving words as they stood on the brink of what he hoped would be a voyage of discovery with an ending they both wanted.

'I think I'd better make us that sandwich,' she whispered, her voice raw with emotion.

'I think you better had, too.' He nuzzled her ear, not wanting to let her go but knowing he mustn't rush her.

'Bring your drink through,' she said. 'Keep me company while I fix us a snack. We need to sort out a few things.'

He nodded, not trusting himself to speak. If he'd been unable to change Andrea's mind about their relationship, he would have gone straight home and emailed his CV to Rhonda

Pierce in Montreal. Andrea didn't need to know that. Not now.

'Ham or cheese?' she said with a straight face.

Keir sucked in his breath. 'Difficult decision! How about we go halves?'

Her laugh was a half-sob. 'All right, and how about I put some salad in? You consultants never eat enough green stuff.'

'That's most unfair. I'm very fond of that pizza topping with the spinach in it.' He found it unbelievably pleasurable watching her smooth spread on bread and lift sliced ham from a dish.

'We really do have to take things slowly,' she said. 'This isn't going to be a conventional kind of romance.'

He did his best to look hurt. 'Who said so? Don't you like being bought flowers and chocolates?'

'What I'm trying to say is, if I wasn't a mum, I could lure you to my boudoir tonight.'

'I wouldn't let you.' He folded his arms, the prim expression on his face concealing a surge of joy. 'I do have my reputation to think of, you know.'

She giggled. What a lovely, carefree, happy sound, thought Keir.

'I love you so much,' he said.

'I know. And I . . . I . . . oh, darn it!'

'Don't tell me you're already regretting your decision?' He pulled a lonely puppy-dog face and she laughed again.

'Definitely not, it's only that I keep on wanting to burst into tears.' She looked round for the box of tissues, waving a knife in her hand.

He got up and fetched the box from the worktop.

'Thank you,' she said, putting down the knife and pulling out at least six paper handkerchiefs.

He wanted to hug her to him again but decided not to crowd her. Retreating to his seat, he took a swallow of his beer. 'The tears are no bad thing,' he said softly. 'Letting them all out, washing away the grief, but holding on to the happiness you shared with Greg. He and Josh are part of you. I feel privileged to be here with you now. I'll never try to stop you remembering.'

She stood still, looking at him. 'Thank you for saying that, Keir.'

'I expect there'll be times when I say the wrong thing.'

She cut slices from a chunk of cheddar. 'We all do that now and then.'

Suddenly he thought of Moira Haynes again. So much had taken place that evening.

The nurse had tried to persuade him into beginning an affair with her and she hadn't been pleased with the outcome. He'd known that surrendering, even briefly, to Moira's seductive tactics would be a mistake even though she'd stressed the 'no strings' tag. Probably certain of his colleagues wouldn't have blamed him for losing his head and pleasing the lady.

In his turn, he'd pleaded with Andrea and cajoled her into seeing things his way. He prayed they were both doing the right thing. Instinct told him they were.

'Shall we eat in here?'

Already she was treating him like family and it felt good. 'No better place,' he said. 'I'll fetch your glass and top it up.'

As he headed across the hall, Keir noticed a movement at the top of the stairs.

'Daddy?' The little figure dressed in colourful jim-jams sounded half-awake . . . puzzled.

'I'm not your daddy, Josh,' Keir said tenderly. 'Just wait there, little mate, and I'll fetch your mummy.'

Andrea had her head in the fridge while she put things away.

'Josh is awake, darling.'

She swung round. 'Is he crying?'

'No. He's waiting on the landing for you.'

'OK.' She headed for the staircase. 'I'm here, baby,' she called. 'Did you have a bad dream?'

'No,' Keir heard the little boy reply. 'My eyes kept opening. Who was that nice man, Mum? Can he play football?'

It was hard to know what to do for the best. No way did he intend following Andrea upstairs, even though Josh's last remark brought a smile to his lips. And suddenly he felt ravenous. Maybe he'd drink another beer. After all, he was planning to take a taxi home, unless he walked. It was a lovely evening and the exercise would do him good.

He looked longingly at the plate of sandwiches, then went to the fridge and took another bottle from the pack he'd brought. He looked around for something to open it with. Andrea had produced an opener earlier. Yes, there it was on the worktop. He prised off the metal top and poured the lager into his glass. If he felt a little lightheaded it was more to do with what took place this evening than with alcohol, of that he'd no doubt.

He couldn't detect any sound from upstairs, nor could he hear any traffic noise. Suddenly he heard his mobile phone bleep out its signal. He'd left his jacket draped over the back of a chair in the sitting room. On his way to retrieve it, he glanced upstairs. There

242

was no sign of Andrea and he guessed she was settling Josh back to sleep again. It was Murphy's law — you mention something predictable, like her son's good sleeping record, and you'll surely be proved wrong. It didn't matter. That was what parenthood was all about. Even he knew that.

He called up the text message.

Sure you won't change your mind?

Keir frowned. He'd no idea who'd sent this and at first his thoughts flew to Rhonda Pierce. He'd given her his phone number at her request, but he hadn't been in touch since. She probably still expected him to send his CV — résumé, as she'd called it. Now that Andrea had reversed her decision about her relationship with him, the last thing he intended doing was apply for a job in another country. No way would Andrea want to move so far away from her mother. Anyway, it was bad enough having his daughter living so far away without compounding the problem.

He hadn't the foggiest idea who might have called him. But the number wasn't an international one and he decided someone must have punched in the wrong digits. He deleted the message and wandered back to the kitchen. Andrea appeared almost at once.

'I'm so sorry about that,' she said. 'You should have started eating. I wouldn't have minded.' She offered him a sandwich.

'It's fine. I poured another beer. How's the little chap?' He tried not to tear into his snack.

'He's asleep again. He wanted to know who you were so I told him you were a doctor, too, and that we'd become friends and I'd find out if you could play football.' The words came out in a rush.

Keir was in mid-bite. 'Brilliant.' He hesitated. 'When Josh saw me first, he called out, thinking I was his dad. I hope I didn't upset him.'

'Not at all,' she said. 'I expect he was taken aback at seeing a man in the house. He was wide awake and a bit annoyed with me for not having your soccer credentials at my fingertips.'

Keir got up, went round the table and folded her into his arms. 'There's so much we have to learn about one another. I may yet astound you with my goal kicks.'

She snuggled against him. 'When shall I see you again? Apart from at the hospital, I mean.'

He didn't even want to think of leaving her that night. 'I'm not going anywhere. What I mean is, I'll be around, so why don't you let me know and I'll fit in with you? I admit it sounds desperately sad, but my social life's virtually non-existent.' He reached for another sandwich. 'These are seriously good.'

She laughed. 'That's only because you're hungry.'

'I'm not half as hungry as I'm relieved,' he said, starting as his phone beeped again.

'You'd better check it,' she said. 'In case it's something urgent.'

'It's only a text — I'd expect to be rung if it was an emergency.' He frowned, his voice tailing off. 'This message can't be meant for me. Someone must have got my number by mistake — transposed the digits or whatever. I'll just delete it. The same thing happened earlier while you were upstairs.'

She took a sip of wine and reached for another sandwich. 'This'll do me, if you want to eat the rest.'

He grinned. 'My appetite's returned with a vengeance. Sorry.'

'And I'm sorry for any anguish I caused you, Keir. We've probably both had enough of that for a lifetime.'

He smiled at her and reached for her hand.

'You must come and have supper with us soon,' she said. 'Maybe not until after I've talked more about you to Josh.'

'I'd like that very much, but only when you feel the time's right, Andrea. I meant every word of what I said.'

'I know,' she said. Softly, softly . . .

His longing for her constricted his throat and robbed him of speech. The wonderful part was anticipating the joy he knew awaited them just around the corner. She watched him clear the plate, a little smile curling the corners of her mouth. He felt as if he'd truly come home.

* * *

It wasn't until later, when Keir searched through his list of contacts so he could ring the taxi firm he always used, that he discovered something odd. Immediately before Hazelwood Cabs a woman's name had been inserted. Keir stared at the letters in amazement. Haynes, Moira now sat among his stored numbers.

He called the taxi company then put his phone away again, shaking his head.

'Keir, is there a problem?' Andrea was sipping mint tea. He'd politely declined.

'No, it's fine. I was only thinking it's great to have your number tucked into my phone and not simply for business reasons.'

'And there was me just looking forward to my good-night kiss. Would you prescribe such a thing for me, Doctor?' She put down her mug and stood up. 'Unless, of course, you've had enough of me for one night?'

He rose too, folding her into his arms and kissing her very thoroughly. When he finished, he repeated the prescription.

'Mmm' said Andrea.

'You'll need more of those. Many more,' he said. 'I recommend starting from tomorrow.'

'Yes, Doctor.'

'Maybe you'd better have a booster now, just in case.'

This kiss was going to make it extremely difficult for him to tear himself away. They'd travelled a long way since Montreal, and not only in air miles.

*   *   *

Keir didn't touch his mobile phone until the cab dropped him off and he'd unlocked his own front door. He kicked off his shoes and walked through to the kitchen where he ran the cold tap and filled a pint mug, drinking half straight away. He sat down at the table, staring at the remaining water, lost in thought.

He didn't need rocket science to figure out how Moira's number came to be saved in his phone. He'd taken off his suit jacket and hung it in her hallway. She'd said something about needing to visit the bathroom and probably carried out her sneaky trick while he

247

sat alone in her sitting room, wondering what the devil he was doing there.

He clenched his jaw, imagining her fingers riffling through his coat pockets, finding the phone then adding her own number. She'd taken a chance. What if he'd decided to make a call and discovered her? Fortunately she'd failed to disrupt the magical events following his visit to her house. Nothing else mattered. If the nurse had rung him while he was with Andrea, instead of texting, he wouldn't have recognised the number, but what if he'd answered? That could have been awkward. No way did he make his personal number known to any of the nurses. Nor did he keep any of their contact details in his phone. His PA did all that stuff at the office and very well too.

Keir decided the best way to make a statement was to remove Moira's number and say no more. He jumped as he reached for the phone because it beeped, disconcerting him, so that he picked it up with a feeling of foreboding. He accessed the latest message, relaxing at once when he saw who'd texted him.

Night night. Love, Andrea XX

One day soon, please let her admit her love for him in three important little words. Maybe she needed to write them before she actually said them. He loved her so very much and he could be patient, feeling as he did that everything would work out for them in the end. He sent his own tender response, then called up his contacts and deleted Haynes Moira from the list. Hopefully that put an end to the matter.

★ ★ ★

Andrea drove to work next morning, having left Josh at the university crèche as usual. The little boy hadn't mentioned anything about the nice man who spoke to him the night before, and he'd slept right through till morning after she settled him down again.

The brief but delicious interlude shared with Keir had convinced her she was ready to take their relationship a step further. She smiled to herself, thinking of the way he'd convinced her to take down the barricades. Once their close friendship became common knowledge, which doubtless would happen sooner than either he or she would wish, there'd be people tittle-tattling, some declaring it was too soon for her to begin seeing a new man. Often, people suddenly made single as she had been swore they could never love again, having found the right partner first time around. But everyone held different views.

She'd battled her own emotions right from that first day when she'd almost ploughed into Keir by the lift. The way their eyes had met ... Looking back, her reaction told her it could be possible for her to find happiness again. She'd used her little son and her mother as excuses, but fortunately Keir had unlocked her capacity to love as well as talked sense into her. He was absolutely right. It would have been terrible to pass up on this chance. He seemed happy to let things happen slowly. All of a sudden she longed to see him again; wished they could sneak away from their jobs and steal a day together. This was silly. She was acting like a besotted teenager. She felt even happier than she had when spending time alone with Keir in Montreal. That had been merely an interlude. Now their future lay before them and it had every chance of proving to be a happy, secure partnership.

There must be something extra bittersweet about a second-time-round relationship. Now that she knew she would never stop loving Greg and it was perfectly in order to do so, as well as express her feelings for Keir, she could consider herself twice blessed. It would be great for Josh, too, growing up with someone around to stop him relying too much on his mother. She smiled to herself as she thought of her clumsy attempts at playing football. Gut feeling told her Keir would be a great role model.

She squeezed her car into a space near the prof's vehicle and grabbed her bag. Richard had beaten her to it this morning and it was time she arrived at her desk. Meanwhile she'd hug her precious secret to herself. Next time she was alone with Keir — really alone, with no one to hear it but him — she'd tell him how much he meant to her. He deserved to hear the words, and only now did she consider it right and proper to say *I love you* and mean it.

Josh had a sleepover invitation for the following weekend. He'd be staying with a family who helped Andrea tremendously in those first dark days when she needed someone living close by, someone who could look after her little boy while she dealt with the unwelcome but inevitable formalities. Josh was as at ease with this family as he was with Kirsty's, and it would be a chance for Andrea and Keir to spend a precious evening together, maybe even a night.

She repeated the words to herself as she strode towards the building where her department was housed. Her silent *I love you* flew from her lips. Next time she said it, she wanted Keir to hear it for himself.

Oddly enough, it didn't feel at all strange. It felt totally right.

11

Andrea read the email and gave a wistful smile. That would teach her to be presumptuous enough to imagine Keir packing his jimjams for a sleepover. Instead of Josh spending the night at his friend Dan's house, Dan's mum had sent a message apologising for changing the plan. A family crisis meant she needed to drive to Devon.

Would it be too soon to introduce Josh to the man she loved? She felt oddly nervous about the idea, even though she had in mind purely a friendly get-together. Lost in thought, she jumped when the prof appeared at her desk.

'These trends are thought-provoking, Andrea,' said Richard, looking over the top of his specs at her.

'Only to geeks like you and me.'

He chuckled. 'Yes, and only I know how much hard work has gone into them. When it comes to digging out detail, I can't think of anyone better than you. You have a forensic mind.' He peered at her. 'Have you changed your hair style or something?'

'Um, no.'

'It's just that there's something different about you. You seem to have a bit of a glow, if you don't mind my saying.'

'I'm taking a lot of exercise these days,' she said hurriedly. 'Josh has aspirations towards the England football team, which means I have to train too.'

'Hats off to you then. Josh is lucky to have . . . Oh heck, I was about to put my size elevens right into it. I'm so sorry, Andrea. Fine friend I am.'

'Don't beat yourself up. You know I don't want you or anyone else to be treading on eggshells every time we talk. Josh and I are lucky to have you and Louise in our lives.'

He beamed. 'Speaking of my lovely wife, she came home yesterday evening with an interesting piece of gossip.'

Andrea raised her eyebrows. 'You're a bad lad, Prof! Is it anyone I know?'

'Well yes, as it happens.' He lowered his voice. 'You know Louise is a friend of the hospital? She did her fortnightly stint on the desk yesterday. Afterwards, she was heading towards her car when she noticed Keir Harrison striding along ahead of her.'

'Uhuh.' Andrea hoped her body language wouldn't give her away.

'Apparently he stopped at the desk the

254

previous time she was there and made himself known to her. I'd mentioned to him about my wife putting in a few hours at the hospital every now and then.'

'He's always very good at singling people out,' said Andrea, wondering where this was going. 'He puts people at their ease.'

'Indeed. Anyway, Louise almost called out to him, just to say hello, but somebody else beat her to it.' He leaned forward. 'A pretty woman with red hair and good legs, Louise's words, not mine, approached him and well, seemed to be pulling all the stops out. Lou said it was the best impression of a damsel in distress she'd seen in a long while. And it worked. The woman was literally hanging on to Keir as he helped her into his car. Lou saw them drive off together. So, how about that then? No prizes for guessing who the redhead was.'

Andrea felt as though a knife sliced slowly and irrevocably through her heart. But wasn't she being stupid? Keir must have been leaving work. If Moira Haynes had been in some kind of trouble, Keir, gentleman as he was, wouldn't hesitate to help. But hanging on to him like that? Suddenly she recalled the way Moira had conducted herself the very first time she'd met her. Andrea had decided the nurse ticked all the boxes in terms of being a man's woman, and got the impression while Moira chatted to her that the redhead's mind was somewhere else and somewhere a lot more interesting. Not, however, while she performed her nursing duties. To be fair, you surely couldn't fault Moira's professional expertise.

'It's easy to jump to conclusions,' said Andrea calmly. 'Look how Keir assumed there might be some romantic involvement between you and me. He couldn't have been more wrong. Imagine how embarrassing it might've been if he'd made his suspicions known to other people.'

The prof took the hint. 'Touché,' he said. 'I'm sure you're right. I sincerely hope it was just a one-off lift. It would seem Keir's had enough trouble in the romance department. Although I suppose if he had a bit of a fling with Moira, it'd probably brighten up his life. As long as they were discreet about it,' he added hurriedly. 'These things happen and they're both unattached.'

'Is that all for now then, Richard?' Andrea wanted to get on. The prof could be a bit of an old woman sometimes with his liking for juicy titbits of gossip, but no way did she intend telling him just how wrong he was. She'd probably sound like a lovesick teenager confessing a crush, and no way would her boss be capable of keeping that morsel of information under his hat.

'May I hang on to this?' He waved her piece of paper at her.

'Of course. I need to look over the latest results for the trial patients now so I'll be next door if you want me.'

'Well, keep an eye on Dr Casanova later, won't you?'

'It's not *Holby City* over there, you know,' snapped Andrea.

Richard looked up in amazement as his research fellow strode out of his office. Her glare would turn a man to stone at ten paces. He winced as she gave the door an uncharacteristic shove.

★ ★ ★

The patients and their carers filtered into the clinic. Moira Haynes was taking her turn to note their attendance, sitting at a small table near the entrance when Andrea arrived.

'Dr Palmer,' said the nurse, giving her a sweet smile. 'How are you today?'

'Fine, thanks, Moira.' Andrea's tone was cool. 'I'm looking forward to this next phase.'

'I know. It's so exciting, isn't it? Keir's amazing, the way he's driving things — all the attention he's created.'

'Indeed,' said Andrea. 'Teamwork's important as well, though.'

'I know. I sometimes wonder if he should delegate more than he does. I was only saying to him last night, when he was round at mine, that I thought he looked a bit tired. I offered to cook supper for him, you know. I told him he should unwind more but — men, what are they like?' She smirked.

Andrea would like to have wiped the silly smile off the nurse's face. She pictured herself hurling a custard pie directly at Moira, then watching as the glutinous mess rolled down each smooth cheek. How childish was that? But what the other woman said didn't tie up with Andrea's experience. Moira's hinted cosy evening with Keir, if it took place anywhere else but her imagination, must have been short-lived. But why hadn't Keir mentioned this visit to Moira's home if it was entirely innocent? She knew she shouldn't let Moira get to her, but a tiny seed of suspicion had been planted.

'I'm not late, am I?' Keir stood, briefcase in hand, immaculate in light grey trousers and lilac and white striped shirt with a dark purple tie.

Andrea's heart did its hop, skip and jump act. She managed to nod in friendly fashion at him, trying not to notice the subtle whiff of citrus and the images it invoked. 'You're not late at all,' she said.

Her eyes moved back to the woman seated at the table. At that moment, Andrea's life still contained an extra dimension, a man-shaped one, and someone with whom she hoped she could find happiness again. She watched with mild curiosity as Moira reached into her pocket and produced a small card, placing it on the surface before her like a gambler playing a trump.

A glance to her left showed Keir watching too. Except his expression displayed not mild curiosity but something verging on panic.

'I believe this is yours, Keir,' said Moira in honey-dipped tones. 'It must have dropped from your pocket while you were at my place last night. Maybe when you took off your jacket? I hope you haven't spent time searching for it. Perhaps I should have rung to let you know where you'd left it.'

How could this be? How could her fragile new happiness crumble so quickly? Like a spectator at a tennis match, caught in slow motion, Andrea turned her head away from Moira and looked back at Keir, noting his still stricken face. A light seemed to click off within her even as a part of her — the practical, sensible part — suspected something very odd about all this. At that precise moment, all she wanted to do was run away and get out of the room before she did or said something she might regret. Except her feet seemed stuck in concrete.

Wide-eyed, Moira looked from one to the other. 'Naughty of me, I know, but I couldn't resist typing Rhonda Pierce into my search engine. With those looks, I reckon she could easily be a model. It appears she's a very high-powered lady — but then, I suppose you met plenty of those in Montreal.'

Andrea watched Moira's gaze flicker between Keir and herself. The nurse was behaving so unprofessionally, so blatantly out of order that she remained lost for words. Why would Moira attack in such a cruel, well-orchestrated manner unless she had revenge on her mind? To her knowledge she'd done nothing to upset the nurse, in which case Moira had it in for Keir. Could he have said something about his feelings for Andrea? But Moira couldn't possibly know how things had moved on regarding their relationship. This wasn't the time or place to make an explanation. There was work to be done.

Keir obviously felt the same. 'I'll be around for an hour if I'm needed,' he said. 'It's a good opportunity for me to speak personally to some of the patients. Excuse me, please.'

He smiled at Andrea but all she could offer

was a tight, frozen smile in return. Moira, meanwhile, greeted the next patient, arriving arm in arm with his daughter. Andrea followed Keir's example but distanced herself from him. She couldn't help but feel angry. It wasn't like him to be rude, but he'd made no attempt to put Moira in her place. He must know how upset Andrea would be, yet here he was carrying on his day as usual. At that moment, their relationship still so new, all she wanted was for him to reassure her. Yet it didn't seem to be happening. Doubt crept into her mind.

★ ★ ★

'Pick up the phone! Pick up the phone, Andrea, please.' Keir prowled the length and breadth of his kitchen. This was such a nightmare. He'd already tried her mobile and discovered she'd switched it off. He'd jumped into his car and driven to the university in his lunch break, ignoring the lift and pounding up three flights to arrive, breathless, in her office. Andrea had gone out for an hour. Keir couldn't hang around. His next appointment was in 45 minutes and no way could he cancel a prearranged meeting with the head of the local authority social services.

Andrea's voice mail requested him to leave

a message after the tone. Keir forced himself to speak calmly. 'Andrea, this is Keir. Could you give me a ring please? I need to speak to you urgently.' He closed the call. He knew she was there. She must be. She was there and she was hurting. And no wonder, given the way they'd parted company the evening before, having allowed their feelings for one another to take them to another level of their relationship. He'd felt as if everything was right in his world, once he'd convinced himself he hadn't dreamed the whole thing.

Now, through the mindless jealousy of scheming Sister Haynes, Andrea's confidence in him, which he'd been thrilled to see beginning to blossom, was shattered. He pictured again that forced smile she gave him before she walked away from Moira's nasty web of half-truths. She'd gone over to speak to her mother and that pleasant woman, Lizzie Dean. Rosemary's condition didn't appear to be deteriorating. Keir had spent time with her after Andrea moved on to another patient, though Mrs Tarrant still seemed to think he was some kind of friendly bystander. No matter. What did matter was Andrea's state of mind. If she wouldn't let him explain everything to her, how could they go forward as they'd decided in such loving circumstances only less than 24 hours before?

He wanted a drink, quite badly as it happened. There was some medicinal brandy in the cupboard and a few beers in the fridge. But he mustn't indulge. He still contemplated driving over to Andrea's house to see her. She'd have to let him in, surely? She wouldn't want to risk the neighbours or Josh wondering what the doorstep discussion was all about. She might yet ring him back. She might be sensible enough to realise how he'd been set up. Or would she? She'd been through too much over the last months. She didn't need this sort of thing. It was precisely the kind of incident to make her reassemble the barricades, and who could blame her?

Keir was in two minds whether to blow the whistle on Sister Haynes, although behaving as she had sent a clear message. She was a very lonely and sad woman who had to be pitied. But why the heck did it have to be him she fixated upon? What she had done was tantamount to stalking. Yet, if only Andrea would let him explain every bit of the whole stupid mess, he'd forgive Moira. Because that would mean that future happiness for Andrea and for him still remained possible.

To think he'd accused Andrea of not trusting him. How laughable was that? He'd insisted he longed to become part of her life — next day she hears he was round at

Moira's house before asking for an invitation to hers. Then up pops Rhonda Pierce — high-powered, glossy, foxy Canadian lady. He had, even to his own ears, been made to sound like a love rat. There were plenty of them around, but surely Andrea wouldn't believe he'd hit the high spots with two women in the same evening?

Suddenly Keir remembered the day he'd spoken to Susie McIntosh with regard to joining the drug trial team. Susie's comments about her colleague had been, well, guarded to say the least. Nobody ever had anything detrimental to say about Moira's work. But, now he thought about it, nobody ever mentioned her in the context of friendship, nice nature or helpfulness except in a strictly professional capacity.

If Andrea wouldn't allow him to explain his version of events then he'd have to find some other way of putting matters right. If Susie could offer proof as to Moira's dubious track record, surely Andrea would take her word?

Suddenly he felt very tired. His emotions had taken a bashing as well as Andrea's, and maybe this was fate's way of telling him to keep away from romantic involvements. Keir wandered over to the fridge and took out a beer. To hell with it — he might as well have a drink while he waited to hear from Andrea.

Surely she wouldn't ignore the closeness they'd already shared?

★ ★ ★

Andrea and her son were sitting in a café eating ice cream. Luscious vanilla ice cream topped with hot fudge sauce, the whole concoction sprinkled with chocolate vermicelli. They'd eaten tomatoes and bacon on a grilled bap apiece before the decadent dessert. She frowned, recalling the last time she'd used that expression. On that occasion she'd been seated opposite Keir, at the restaurant in the French Quarter where he took her on their last night in Montreal. She'd always been scornful of people using the term 'rollercoaster ride.' It was such a cliché. But right now, she couldn't think of anything to surpass that expression to describe what had happened to her since joining Dr Keir Harrison's team.

He'd seemed so sincere. *Stop it, Andrea!* She swallowed another mouthful of ice cream, enjoying the gloopy chocolate heaven in spite of her churning emotions.

'This is lush, Mum.'

'It certainly is, Josh. Don't expect it too often,' she said. 'This is a special treat today because I'm so pleased with Gran's progress.'

'Are they making her better again? Will she be able to take me to the park soon?'

'Probably not, sweetheart.' She patted his arm. 'Sorry. What we're hoping is that she won't get any worse. She's quite old, you know. That's why we're trying to help her.'

'Will she die soon?' Josh wore a smear of fudge sauce on his chin. Andrea felt love well up inside her. Death had danced into their lives when Josh was far too young to lose his dad. No way should she be putting a new relationship ahead of her son. She should have known better. What kind of a mother was she?

'Mum?'

'Oh, I hope not, Josh. But dying is something that happens to all of us one day,' she said, trying to sound matter-of-fact. 'Your dad was in a high-risk occupation.' She swallowed. This was getting heavy. 'You remember Aunty Kirsty's dog dying?'

'Luis cried loads. Nearly as much as you did when Daddy died.'

'I know. Sometimes sad things happen and people don't cry. Sometimes they do. I can't explain it. It's all about something we call emotion.'

'Are you sad, Mummy?'

For a moment he sounded ridiculously mature. Andrea took her serviette and wiped his chin. 'How could I possibly be sad when I'm with you, scoffing chocolate sundaes? When we've finished, how about we go to the park and see what the ducks are up to? Then it's home to bed. Saturday tomorrow, so no work for Mummy.'

'Wicked,' said Josh. 'Can we go to Auntie Kirsty's? Please, Mummy?'

Why not? It seemed the perfect solution. The thought of Keir turning up on their doorstep did not appeal. She couldn't bear the thought of her emotions in the blender again. Andrea took out her phone and called up her friend's number.

'It's ringing, Josh,' she said. 'But if they're busy, we'll find somewhere else to go. Somewhere you can run around and have fun. That's a promise.'

She was wondering which of Josh's little friends might be free to come along with him, when Kirsty picked up the phone. Moments later Andrea gave her son a high-five. Their day out was arranged and they'd be well away from Hartnett, just in case Mr Wolf came calling.

★   ★   ★

Keir spent a fractured night agonising about his next move. He even wished Andrea would

267

ring him and give him a tongue-lashing. Anything would be better than this awful silence hanging like a toxic cloud between them. Imagining her deleting his answer phone messages hurt more than he would have believed. Also on his mind was the meeting he'd attended that morning. Everyone had cost-cutting as a prime target. Keir's trial was a matter of great interest and at this point in his life, whatever else was changing into a pear shape, his career seemed right on course. It was ironic. Despite all his hard work and his recognition of his former mistakes, a happy, lasting relationship still appeared as likely as him winning an Olympic gold medal.

Seated at his kitchen table, drinking yet another cup of tea, Keir resolved to write a letter to Andrea, then get in the car and deliver it to her house. If she didn't answer the doorbell, he'd push the envelope through her letterbox. Surely she couldn't possibly believe he was a . . . whatever today's word for womaniser was. Love rat? That'd be the one.

Absent-mindedly, he rose from his chair and took out a couple of wholemeal bread slices. Andrea's cheeky remark aimed at consultants being careless over the recommended intake of fruit and vegetables swam into his head. While the bread browned beneath the grill, he unpeeled a banana and bit into it, standing in front of the cooker. If he wandered away, he'd be eating charcoal for breakfast.

★　★　★

By the time Keir finished his morning chores, Andrea and Josh were setting off for their day out. Josh insisted on bringing Becks, his battered but favourite teddy bear, with them. Becks wore a miniature Manchester United strip and a manic grin. The little boy chattered as his mother drove them out of the town and on to the dual carriageway.

'When's that nice man coming to see us, Mummy?'

Andrea's stomach lurched. 'Um, the man who called round the other evening, do you mean?' As if legions of men often parachuted in for tea and biscuits.

'The doctor man.'

Sometimes Andrea felt her son's memory was a little too retentive. 'Ah, Dr Harrison,' she said. 'Well, he is very busy, Josh. He's helping Gran to stay well, so maybe it's best not to interrupt him just now.' Mentally she crossed her fingers. Keir had made it plain he wanted to meet her son, but in view of recent developments, surely he hadn't really meant what he'd said? It stung to think he might have played on her sympathies in order to lure her into what might be called his harem.

'Boy, but I must have become a rotten judge of character,' she muttered, forgetting Josh's sharp ears.

'Are we nearly there yet, Mummy?' Fortunately her son had other things on his mind.

'You need to be patient a little longer, Josh. Tell me what you hope you'll be doing today with Uncle Rafa and Luis while I have a lovely chat with Aunty Kirsty.'

This got Andrea off the hook, though the football theme still shone through. Today, she thought ruefully, might have presented the perfect opportunity to introduce Keir to Josh, the occasion being diluted by a fun time with her son's and her favourite people. That wasn't to be. Fate continued to reshuffle her life cards but no way would she allow herself to wallow in depression. Too many people depended on her, including the members of the trial team.

While Josh chattered his way through a goal-scoring scenario involving Becks poised on his knee and shooting imaginary goals into the glove compartment, Andrea's jaw set as if she'd slapped on a mud pack. The thought of rubbing shoulders not only with Keir but with that red-haired siren made her wish she could whisk Josh away and fly back to Montreal. In spite of what had happened since, she'd fallen in love with the city and felt a definite bond forged with Pierre and Lisa. They were her kind of people. To have such a holiday in view would give her something to keep her mind off her emotions. And Josh was just old enough to appreciate the trip.

Andrea crossed the boundary of the town where Kirsty and family lived, cheering Becks as he headed in the winning goal. She remained of course completely unaware that Keir Harrison stood on her front doorstep at that precise moment, finger about to press the bell. If she could have seen the expression on her star-crossed lover's face, she might possibly have felt a twinge of compassion.

★ ★ ★

Ignoring the space on the driveway where the car should have been, Keir rang Andrea's doorbell a second time. Her vehicle might be in for service. Or she could easily have lent it to Mrs Dean, especially if Lizzie needed to drive Rosemary somewhere. Who was he trying to convince? Andrea wasn't at home, and he wouldn't be surprised to discover she'd no intention of being at home to him ever again. He puffed air through his cheeks and felt in his jacket pocket for the letter he'd written to her. Fingering the envelope, he closed his eyes, wondering the wisdom of hammering his point home. Andrea wasn't exactly making it easy for him to explain the situation.

Shooting one last despairing look over his shoulder at the impassive house, Keir strode down the driveway towards his car. What now? This depressing situation nagged at his brain and left him feeling unco-ordinated and restless. Shopping? His fridge had been recently well-stocked. Household tasks? The cleaner he employed so his house didn't end up resembling his long-ago student digs would be coming in after the weekend. As for the garden, he could mow the back lawn, but the shrubbery looked after itself and the front garden needed little attention, having been immaculately paved by the previous owners.

He drove out of Andrea's road, wondering if he'd ever have cause to visit it again. Keir frowned. What was that song one of his elderly patients had been singing to him yesterday? At the time it seemed absurdly appropriate. Now the sentiment expressed in it seemed too poignant to think about. 'This Nearly Was Mine'. That was the song, but he wasn't sure where it came from. It didn't matter.

He needed to take a hold of himself. If Andrea really, really wanted him, she'd have reacted to his phone messages. Surely? If she'd written him off, she would continue to ignore them. Maybe he should give her 48 hours to respond. That should allow her plenty of time to confirm her feelings. How fantastic it would be if she missed him as much as he missed her. How fantastic if she returned from wherever she'd gone and rang him later that day. If she didn't, how difficult would it be for the pair of them, forced to meet professionally and pretend to the rest of the world they were nothing but colleagues . . .

Keir drove straight home. If the worst happened and Andrea didn't want to know him, he'd go off next weekend somewhere on his own. Maybe look up one or two people he'd not seen in a while. If she decided to draw a line beneath Moira's pathetic theatricals, maybe he could look forward to a family weekend with Andrea and Josh. Keir didn't often pray, but on this occasion he unashamedly spoke his thoughts aloud, as if he had a direct line to some higher authority.

'Phew!' Kirsty dropped into the chair beside Andrea. 'I'm beginning to wilt.'

Andrea cast a professional eye over her friend. 'You look fantastic — textbook stuff. Are you sleeping?'

'Pretty well, thanks — but I want to know about you. You sounded very cloak-and-dagger on the phone. While the guys are at the leisure centre, why don't you tell me what's bugging you?'

'I don't want you to think I come running over here just to unburden my woes,' Andrea said.

Kirsty shook her head. 'If you and I didn't have each other to confide in, we'd probably end up talking to ourselves. Not that I don't do that anyway,' she said thoughtfully. 'Come on. Let's take advantage of this rare oasis of peace.'

She listened in silence as Andrea related the events of the past few weeks, beginning with the meeting at the elevator. Listened in fascination, learning what a good sounding-board Keir had proved to be on the flight to Canada and how he'd been the perfect gentleman despite the time he'd grabbed her at the top of the lecture room staircase, making her feel, Andrea admitted with a grin, like the heroine from *Gone with the Wind*.

'How does he kiss?' Kirsty leaned forward.

'I can't tell you that!'

'Of course you can.'

Andrea looked heavenwards, then relented. 'Like the world has stopped spinning? Like the two of us are about to float off together somewhere warm and sunny? Slow burn at first then — oh, heck. It's all past tense now.'

'That well, ay? And you still decided to keep things on a professional level, even after such a heart-stopping kiss?'

Andrea craned her neck to look at the leafy branches of the gnarled old lilac tree. Sunlight created a kaleidoscope of light and shade. 'I didn't think it wise to encourage him any further,' she said.

'Flippin' heck, if you were wearing a bonnet, I'd think you'd stepped straight out of a Jane Austen novel,' Kirsty said. Rather tartly. 'You're two single adults — this consultant of yours is single, I hope?'

'He's not mine, Kirsty!' Andrea bit her lip. 'At first I assumed he was married, but he's actually divorced.'

'Keir told you that himself?'

'His friend Pierre spilled the beans while we were having lunch together in Montreal. Keir has spoken to me about his failed marriage since though.'

275

'Let me get this straight. When you kissed him back that time after the lecture, you were still under the impression he was a married man?'

Andrea shifted in her seat. 'Um, yes, I suppose so.'

'That tells me the attraction between you two must be pretty darned powerful. Unless you've been concealing a secret scarlet woman persona, you're just not the type to go round snogging other women's husbands.' Looking smug, Kirsty folded her arms over her bump.

Andrea didn't laugh. 'I felt sure my reaction was all down to the rebound thing. I didn't want to complicate my life any more than I had to. While we were in Montreal, I realised — and this sounds terrible — I realised how much I wanted to go to bed with him.'

'I'll make us something to drink.' Kirsty eased herself from the chair. 'But I want to hear more. I can't believe you'd have reached such a huge decision about this man unless he was pure gold. Your judgement was certainly spot-on with Greg,' she added gently.

Left alone, Andrea recognised the truth in what her friend said. She also knew what Kirsty would say once the whole episode had been related. Kirsty would tell her she was crazy to allow Moira Haynes to muddy the waters. Kirsty would tell her she was crazy not to give Dr Keir Harrison one more chance. At least let him explain his own version of events.

In the kitchen, waiting for the kettle to boil, Kirsty heard the beep of a text message arriving. The sound came from Andrea's short-sleeved white linen jacket, hanging on the back of a chair. She slipped her hand in the pocket and drew out her friend's mobile, weighing it in her palm and staring at the little screen. Could this be a message from the man they'd been discussing? Dare she access it? Ring him back and tell him to get the hell over here and talk some sense into the unhappy woman sitting under her lilac tree?

Kirsty shook her head and placed the phone on the drinks tray. She might believe her friend was a knucklehead, but no way should she influence her very important decision. No way did she believe Andrea really doubted Keir's sincerity. It was the understandable instinct for self-preservation making her pull back from the possibility of further hurt and disappointment. Pull back from what seemed to be the promise of a wonderful happy ending for both Andrea and Keir.

She made a single mug of coffee and poured herself a glass of orange juice before returning to the garden and handing over Andrea's phone.

★   ★   ★

Keir dumped a pile of grass cuttings behind a bush laden with fat fuchsia blossoms. The job was done, despite the man who lived next door waylaying him to talk about the English cricket team before he'd even switched on his mower. He needed a shower, a cool drink and something to eat, but not necessarily in that order.

Sweaty and hot, he walked through the back door into the kitchen just as his landline shrilled. He hurled himself at the phone, willing it to be Andrea on the other end, wanting it to be her with an intensity that shocked him.

'Keir Harrison.'

'G'morning, Keir. How are you?' Richard's voice.

Keir swallowed his disappointment, closed his eyes briefly and muttered something in response.

'Good, good,' said the prof. 'Louise wants to take advantage of this lovely weather. I get the job of ringing round. Would you be free to come to our house around six o'clock? A few drinks and nibbles. She's already made a quiche the size of a cartwheel. We don't usually do impromptu — must be the sunshine getting at us.'

Keir swallowed his dismay. He didn't much like parties. But what about Andrea? Surely she would be invited? Richard and Louise were close friends of hers. All of a sudden it seemed to be a no-brainer.

Richard picked up on his silence. 'The guests are a mix of old friends plus a handful from your team. So you won't be among strangers.'

'That sounds very good,' said Keir. 'Shall I bring a bottle?'

'No need, but thanks for the offer, old chap. Got a pen handy? I'd better let you have our address.'

Richard closed the call and padded back into the kitchen where his wife had another job waiting. 'Keir's accepted our invitation. I hope we're doing the right thing here.'

'By not telling him we've invited Andrea? We still haven't heard back from her though, have we? She may not be able to make it.' Deftly, Louise stretched cling-film over a bowl of rosy radishes.

'She hasn't responded yet. I do wonder if, by inviting the pair of them,' her husband said

279

thoughtfully, 'they'll think we're matchmaking.'

Louise shook her head in exasperation. 'Oh, come on! They were thrown together on that trip to Canada. If those two happen to be attracted to each other, they've got plenty of opportunity to meet without waiting for chance invitations to arrive.' She reached for a whisk. 'We'd have invited Andrea and Greg if he'd been around, wouldn't we?' She paused. 'Oh dear, that sounds so flippant. I should have said, in other circumstances.'

'It's all right,' said Richard, moving round the table to give her arm a little squeeze. 'I knew what you meant.'

'Anyway,' Louise spoke in a brisk tone. 'I'd like to get to know Keir better. He seems a lovely man.'

'He's a great bloke and my respect for him isn't in question.' Richard sneaked a radish before his wife could cling-film the second bowl. 'But I very much doubt Andrea's ready for another man in her life just yet. Even a squeaky-clean one like Keir.'

'Squeaky-clean doesn't always do it for a woman, you know,' said Louise. But Richard didn't respond.

★ ★ ★

Only after Keir put the phone down did he start wondering whether Moira Haynes's name might be included on the guest list. Could he cope with that? Maybe he should take the defensive option, ring Richard back and pretend he'd totally forgotten another engagement. He frowned. No. No way would he allow the woman to interfere in his personal life any more than she already had. A bit of company would be good for him and stop him brooding. And if Andrea did happen to be there, he'd find a way of cutting through the barbed wire. After all, it would be difficult for her to spend the whole evening avoiding him.

* * *

'It's an invitation.'

Kirsty looked across at Andrea. 'Don't sound so thrilled. If it's from that hot guy who played Mr Rochester in that TV series, I shan't speak to you ever again.'

Andrea didn't come up with a jokey response. 'Richard and Louise are having a party this evening. I'd better give them a quick ring to say I can't make it.'

'Excuse me? Do you have some other bash to attend after you leave here?'

'Well, no, but I can't possibly get a sitter for Josh. Impromptu's great for those two — not

281

so great for someone with a young child.'

Kirsty steepled her fingers and glared at Andrea. 'So why not leave Josh with us? He's already got a toothbrush and jim-jams here. It'll do you good to go somewhere where you can chat to people without keeping an eye on the clock.'

Andrea bristled. 'I'm always chatting to people at work. Plus I've just had that trip to Canada.' The thought of certain events related to that trip silenced her for a moment.

Kirsty cleared her throat.

'Besides . . . '

'Besides what, Andrea?'

'Richard might have invited Keir.' Andrea's words were almost a whisper. 'I don't really want to see him outside of working hours. Not at the moment.'

'Why not?'

'Everything's topsy-turvy. You've saved Josh from disappointment about his cancelled sleep over. I just need some quiet time tonight.'

'Prolonging the misery?'

'The two of us meeting in public could be very embarrassing for him.'

'For him or for you?'

Andrea inspected her nails as if she'd never noticed them before. 'What if he's there and he brings that woman?'

'Ah. What if he rubs your nose in it, you mean?'

'Yes.' Andrea suspected she sounded like a small, hurt child.

Kirsty picked up her orange juice and swirled the glass gently so the ice clinked against the sides. 'You know, from what you've said, I think Dr Keir Harrison seems way too nice a guy to behave in such a despicable way. Can you put your hand on your heart and tell me you really believe he's a Jekyll and Hyde character? I'm thinking back to that time he rescued your mum when she waltzed off with those plants.'

'Don't remind me,' Andrea wailed.

But Kirsty's logic was relentless. 'I think I should remind you. He went out of his way to look after Rosemary. And that was a huge confidence boost he gave you, insisting he wanted you to attend the conference with him. From what you said, he couldn't have done more to make you feel at ease.' She watched her friend's cheeks turn fondant-pink. 'Hmm. You came back with an open invitation to go and stay with those friends of his. How lovely is that?'

'Of course it's lovely. I can't argue with anything you say. But this evening, I'd really rather head for home around seven o'clock.'

'Really, really?'

'Yes. Now, excuse me while I ring Richard and make my apologies. Then you can tell me what needs doing about lunch while you sit there, making the most of being able to keep your feet up. It's the least I can do.'

*　*　*

Keir didn't totally relax again until his hosts began serving supper. Clearly, neither Andrea nor Moira could be expected to turn up after that. It wasn't the kind of party where people piled in, drinking from cans of lager after the pubs closed. He left Richard and Louise's house at around nine o'clock. He'd enjoyed the food, drunk a little wine and accepted a lift halfway home from a pleasant couple he'd spent time talking with.

He walked the couple of miles on to his place and let himself in. There was no tell-tale red light on his house phone. He usually switched off his mobile on the rare occasions when he got into his sparklies, but as the screen returned to life, nothing claimed his attention. He hadn't switched off his computer before going out, but on sitting down to check his mailbox there was only one personal email and that was from Rhonda Pierce in Montreal. Its heading was *Decisions, decisions!*

Keir frowned and sat forward in his chair, wondering what all that was about.

Hi Keir. Hope all's well with you. This is to say I've handed in my notice at the hospital. The board are anxious to commence interviewing applicants for my job like yesterday. What's keeping you? May I expect your CV? I'm attaching the job description and with apologies, a very detailed application form, hopefully to speed things up. Of course your salary would be between you and the big cheeses. When you come out for interview, you must have dinner with Patrick and me.
Regards, Rhonda

He sat back and gazed at the screen. Was this what fate had in store? He got up and walked through the kitchen for a drink of water. He'd thought fate had brought Andrea into his orbit for a purpose. He'd never imagined the kind of happiness they'd so recently shared ever being his again, and hey presto, he'd been proved right about that. The hours spent in her company once they'd got over that initial barrier had been like an oasis. Then he'd gone and blown things. The whole thing was a farce, but Andrea appeared to have made her decision and now it was time for him to make his.

Keir called up his CV from his personal file and realised he needed to do a quick makeover to include details of the position he held at Hartnett General and how he'd got the trials up and running. He could see no reason why his team shouldn't cope without him and if he got on with things, and if he was offered an interview date soon, he could take a few days' leave and be back at Hartnett well before the next stage of the trial commenced. Living overseas wasn't something he really wanted to do, but he could probably rent out his house and Pierre would help him find somewhere to stay in Montreal until he adjusted to his new position. Providing, of course, he got the job.

He groaned as a thought struck him. Andrea had seemed delighted when his Canadian friends offered her an invitation to go and visit. He wouldn't want her to miss out on such an opportunity. But that was thinking too far ahead. It was unlikely their paths would cross because he'd make it plain to Pierre and his wife that no way would Andrea wish to make up a foursome should she decide to visit Montreal after Keir took up residence.

His PA always emailed him his appointments list on a Friday. When he saw her on

Monday, he'd ask her how the next couple of weeks were looking, then mention the possibility of his taking a few days off to catch up with family matters. He could tell a little white lie. If Montreal did as Rhonda insisted they would, and called him for interview, he'd be foolish not to accept.

★　★　★

When Andrea returned to work the following Monday, she found herself staring at her computer screen as if her usual messages arrived via carrier pigeon. Seeing the bullet points before her, scrolling down to read the comments and overall positive summing up of the drug trial so far, she felt like she knew she should feel, and that was just another member of Dr Harrison's highly skilled team.

Well, what else did she expect? Hadn't she blocked his personal texts and phone messages? Hadn't she replaced the iceberg between the two of them? No way would he be calling round with wine and roses any time soon.

In spite of her decision, in spite of the way he'd clearly taken it on board, Andrea felt depression settle upon her like a black shroud. She'd worn a metaphorical one for too long and Keir had succeeded in ripping it away. His kisses; his generous, tender lovemaking — it was no good. She didn't need to keep torturing herself like this. The interlude had been sweet, but she shouldn't have taken him seriously. Thank goodness Josh hadn't got to know Keir, grown fond of him, and ending up hurt by the appearance and disappearance of a father figure in the life he and his mother shared.

Nor did it help when the prof ambled into her office, bearing goodies. 'Sorry we didn't see you on Saturday, my dear. Good weekend, was it?' He held out a plastic box. 'Louise catered for a banquet, as usual. She sent a slab of gateau for you and Josh.'

'That's very kind, Richard. My goodness.' Andrea held out both hands. 'That'll be three evenings' desserts for the boy and me. Did — I mean, how did the party go? I was at Kirsty's house. Things are a bit complicated, what with one thing and another. I like to help out a bit now her bump's so much bigger.'

'Understood. Yes, it all seemed to go well. Keir came, but to be honest he looked a bit like a fish out of water. Fortunately our friends from the golf club took him under their wing. I believe they gave him a lift home afterwards.'

'He was on his own?' she blurted.

Richard stared at her. 'He didn't bring anyone with him, if that's what you mean. Louise's cousin seems to have enjoyed talking to him, but she won't see seventy again. She did tell me how charming he was though.' He pulled a face. 'Can't imagine him as someone's toy boy, but you never know.'

Andrea felt ridiculous relief. 'I didn't mean to sound nosy. Sorry!' She gestured at her monitor. 'He must have been moonlighting over the weekend.' She kept her tone light. 'Have you read his update yet? It's very heartening. Even without my mother's involvement, I'd be picking up positive vibes from the results so far.'

Richard nodded. 'The results are very encouraging. Excellent in fact.'

Andrea thought he had something else on his mind, but his PA put her head round Andrea's office door, pre-empting further comment. 'Sorry to interrupt but I have Dr Harrison on the phone for you, Richard.'

The prof nodded at her. 'I'll take it in my office. Talk of the devil, ay, Andrea?'

He hurried out, leaving her alone with a large invitation to death by chocolate and a huge helping of curiosity. So Keir had been out partying, however sedately, and without a plus-one. What did she care? The odds were on Moira playing hard to get now she'd succeeded in shattering Andrea's trust. It was probably just as well all had been revealed before things developed too much too soon.

Andrea forced herself to concentrate. Keir's social life was no longer her concern. But the pink cloud of joy, having so recently wrapped itself around her, left her feeling like Josh's punctured space hopper. Life seemed very drab.

★　★　★

'Good morning, Richard,' said Keir. 'I just wanted to say thanks again for a very enjoyable evening.'

The prof settled back in his chair. 'Glad you could make it, old man. I've been telling Andrea we were sorry she couldn't join us. Louise is good at parties.'

'Indeed she is.' Keir hesitated. 'Look, Prof, the fact is, I'm thinking of taking a short break. It will mean my missing a couple of clinic sessions, but nothing will be delayed. The schedule remains in place. I just wanted to assure you on that score before I confirm my travel arrangements.'

'Holidays are important. Going anywhere special?'

'I might catch up with some old friends. Nothing's finalised yet, but it'll be very helpful if you can maybe drop in on a clinic session or two. Keep an ear to the ground for me.'

Richard frowned. 'Won't Andrea do that? I don't want her to feel I'm breathing down her neck.'

'Understood, and I'm sure she won't think that's the case. I just don't want her to feel I expect her to carry any extra responsibility, that's all.'

'How long will you be away?'

'Only a week. That'll be plenty.'

'Let me know when you're off and don't give it another thought.'

When Keir put down the phone, he sat thoughtfully tapping his pen against the edge of his desk blotter. He'd felt strange during the brief conversation, not his usual assured self. He could tell Richard sensed something, especially when Keir mentioned Andrea. It proved what he'd always thought. Relationships between men and women in the workplace were like old flames at weddings — needing to be doused before they could do any damage.

12

Keir watched a spoof horror movie on the flight over to Montreal, hoping its dreadful but comical script would help block the memory of his last trip, when Andrea had started to let down her guard. On that trip, his instincts had led him to believe he might, just might, be laying a foundation for a deeper personal relationship. Despite the bizarre film, his thoughts roamed dangerously. How did he know he was doing the right thing, setting in motion a chain of events that could lead him to live on a different continent from the one where he'd spent all of his life so far?

He didn't. Fate, or whatever higher authority dictated events, would no doubt take over. All he knew was, he could not be around Andrea and treat her as an ordinary colleague, while his emotions shrieked distress signals at him whenever he came within her orbit.

Maybe, thousands of miles away from her comfort zone, she'd found it easier to unwind once the business part of their visit ended. Whilst on their flight home, the uncertainties wormed their way back. When she'd made her feelings plain, it was if the gremlins stuck two taunting fingers at him. But his determination not to let her pass up a chance of happiness had swayed her. Two steps forward, three steps back. Along had come another gremlin. One with red hair and an attitude spikier than her gleaming fingernails.

Canada could be the way forward at this point. No way could he sustain another emotional tsunami such as the one endured so recently. Neither could Andrea, as he very well knew. He felt a surge of pity, picturing her stricken face as Sister Haynes spun her little melodrama. It was all so crazy. Placed in an invidious position, he'd taken refuge in work. The unfairness of it ate away at him so much that when the stewardess appeared again, he ordered a brandy. That wasn't the answer, but it would do for the moment. Maybe afterwards he'd be able to take a nap and wake up feeling more kindly disposed to the world.

★　★　★

Rhonda Pierce talked. Keir listened. Each of them sat in a low leather chair, a glass-topped table between them bearing a jug of iced water and two tumblers. He nodded as she outlined the important aspects of her role. His eyes widened as he heard how much importance was attached to the exchange of findings within the various teams. His enthusiasm increased as he realised how much that centre of excellence had to offer someone with his qualifications and experience.

'This is a fantastic branch of medicine to be in,' said Rhonda. 'Of course you already know that, but I've never before encountered such dedication to sharing and comparing, with all of us striving for the ultimate. And that is, all of us striving to benefit the patient.' She paused. 'Do you know we have trainees from around sixty different countries working at this hospital?'

Keir gave a low whistle. 'I did a little homework on the flight over, but hearing it from the horse's mouth makes a far greater impact.'

Rhonda chuckled. 'Well, I've been called a few things in my time but that takes some beating.' She glanced at her watch. 'How about the horse takes you to lunch and introduces you to a few of the team?'

His eyes narrowed. 'Lunch sounds great, but isn't it a little premature for me to start meeting people?'

'I don't think so. You're on the shortlist, Keir.'

He nodded. 'I get it. So lunch is part of the selection process? If I eat peas from my knife or shower my food with salt, will your colleagues be mentally awarding me marks out of ten?'

Po-faced, she looked him in the eye. 'Be very afraid. It's only the big boss who gets to slurp his tea.' She got to her feet and Keir immediately stood too. 'We can freshen up on our way to the dining room,' she said. 'I'll just collect my purse, then we'll go throw you to the lions.'

★ ★ ★

Some days were like that. Andrea's mother was being a tad tetchy. No matter how tactfully she tried, Lizzie Dean could not persuade Rosemary to stop dawdling and prepare to travel to Hartnett General for the morning clinic session. At last the elderly woman came out of her bedroom but still wearing slippers instead of her summer sandals.

'Rosemary, the colour of your dress is very pretty but I'm not sure the slippers go with it.' Lizzie held her breath, hoping this was a wise remark.

Rosemary looked down. 'Oh dear,' she said. 'I'd better change.'

'You look lovely in the dress. Why don't I fetch your navy-blue sandals and you can just slip into them?'

'That's a grand idea,' said Rosemary. 'Do you know where to find them?'

Lizzie left her in the hallway while she collected the sandals. They weren't on the shoe rack inside the big wardrobe, and she needed to check under chairs before locating them neatly parked beneath the bed. She returned to find the hallway empty.

It was too much. Lizzie's good humour and patience were often sorely tested, and that morning she'd awoken feeling slightly out of sorts. 'After all, I'm human too,' she muttered to herself. 'Rosemary,' she called. 'Where are you?' A quick glance showed her the door chain remained in position. But that mightn't apply to the kitchen.

'I'm in here!'

Lizzie raised her eyes to the heavens. Panic over. Then she saw the funny side. Rosemary was leafing through a dictionary she kept on the table beside her favourite chair.

'Do you think you could leave the crossword until later, please?' Lizzie crossed her fingers behind her back. 'We really need to get going now.'

Rosemary looked up indignantly. 'But this

is very important.'

Lizzie walked towards her charge. 'Why don't we take the crossword and dictionary with us? Then we can solve some clues in between the games and things you'll be doing.'

The older woman's face broke into a smile. Still clutching a handbag roomy enough to hold a bundle of kittens, she followed Lizzie through to the front door. Today, Lizzie would have to leave the session early in order to reach the school on time. Andrea would take an early lunch break and drive her mum home. Two ham salads sat under wraps in the fridge. The kindly neighbour who came in to keep an eye on Rosemary at odd times would take over so Andrea could return to the university. It was a highly organised schedule, rather like a line of dominoes with everyone hoping the first one wouldn't fall.

Lizzie fully appreciated Andrea had had a tough time over the last months. But she couldn't help but wonder what kept her so preoccupied lately. You'd have thought she'd be satisfied now her mum's care was sorted and her job involved working with such a charming man.

★　★　★

Keir stood beside Rhonda Pierce at the elevator on her office floor.

'You see, Keir, your visit today has left me more convinced than ever that you're the right person for the job.'

'Because when the big boss talked about ice hockey, I understood at least ten per cent of what he was saying?'

She patted his arm. 'That too. I was thinking more of your ability to talk easily to all kinds of people — orderlies, patients, consultants, lab technicians. You don't do hierarchy, do you?'

He shrugged. 'Not if I can help it. I have to say there's a great atmosphere in this department. Unless you're all on your very best behaviour today.'

'Believe me, I think you're home and dry.' She glanced upwards. 'The elevator's about to swallow you up. Are you still OK for dinner later?'

'If you're sure it's no trouble.'

'We love entertaining. Patrick's very much looking forward to meeting you.' She hesitated. 'I hope you don't mind but I've invited an old friend of mine, Carrie Michaels. She's in Westmount visiting her folks and it just seemed a good idea to invite her over to keep us company.'

'It might also keep the three of us from

298

talking too much shop,' he said. 'Unless your friend happens to be another medic?'

'She's a musician,' said Rhonda. 'A very sought-after violinist.'

'Sounds interesting. OK, I'll see you at seven then.'

'Sure you can find your way?'

'Positive.'

Keir rode to the ground floor, acutely aware that each time he got into a lift, Andrea's face floated across his vision. He didn't think it was likely he'd be cured of this phenomenon too soon, even if Rhonda Pierce produced a whole strings section of glamorous friends to eat dinner with him. But maybe this was what he needed. If he wanted to make a complete clean break after the tempestuous times of the last weeks, meeting a female he was unlikely to come across again might help him banish some ghosts. Unless she happened to be looking for a soulmate, in which case she'd be disappointed. It would take him a long time to exorcise from his thoughts the only woman he could envisage in that role.

He walked to the nearest cab rank and stood a moment, looking back at the huge hospital complex he'd so recently visited. It put him in mind of a stack of gigantic blue and white egg boxes, but its somewhat unprepossessing exterior shielded hundreds of talented, caring professionals going about their everyday tasks. In many cases that would be saving lives, then. Could this be the right place for him? How much was he allowing his emotions to influence his career? His first concern had been the impact such a move might have upon his former wife and daughter in terms of seeing Naomi. But when he checked the distance between London and Melbourne, he discovered it was only marginally less than that between Montreal and Melbourne.

He reached the head of the queue for cabs. As he got into the next one to arrive, he told himself to stop worrying and enjoy the rest of his stay. Despite what Rhonda said, she wasn't the decision-maker. He might be shortlisted, but that didn't mean he would receive even the sniff of an offer. The board might be looking to put a younger person in post. They might even be looking to replace one woman with another. Everyone knew it would be very challenging to take over from such an impressive boss lady.

★ ★ ★

'Don't worry, Keir, I'm not looking to find a husband.' Carrie Michaels flashed an impish grin at him. 'Those guys don't ever believe me though.'

He'd immediately taken to this quirky woman with the tiny diamond nose stud and the cap of corn-gold hair. Patrick and Rhonda left them alone after the former had produced tall glasses clinking with ice cubes and filled with a delicious fruit concoction he swore was virtually alcohol-free.

'I know the feeling,' Keir said. 'If I'm invited anywhere, I immediately start wondering which poor soul's been earmarked as my potential partner.'

'Strikes me that wouldn't spoil anyone's evening,' she said. 'You're presumably single, undeniably attractive, and doubtless solvent?'

He burst out laughing. 'You don't stand on ceremony,' he said. 'And I couldn't possibly comment on what you've just said, except it's true to say I live within my means. I'm incredibly boring, in fact. And divorced, to answer your first question.' He put his drink on the patio table. 'So where's the current Mr Carrie Michaels, if I may make so bold? Or are you between boyfriends, perhaps?'

His companion sneaked a glance over her shoulder and leaned closer.

She smells of violet cachous, he thought. It was like a blast from his childhood when his sister used to buy tubes of the little sweets.

'I'm going to entrust you with a deep, dark, secret,' she said.

'Isn't that rather rash? After all, you hardly know me.'

'I know enough about you, Mr James Bond. And we're ships that pass in the night, though I really would appreciate your keeping this particular bit of information under wraps.'

Keir nodded, highly intrigued now. Carrie's turquoise-blue eyes sparkled. He could easily imagine her dressed in an elegant black gown, lost in the melody as she drew music from her violin in harmony with the rest of her orchestral colleagues.

'I don't do commitment,' she said.

'Ah.'

'You don't sound in the least shocked.'

'It's not my business to be surprised or otherwise. You're a beautiful woman. You're single, intelligent, and presumably solvent, and it's my pleasure to be in your company for the next few hours.'

She sat back in her chair. 'Touché, monsieur. You're certainly not boring. *Tu es très gentil.*'

He put up his hands. 'I thought this bit of Montreal was pretty much English-speaking. My French isn't great. As to whether I'm kind or not, well the jury's out on that one.'

Carrie frowned. 'So, did you beat your first wife? Do you drown helpless kittens?'

'God, no!' He had to laugh at her. 'The truth is, I just don't seem able to do relationships.'

He couldn't believe he'd said that. How long had he known Ms Michaels? Ten minutes? Suddenly he wanted to see this woman again. Whether she considered him to be bland and boring or totally bonkers, he'd a hunch she might be able to point him in the right direction. She sounded as if she'd got herself sorted. What did he have to lose?

'Before our hosts come back, I couldn't entice you to have lunch with me tomorrow, I suppose?'

'I may be a commitment-phobe, but I'm not interested in one-night stands, Keir.'

'Nor me. But I'd like your advice on nose piercing.'

When Patrick and Rhonda emerged from the kitchen, Patrick carrying a tray on which sat a jug of his innocent, wicked cocktail, they found their guests laughing together as if they'd known one another years, not minutes.

Rhonda jabbed her husband in the ribs. 'See? I told you these two would get on.'

Patrick's expression was neutral. 'Let's just enjoy the evening, honey.' He went through to the patio. 'How about I freshen your drinks?

Dinner's going to be in a half hour. Keir, I hear we have an acquaintance in common. Pierre Duval? Our paths have led us different ways but we went through med school together.'

'Small world again,' said Keir. 'I met up with Pierre and Lisa when I came over for the conference.'

'The conference where my lovely wife buttonholed you. What did you think of the hospital?'

Keir glanced at the two women.

'It's OK,' said Patrick. 'Those two are catching up on the local gossip.'

Keir nodded. 'I haven't said anything to Pierre about coming over here again.'

'Is that wise? If he does happen to hear about it, won't he be hurt?'

'I can't believe my life would be of such interest.'

'No? You'd be surprised. This is quite a high-profile position you're up for. Rhonda and I haven't mentioned the famous Dr Keir Harrison possibly taking over from her. But you better believe the old grapevine's working overtime.' He smiled. 'Don't look so worried. Aren't things like that back in the UK?'

'Is the Pope a Catholic?'

'Well, there you go, then.'

'Maybe I'll give Pierre a ring tomorrow.'

'I would. He's a friend. And if you do end

up working here, you'll surely need friends to help you over the first hurdles.'

Keir stared at his host. 'I hadn't thought of it like that. But I understand where you're coming from. I was, erm, trying not to make too much of it. While nothing's decided, I mean.'

'Pardon me, but I don't believe you'd have flown all this way unless you were a little bit interested in this job.'

'I'm very interested, Patrick. Frankly, I think it could be a very good move for me. If they offer it, that is.'

'Are you considering applying elsewhere? Hell's bells, Keir, I don't mean to pry. You must think I'm some piece of work.'

Keir grinned, thinking of Richard and his appetite for gossip. 'You're all right. I imagine you feel quite protective of this position — Rhonda being such a terrific role model and so on?'

'I guess I do. It hadn't really occurred to me before. I was pretty surprised when she told me she'd no intention of living apart from me. She's a lovely, loyal woman and I know she'll be missed at the hospital. Realising how much she admires your work makes me hope she can hand over the reins to you, I guess.'

'No pressure then,' said Keir.

When he heard the buzz of the phone he'd
left on the desk in his hotel room, Keir
scrabbled to reach it from his seat beside the
window. Even though he was alone, he felt
foolish and swore softly at himself for being
such an idiot. Of course it wouldn't be from
Andrea. The lady with whom he was lunching
later that day had sent a short and succinct
message regarding where they were to meet.

*Hi Mr Bond. Rehearsing till 2. Meet you in
Nijinsky's. Google it.*

Carrie Michaels delighted him, though he
wondered what some of his colleagues back at
Hartnett would think if they knew he was
lunching with her. He'd already typed her
name into his search engine and discovered
her mind-blowing musical background. She
was in great demand as a soloist and she'd
performed in just about every top concert
hall worldwide. He wondered what else he'd
learn about her. If he did come to Montreal,
she wouldn't be around very much, that was
for sure. Her orchestra was touring at the
moment but normally she was based on the
west coast.

He replied to her text, then checked the
time. He'd left his hire car in his hosts'
driveway the evening before and shared a taxi

back with Carrie. Her folks lived not far from Patrick and Rhonda. He hoped they wouldn't resent some strange Englishman stealing their daughter's precious leisure hours like this. Patrick had told him he'd come and pick him up so Keir could drive his car back to the hotel. Keir had chuckled when Carrie told him it wouldn't hurt to let slip the two of them had a lunch date.

★ ★ ★

'My hectic schedule just wouldn't fit married life,' said Carrie while she and Keir sipped ice-cold beers at a table on the restaurant's terrace.

He nodded. 'Fair enough, but if you keep yourself at arm's length, mightn't you wake up one day with regrets? I imagine your parents would love to see you find a life partner.' Her attitude intrigued him.

She shrugged. 'My parents and my friends respect my status as a musician. They're pleased to see me following a career I love.' She moved her glass slowly round on its coaster.

Keir smiled at her. 'You sound like you have a good relationship with your parents.'

'I think so. And if settling down doesn't happen for another couple of decades, I just hope they'll still be around to see it.'

They sat in silence, enjoying the cool green oasis beneath the huge umbrella sheltering them from the sun. After they'd placed their orders for what Carrie told Keir were the best burgers and fries in Montreal, she sat back and looked him in the eye.

'So, what's next for the sexy Brit Doc?'

He shook his head at her. 'Lunch? Coffee? You tell me you have to get back and rehearse. I'll probably visit a gallery before meeting up with an old friend for a bite to eat. Tomorrow, I fly back to the UK.'

She crossed her eyes at him. 'Thanks for the diary detail, but I think you know what I really mean.'

He picked up a pretzel and bit into it.

'In your own time.'

'Persistent so-and-so, aren't you?'

'You better believe it.'

'If I get this job offer, I think I'm going to accept it.'

'You think?'

'I'm not counting my chickens.'

'Understood, but let's say they offer it and you accept. Will you be saying yes for all the right reasons?'

'To be honest, without blowing my own trumpet, I'm on a bit of a career high at the moment. I'm not in any way unhappy with my job back home. Ideally, I suppose I shouldn't move on for at least another couple of years. But — '

'Something's bugging you, and it's not a career thing.'

'You got it.'

She sighed. 'So this whole trip is predicated on your emotions. It's a heart not head thing.'

Keir winced. 'That sounds terrible. For a start, you make me sound such a wimp.'

'I didn't mean you were a coward.'

He considered for a moment. 'Some would say I'm running away from a situation.'

'Is this situation like a relationship thing?'

Suddenly he wanted to tell her everything. She made a good listener. The restaurant was busy and their meal didn't arrive for a while, by which time he'd given the basic details to Carrie and he knew she'd filled in the rest for herself.

'Do you want to know what I think?'

'Hit me with it,' he said. 'I can handle it and I have a hunch you'll be honest.'

'I think you'd be doing the right thing if you moved to another position to better yourself or to pursue a different career path which you could only achieve here in Montreal. I think you'd be crazy to move just because you can't bear to be around the beautiful lady doctor.'

Carrie smiled up at the waitress bringing their orders. The young woman was flustered, apologetic and extremely pretty. 'Don't worry,' Carrie told her. 'We're cool.'

Keir waited. No way had his companion finished with him. Even with appetising but worryingly sky-high portions of food in front of them.

'It doesn't matter to me what Dr Harrison does with his life. I'm not likely to see the guy again after we finish our lunch. But it very much matters to him what he does. He'd be well advised to remember what my dad once told me.'

'Which is?' Keir took a bite of burger.

'You can change your job and you can move house. You can buy a whole new wardrobe and get a ritzy haircut and teeth like a Hollywood movie star's, if you've got enough dollars. But you can't change your memories. You can't shut down your emotions and convince yourself to stop caring about someone.'

Keir put down his fork. 'What about out of sight, out of mind?'

She dunked a chip into the pot of salsa verde. 'You cannot be serious. I'm trying to tell you, you can't run away from Keir Harrison.'

'OK. If you know so much about this kind

of thing, what do you think I should do to win over the beautiful lady doctor?'

She pointed to her steadily moving jaw and rolled her eyes at him.

'OK. Your mother told you never to talk with your mouth full,' he said. 'Just bear in mind, Andrea refuses to answer my text messages, respond to my telephone messages or the dozen or so emails I've agonised over.'

'What about pushing a letter through her mailbox? You do still have those in England?'

'Already tried that and it didn't work.'

'Ah.' She finished her fries and began on his. He waited patiently.

'Got it,' she said at last. 'Call a meeting. Get your PA to book a room and invite Andrea in the usual way. But when she turns up, you and she will be the only ones there.'

He groaned. 'What are you trying to do to me? The regular team meetings happen as and when. Andrea would be sure to ask her boss about the extra one and he won't know what she's talking about. She'll smell a rat and that rat will be me.'

Carrie daintily dabbed her mouth with her paper napkin. 'Her pride has been hurt. Her heart's broken. Why would she want to meet you? Don't answer that!'

He waited while she thought.

'You must find a way of breaking down her

resistance. Can you not camp on her door-step?'

He heaved a sigh and pushed his plate aside.

'Don't you have a friend who can put a word in?'

'What, like in the playground? I don't think so.'

She checked her watch. 'Keir, I'm afraid I must get back soon. Let me split the bill with you.'

He put his hand over hers, to stop her reaching for her purse. 'No. Lunch is on me, Carrie. I've enjoyed your company and you've helped clarify my thoughts. You really have.'

She looked unconvinced. 'I'm pleased but I can't think why you say so. Short of abseiling down the lady's chimney, I can't suggest any magic formula.'

'Whatever happens, you've sorted my way forward. Regarding my career, I mean. There is no magic formula.'

She rose and bent to kiss his cheek. Keir stood up, too, and gave her a hug.

'You have my card and I've tucked yours in my wallet. Let me know what you decide.' She held up her hand. 'Remember, the real decision has to wait until they actually make that job offer. When the crunch comes, that's when you'll have to say yes or no. That's when you'll know whether to pack up and run or whether to keep fighting for what you really want.'

He watched her walk away. The waitress arrived with his tab and he dealt with the payment, calculating the service tax. He left the restaurant deep in thought. His problem was deep-rooted. It had taken another trip to Montreal to clarify his thoughts, but he knew now what he had to do. Somehow he'd known Carrie Michaels would cut to the chase.

13

When the prof walked into her office, Andrea was staring into space. Richard cleared his throat. 'Keir has got back from his break. We've just spoken.'

'Sorry, Richard, I was thinking about the next clinic session.'

'Well, Keir will be attending. He asked after you, by the way.'

She looked anywhere but at him.

He shifted his feet. 'Andrea, tell me to mind my own business if you like, but I have the impression you two are treading warily around each other.'

'I don't intend it to cause problems. If that's the case then I apologise.'

He threw his hands up in the air. 'Damn it, I don't need you to apologise. I've a rough idea what this might be about and I just wanted to say if there's anything I can do to help, I hope you won't hesitate to ask.'

She nodded. 'Thanks, Prof. That's very kind of you. But these things happen.'

'Misunderstandings, you mean?'

'Mistakes is more like it.'

'We're all capable of making those, Andrea.'

'Richard, if you're trying to cheer me up, it's not going to work. I just need time to get over him. It. Whatever.'

'Is that what you really want? To walk away from him? I don't know too much about it, but I care about you enough to risk you snapping back at me.' He rubbed his chin. 'Are you quite sure you're not making a big mistake?'

She stared at him. His tone was gentle and his hooded grey eyes beneath a pair of giant shrimp eyebrows shone with compassion.

She slumped, head in hands. 'It doesn't seem I have any choice.'

'What rubbish. The man thinks the world of you. Any imbecile can see that.'

'Is that so? Well, the man has a funny way of showing it.'

Richard turned to leave, muttering something that sounded like, 'We'll see about that, won't we?'

She called after him. 'It's driving me crazy, Richard. How the heck did I get in so deep?'

He stopped but didn't turn to face her. 'It's called love, Andrea. Ring him. Better still, go and see him. Kick the fellow's butt if that's what it takes! So long as it puts you, him, and all of us out of our misery.'

When Keir reached for his mobile again,
this time he didn't call up Dr Palmer's
number.

'Keir?' His PA sounded anxious. 'Is
everything all right?'

'Lyn, I'm sorry to disturb your evening, but
I'm anxious to get in touch with Sister
McIntosh. You wouldn't happen to have her
home number on that laptop of yours, would
you?'

'As it happens, I do. Hang on, Keir. I was
just looking up volcanoes for my daughter's
school project.'

Keir closed his eyes. If only this worked out
right for him. Susie McIntosh would think
he'd lost his senses, ringing her at home to
talk about his love life. Or would she? She
was unflappable, unshockable and indomi-
table. And like his PA, she was also more
discreet than a plain brown paper bag.

'Here it is,' said Lyn. 'Got a pen?'

'Just a minute.' Keir looked round. Why did
he seem incapable of keeping pen and
notepad on the kitchen table? 'Lyn, call it out
slowly, would you please? I'll put her straight
into my phone.'

* * *

Susie McIntosh and Keir sat across from each other on her garden patio. It wasn't an evening for bare arms and she'd gone inside, to re-emerge wrapped in a three-sizes-too-big fleece.

'Your husband must have wondered what the devil was going on, Susie,' said Keir. 'I'm grateful to you for letting me call round.'

'I'm only sorry I can't entertain you properly. But Friday is Rob's cards night and it's our turn to play host. We'd have got no privacy in the kitchen with that lot popping in and out for beer and wondering when the sausage rolls might be ready.'

'It's a lovely house you have here.'

'We downsized. We trip over the dog sometimes but it suits us. So, what can I do for you? I guess this isn't purely a social call.'

'It's a rather delicate situation. I'd better start right at the beginning.'

'That's probably a good idea.' She settled back in her seat.

'It began when I was trying to get out of a lift.'

'Tell me more. It sounds fascinating.'

Minutes later, Susie shook her head in disbelief. 'You walked right into the honey trap, didn't you? I can't believe you were so naïve. Surely you must have read the signals?'

Keir winced. He'd told Susie to speak her

mind, not gloss over anything for fear of retribution. He didn't unburden his soul lightly and he trusted the older woman's good sense. 'I'm not a man of the world, Susie,' he said. 'Not where females are concerned anyway.'

Her face softened. 'No, I realise that. It's one of the reasons people like you. And I understand how, when you offered to drive Moira home, you were still smarting as a result of Dr Palmer's original decision. Your defences were down.'

'It's such a mess. I feel like an actor in some kind of bad drama but without having learnt the right lines to say.'

'Yes, but remember you're in possession of the full facts. Dr Palmer isn't. After a command performance like Moira's, how must Andrea be feeling? It's pretty much agreed Sister Haynes is a minx, but she's nothing if not plausible. You didn't deny anything, did you? Not at that point. Think about it, Keir.'

He groaned and propped his chin between his hands, gazing gloomily at Susie. 'You're right. I walked away because I didn't want to cause a scene. Not in front of staff and patients. It was embarrassing enough as it was. I let Andrea down. So, what should I do?'

'Phew! That's the million-dollar question. Putting myself in her shoes, I'd probably refuse to see you outside of work, just as she's doing. On the basis of damage limitation, if you know what I mean.'

'I'm bad news?' His shoulders drooped.

'Not necessarily but Andrea has had a very tough time. Bereavement affects people in such different ways. It's highly likely her attitude is all about self-protection. Who can blame her?'

He nodded.

'Tell me, Keir — just how much do you want Andrea? Do you think she still wants you? That has to be established. Otherwise it's pointless agonising about it, don't you think?'

'I know I want her. I hope she wants me.'

'It sounds as though you and Andrea are soulmates,' said Susie. 'She obviously decided she wanted you in her life but justifiably remained on the defensive. Don't underrate her courage though. She decided to trust you not to play fast and loose with her feelings. You and I know both you didn't betray that trust but after Moira's scheming, you can't blame Dr Palmer for deciding she's made a very bad mistake.' Susie hesitated. 'Although — '

'Although what?'

'From the way you described Moira's actions, including the conjuring trick with the card, it does sound like smoke and mirrors — like an OTT soap opera plot, as you say.'

'Nothing against soap operas,' he said. 'But yes, in my position I collect dozens of business cards wherever I go. Some of them are handed over by women who have important jobs in medicine or pharmaceuticals. Rhonda is professionally my equal and she'd expressed interest in the Hartnett Trial. Honestly, Susie, Andrea would find a whole raft of cards in the top drawer of my desk.'

'I'm sure you're right. But this is all about the way Moira has ratcheted up the situation. You drive her home because her car's broken down. You go in, with the intention of staying for just one drink?' She raised her eyebrows at him.

'Yes, of course! Hell's bells, Susie, you surely don't think for one moment I had designs on the woman, then got cold feet and upset her by backing off?'

'You're too much of a gentleman to fabricate this story, Keir. Also, when you talk about Dr Palmer, your whole demeanour changes. Your face softens, and it's obvious how you feel about her.'

'Thank you,' he said. 'You could put it that way. She means everything to me.'

'I imagine Moira must have had her devious little plan in mind, just in case you behaved in a more gentlemanlike way than she hoped.' Her eyes twinkled. 'You were dead in the water. But so is she, because I, too, have a cunning plan.'

★ ★ ★

Andrea was reading the notes from the previous day's session at the hospital. Her mother had interacted well, appeared calm and comfortable in her surroundings and, as Andrea already knew, Lizzie Dean had no concerns she wished to highlight. It was a terrific result and very heartening. But, for all sorts of reasons, Andrea hadn't slept well the night before, mainly because that surreal pantomime at the clinic kept invading her thoughts. Intimate images of Keir and Moira drifted into her mind's eye as if they were a couple of scantily dressed *Strictly Come Dancing* contestants.

She mustn't torture herself like this. Since the regular arrival of message after message from Keir, she'd received that notification of his absence on leave and although she knew he was back again, he hadn't resumed his attempts to reach her. She thought of the note he'd pushed through the door, probably

321

when she and Josh were at Kirsty's house that Saturday. She'd immediately shredded that letter on returning home. Self-preservation was the name of that particular game. But the memory of the fleeting happiness she'd known with Keir continued to taunt her.

Now Richard was nagging her to rethink her attitude. If only she knew whether that was the right thing to do.

When her office phone rang, she picked it up absent-mindedly, eyes still on her computer screen.

'Dr Palmer? It's Susie McIntosh here.'

'Hey, Susie, why so formal? What can I do for you?'

'I'm not at the hospital today. I wonder whether you have half an hour free some time, because I really need to talk to you.'

Andrea fidgeted with her hair. 'Can't it wait until the next clinic session?'

'No, Andrea, it really can't. Please trust me. I feel bad enough as it is, ringing you about a non-medical matter.'

'I see. Well, you won't want to trudge all the way over here on your precious day off. What about Lydney Gardens at half past twelve?'

'The park will suit me well. I need to go into town. See you by the lake then.'

Andrea was finding difficulty in concentrating on her work as it was. It had been difficult resisting the messages while Keir tried to contact her. Now, the lack of them depressed her. Was he really prepared to give up on her so easily? She sucked in her breath as she realised not only had she not checked her mobile that morning, but it was still switched off from last night.

She reached for her bag and pulled out the phone. There was one text message from Kirsty but nothing from Keir. Well, that was it then. She shook her head ruefully, recalling the stricken expression on his face when Moira launched her bombshell. At that moment, she'd almost felt sorry for him. Almost.

Andrea had her own take on things. There'd been no mistaking his sincerity when he came to her house and expressed his true feelings. But she was miffed. Moira had been well out of order and it was down to Keir to dig himself out of the deep hole he'd excavated. It was all very well for Richard to dole out advice. She didn't need to take it. Meanwhile, it would be interesting to discover what had rattled nice Sister McIntosh's cage. For the life of her, she couldn't imagine what all the mystery was about.

★　★　★

Andrea grabbed her umbrella from the back seat of the car. Josh had been using it as a telescope to spy out baddies and when she tried to open it, the brolly didn't function quite as she would have hoped. But as she hurried down the path towards the lake, the raindrops petered out and a watery sun emerged.

Susie McIntosh was gazing at the water-fowl. 'The benches are all wet,' she said, noticing Andrea. 'Shall we stroll around the lake?'

'Why not?' Andrea looked up at the sky. 'Look at that perfect rainbow.'

'It's gorgeous,' said Susie, barely giving it a glance. 'I hope it's in order to talk woman to woman?'

'Absolutely,' said Andrea. 'I hope this isn't something to do with my mother.'

Susie stopped walking. 'Andrea, of course it's not. What an idiot I am — I'm so sorry for not making it clear this wasn't about Rosemary. For what it's worth, I think she's doing very well indeed. But Dr Harrison would be the one to talk to you if something was upsetting her.'

'Yes. Well, so far it's very encouraging. Forgive me for jumping at you. You did say it was a non-medical matter. I suppose I'm a bit on edge what with one thing and another. So come on, what's bugging you?'

They watched a group of Grey Back geese swoop and settle on the lake, greedily eyeing up passers-by in hopes of food.

'I feel so embarrassed about this, but I also feel very strongly so I'm going to charge straight on. Please hear me out. Keir Harrison has, I believe, been set up. The person in question has history, shall we say, and I want to try and put the record straight.'

'We're talking about Nurse Haynes,' said Andrea.

'We are indeed. She's a brilliant nurse, but not someone to cross.'

'Hey,' said Andrea. 'To my knowledge, I've done nothing to upset her.'

'I'm sure you haven't, but Dr Harrison has, so by default you're part of this. She's had her eye on Keir for a while now, with no progress, I might add. Your accompanying him on the Montreal trip seems to have aggravated her jealousy. I gather she performed her little-girl-lost act on him recently, with the object of begging a lift home. Oh, I know she could outdo any of the TV soap divas, but Dr Harrison seems to have walked into her lair without having his radar switched on. Typical man. And this is a specially nice one.'

Andrea frowned. 'Am I being a bit thick here, Susie? Has Keir put you up to this?'

Susie nodded. 'That must surely tell you something? If he was blissfully in lust with the copper-haired bombshell, he wouldn't have needed to cry on my shoulder.'

Andrea gulped. 'Cry on your shoulder? Obviously you've known him far longer than I have — is he so terrified of me? Would he knowingly not tell me stuff?' Her eyes showed her distress and confusion.

Susie cleared her throat. 'I gather you've been less than receptive to his attempts to contact you. Also, he's scared of hurting you even more than he believes he already has. As for being terrified — he's terrified of losing you, Andrea. Correction: he's terrified he's already lost you for good.'

'I'm not going anywhere,' she said. 'His timing's out, I think. Or else, he doesn't credit me with much common sense.'

'Sorry?'

'The pieces are falling into place now. I see what happened. When he gave Moira a lift home and she invited him in for a drink, supper, whatever, he still thought he and I had no future together.'

'You don't have to tell me anything, you know. I'm here to explain Keir isn't the first doctor to find himself getting into a pickle with Moira.'

'I'm not surprised. She's maybe a bit too

anxious — comes over as a bit too possessive?'

'That's very charitable, Andrea. As a nurse she's Florence Nightingale. Where the opposite sex is concerned, she's a 24-carat bitch. And consultants are her speciality, if you'll pardon the pun.' Susie turned to face Andrea. 'So you're not actually as upset as Keir thinks you are? You've known all along that he wouldn't deliberately hurt you?'

Andrea squeezed Susie's elbow. 'At first I didn't know what to think. Then I was cross with him for not telling me later that evening, after he left Moira's. It would've made things so much easier.' She paused. 'You won't tell him though, will you?'

'Not if you don't want me to. So, what am I to say to him?'

'Nothing yet, please. If your paths cross this afternoon, could you maybe tell him you did all you could but you're not sure you convinced me?'

'No problem,' said Susie. She chuckled. 'I couldn't help but feel sorry for him. In spite of his status and all that, I felt as if I'd jumped back in time. It was like I was trying to console my teenage son when his first relationship fell apart, though in that case my son didn't take long to find someone else. I have a feeling the two of you mean rather more to one another.'

'You could say the situation between the two of us did move on fairly rapidly.' She hesitated.

'You don't need to worry about me gossiping, Andrea. If it helps, let it out. I'm totally unshockable after the career I've had.'

'Some might say certain things happened too quickly. I don't want to sound as if I'm trying to write a romantic novel but being in Montreal, away from our everyday lives, we created a little world of our own. I never ever imagined I could find that kind of happiness again. I never ever thought I could love another man after what happened to Greg.'

Susie produced a pack of paper tissues from her jacket pocket and passed it to Andrea, who shook her head.

'Thanks, but I'm not feeling tearful. I'm feeling very strong and very sure of my mind.'

'I'm so pleased for you. It's obvious to me how Keir feels about you.'

'Thanks, but I pushed him away, you see. Just like Cinderella losing her slipper at midnight, I lost my confidence on the flight back to Heathrow. The demons popped into my mind and I started worrying about what people might think about me, beginning a relationship so soon after being widowed.'

'It's not that soon,' said Susie.

'That fits with Keir's opinion. He was so lovely, so caring, yet somehow I couldn't bring myself to let him into my life. Did he tell you how we got together the night he gave Moira that lift home? That's what I meant when I said he should have told me what happened. She sounded so, so convincing.'

'He knows that now. In my humble opinion, both of you have been through the wringer. If Sister Haynes had pulled that trick with him a bit further down the line, he'd have run a mile. After he'd called a cab for her no doubt! Keir is indisputably a gentleman.'

'And I'd have to be totally stupid not to take this chance of happiness.'

'The answer is yes and if anyone deserves it, you do, Andrea. I'm rooting for you but my lips are sealed.' She checked her watch. 'I must let you go. Thanks for meeting me.'

'I can't thank you enough. I have to make a little purchase before I go back to work. Thanks for taking time to talk to me, Susie, but most of all, thanks for caring about Keir and me.'

Susie gave her a quick hug and turned away quickly. But Andrea had noticed the tears glistening in the nurse's eyes. She'd be rooting for a happy ending. Andrea muttered a swift prayer to herself before hurrying towards the gates opening on to the shopping precinct.

★ ★ ★

Around seven p.m. Keir sat gloomily at his kitchen table, newspaper propped up against a bowl piled with fruit he kept forgetting to eat. He glared at a mottled banana. He'd read one particular article twice, without absorbing one single word. He was prolonging the frightening finality of responding to the email recently received from Rhonda Pierce when he jumped at the sound of the doorbell.

'Please don't let it be Moira Haynes,' he muttered. Maybe if he stayed where he was, she'd go away again. Except his car stood in the driveway. Anyway, why on earth should he be so neurotic? The nurse couldn't possibly know where he lived, and his caller could well be one of his neighbours. They weren't to know he'd rather mud-snorkel than socialise.

Reluctantly he rose and padded barefoot towards the hall. He couldn't be bothered to put on his shoes and no way would the visitor, whoever he or she turned out to be, cross his threshold. He opened the front door, peering suspiciously around it like a lonely pensioner longing for someone to share a pot of tea with, but dreading a nuisance caller.

14

Keir's gaze took in the sight of the woman he loved standing on the driveway, clutching a large plastic bag in one hand. She wore a skimpy pink linen dress and sandals that reminded him of the kind of footwear you saw in pictures of Roman soldiers. His heart felt like a rabbit bouncing around inside a cardboard box. All he could think about was how much he loved her and how depressed he felt.

Neither acknowledged the other until at last she said, 'At the risk of making your neighbours gossip, could I maybe have a word with you in private?'

He looked over her shoulder at the road and saw her car. 'Have you brought Josh? Is everything OK with you?'

'No, everything's not OK with me but Josh is fine, thank you. He's with Lizzie and my mother.' Her eyes danced. 'They're fine, too. Or they were when I left them a short while ago. May I come in, please? This won't take very long.'

'No. I don't expect it will,' he said gloomily, making way for her. 'I'm well aware I deserve to be hung, drawn and quartered.'

'Really? That sounds a bit harsh. Have you done something very wrong?'

'You mean apart from badly hurting you, letting myself down, letting you down, in addition to totally ruining my life? You can probably add more vices to that list. All I can say is how sorry I am, Andrea. I'm so, so, very sorry. You must think I'm some kind of a louse. I expect the prof would have me horse-whipped if he knew the full story.'

He led the way into the sitting room, unaware how difficult she found it not to laugh. 'Please sit down,' he said. 'I'll stand, if you don't mind. I've already spoken to Susie so I've a rough idea what you've come to say.'

She settled herself on the settee with the plastic bag placed carefully beside her as if it contained a precious artefact. She sat, hands clasped round her knees, while her eyes roamed the decor. 'This is a very comfortable room,' she said.

He spread his hands in a gesture of helplessness. 'I'm sorry your first visit isn't due to happier circumstances. But thank you for giving me the chance to say sorry.'

She sat back against the crimson sofa cushions.

'I really can't apologise enough for my

stupid behaviour,' he said, 'but I'm not going to waste your time with excuses. You won't have to put up with me hanging around and embarrassing you for much longer. I've reached a decision which I believe is the right one.' He sucked in his breath. Talk about burning his boats.

'Is it that you won't ever trust a woman again? You won't ever again allow yourself to be placed in any kind of compromising situation? Well, I find that rather disappointing.' Her lips twitched.

He glared at her. 'It's not funny, Andrea. I've made a big mess of things and I'm well aware it's pointless trying to talk my way out of it. Why should you bother to listen? You must feel you've had a lucky escape.' His gaze travelled to the plastic bag, registering it but not recognising its significance. 'I should have known it was no good hoping Susie McIntosh could work miracles. The best thing for me is to pack up and take a job elsewhere. There's no way I'll ever forget what we might have had together, but you won't want me hanging round here.'

Andrea raised her eyebrows. 'But where exactly are you planning on going?'

'To Montreal, as it happens. You already know Rhonda Pierce gave me her business card while you and I were over there for the conference. Since then, rather a lot has happened.'

He expected some response but Andrea waited for him to continue, her solemn grey eyes fixed on his face. Sending little shivers of longing down his spine.

'I won't bore you with all the details. It was pointless telling you I was headhunted in Montreal. Pointless because I thought — I thought you and I were — '

She took hold of the mysterious carrier bag and stood up, keeping her distance. 'Ah, so you were being lured by the high-powered woman who handed you Moira's little trump card. That'd be the woman who's very glamorous as well as successful. That's a very potent cocktail.'

He shot her an anguished look. 'Glamorous? I suppose so, if you like wafer-thin females. I saw Rhonda for a brief chat in the park while you were shopping on our last afternoon. I had no idea why she suggested I met with her away from the conference. To my surprise, she wanted to sound me out regarding a position becoming vacant at her hospital and she handed me her card so I had her contact details.'

'And this job is better than the one you already have?'

He ran his hand over his hair. 'Not better,

necessarily. Swings and roundabouts, I imagine, now I've actually been interviewed. Excellent facilities, as you'd expect. And you know how fond I am of that part of Canada.'

She nodded. 'So, let me see. At first, you opted not to take up Rhonda's offer because you thought you and I might have something going for us.'

He groaned. 'Yes of course, though I did agree I'd at least consider applying. Then on the flight home, it seemed you weren't singing from the same hymn sheet as me. The evening you let me call round to talk to you, I thought we'd finally sorted things. After Moira Haynes kicked off in the clinic, I knew I must have totally blown it as far as you were concerned.'

'That was such a fiasco.'

'It certainly was. With hindsight, I should have frog-marched her from the room, but no way did I want to cause a fuss.' He smacked one fist into the other palm. 'After that you wouldn't let me explain so I thought it best to back off and explore my options. It's Rhonda's own position that's up for grabs, by the way.'

Andrea whistled. 'So she really is holding down a top-notch job?'

'She's extremely able, yes. But her husband's accepted a position over on the west coast and Rhonda's decided she won't be left behind. She told me I'd been shortlisted while I was still over there, but before I flew home she told me something prevented them giving me their decision before I left Montreal. It involved one of the board members.'

'Probably just a technicality — you must feel pleased to have got this far. But you're still waiting to hear?'

'Not anymore, because Rhonda has since emailed the good news. A letter offering the position is being sent to me.'

'Congratulations.' Andrea's voice sounded surprisingly flat.

'Thank you. I'm sure it's the best thing for both of us, given the circumstances.' He paused. 'I wish you'd tell me what's in that darned bag you're clutching. I don't remember leaving anything at your house.'

'You didn't. But before I tell you what's in here, I need to say something about your innocent escapade with the lovely Moira Haynes. When she put you into a compromising position, you and I were still in, shall we say, a state of limbo as to our relationship.'

He stood there, looking as if she'd suddenly started addressing him in ancient Greek.

'I'd given you my decision not to allow our

relationship to progress in the way you wanted,' she said. 'That was while we were flying back.' She spoke slowly and deliberately, as if he'd just awoken from a coma. 'And that was days before you gave Moira a lift home and she invited you in. For what it's worth, nobody in the world would have blamed you if you'd decided to, um, accept her hospitality. You were at that point totally single and unencumbered. Although I'm really pleased you didn't get too friendly with her.'

He still looked blank.

'It's me that's made a mess of things, Keir. With hindsight, you maybe should have said you'd been to Moira's house. When you rang me that evening after you'd left her, you sounded so unhappy and lonely, my heart just melted. I wanted you so much. I thought everything would be fine. Then as you say, she kicked off at the clinic session and you seemed to go along with what she said. Little doubts crept in.'

'I'm not proud of the way I handled that situation.'

'You didn't have a lot of choice. She was so out of order. Everyone says she's such a professional but on that occasion she really let herself down. I don't want to sound like a grumpy old bat but she really should be reprimanded.'

'I think that's been dealt with, actually. I didn't want to lodge a formal complaint, as you can imagine, but I heard through the grapevine Susie McIntosh made her views clear.' He managed a faint smile. 'Grumpy old bat indeed! You're absolutely right. Sister Haynes betrayed her profession.'

Andrea nodded. 'Even so, I let you go on sweating and before I could come to my senses you sent round that bleak little message informing everyone you were going on leave. I cried myself to sleep that night.'

He took one step towards her. 'You what?'

'I wanted to come and give you my side of the story. I heard your side of it from Susie McIntosh. She's a lovely woman and she thinks the world of you, though I can't think why.'

She was smiling at him. He longed to take her in his arms but still didn't move from the spot. 'So, where do we go from here? I need you to tell me, Andrea.'

She shrugged. 'I never wanted just a fling. You know that. I've been acting like a teenager with raging hormones. But now, if it's a case of just a short few weeks with you before you leave, if you're still interested, I'm going to have to accept it. I'm very much to blame when it comes to this decision you've made.'

'Hello? Don't you get it, darling dunderhead?' He moved another step closer. Now he could almost smell that floral scent he associated with her hair. She'd got a sprinkling of brand-new freckles on the bridge of her nose.

'Get what?' She looked enquiringly at him.

He folded his arms across his chest. 'I refuse to tell you until you explain what's so important about that darned plastic bag.'

Andrea's eyes sparkled as she thrust her hand into the red carrier bag and whipped out a new white football. 'I'm sorry it's not a romantic gesture like chocolates or flowers,' she said. 'But I'm hoping you'll come round to meet Josh as soon as possible. My dribbling skills aren't what they should be.'

He watched her face crumple.

'Darling Keir, I love you so much. I don't know how I can bear it once you go away. But now it's too late to beg you to stay.'

The ball fell to the floor and rolled gently into a corner as Keir took three steps towards Andrea and wrapped his arms around her. She nestled against him.

'I've been such an idiot,' he murmured in her ear, his spine tingling as his lips brushed her hair.

'So have I. If I hadn't acted as I did in Montreal, things wouldn't have accelerated as

339

they did. I was totally out of order and I'm afraid I've hurt you very much and I'm sorry, Keir. How long will I have with you before you leave Hartnett?' The words ran one into the other, punctuated by little gasps for air.

'You know what?'

'What?' She took a deep, deep breath and snuggled closer.

'Don't you think we should stop wasting time apologising to each other and get on with the rest of our lives? Listen carefully, Andrea. I said we.'

'But, I don't understand. Haven't you already accepted this job? Much as I want to be with you, I can't abandon my mother to allow Josh and me to follow you. I'm so sorry.'

He kissed her hair, her forehead and the tip of her nose. Then he kissed her on the mouth. Softly at first but gathering momentum as he met with a more than satisfactory response.

This kiss kept them both occupied until at last she broke gently away. 'You haven't answered me yet.'

'I was far too busy. As if I'd even think about asking you to abandon your mother! The answer is you arrived just in time, my darling. I haven't signed anything yet. And when I've finished kissing you, which may take quite a while, I may add, I shall ring

Rhonda Pierce, grovel as much as I think necessary and tell her I'm sorry to have wasted her time but my circumstances have changed and I can't move to Canada. Is that all right with you?'

She showed her concern. 'Are you totally certain you should turn down this job?'

He picked up his wallet from the coffee table and pulled out a little cream card. Andrea took it from him, reading the elegant dark red script. 'Carrie Michaels,' she said. 'Isn't that the violinist? The one that crosses over from classical to pop?'

'I didn't realise I was taking such a famous musician out to lunch,' he said.

'How many more Canadian conquests has the man made?' Her eyes danced.

'Off the top of my head, one old lady on a hospital bench and a golden retriever in the park, though actually I think the retriever was a boy. Carrie's a friend of Rhonda and her husband. We met at their home then she and I had lunch next day. I told her all about you.'

'You certainly made her earn her lunch, poor soul.'

'I told her I was considering moving to Montreal because I couldn't bear seeing you at work without the prospect of becoming close to you. Without the prospect of ever coming home to you in the evening and being part of a family.'

Andrea's eyes were solemn. 'So, what did Carrie think?'

'She told me it was pointless trying to escape my feelings. In other words, she told me changing my job and living on a different continent wouldn't work because I could never leave myself behind.'

'I see. But you'd have been prepared to go?'

'Only because I thought it would make life less complicated for you.'

She traced the outline of his lips with her forefinger. He closed his eyes, groaned and gently licked her fingertip. Squillions of seconds went by.

'I need to tell you something,' said Andrea, as soon as he allowed her to breathe again. 'Before we met in your office, I had my own nickname for you.'

'Before you even got to know me?' He looked incredulous.

'Yes. I heard stuff about you that led me to call you Dr Shiny Pants.'

'Is that right? He smoothed away a lock of her hair. 'And do you still call me that?'

'Not anymore. I soon discovered your human side.'

'When I saw you for the very first time I

thought of you as Ms Torpedo.'

'You had a nerve.' She screwed up her nose. 'I suppose I was in a bit of a hurry that time at the lift.'

'What about now?'

'I'm not in a hurry. Josh is with Lizzie and Mum.'

'Uhuh. I suppose I ought to let you audition my soccer skills.'

She stroked his ears, melting his bones. 'I need to say something else to you.'

'You think I forgot to put my shoes on?'

'I love you, Keir.'

The power of speech temporarily deserted him.

'Well, that went down well,' said Andrea.

He held her very close, very close indeed. 'Thank you,' he whispered. 'One day, when you tell me you're ready, I want to hear you say 'I do' again. Until then, 'I love you' will do very nicely. Very nicely indeed, Dr Palmer.'

We do hope that you have enjoyed reading this large print book.

Did you know that all of our titles are available for purchase?

We publish a wide range of high quality large print books including:
Romances, Mysteries, Classics
General Fiction
Non Fiction and Westerns

Special interest titles available in large print are:
The Little Oxford Dictionary
Music Book
Song Book
Hymn Book
Service Book

Also available from us courtesy of Oxford University Press:
Young Readers' Dictionary
(large print edition)
Young Readers' Thesaurus
(large print edition)

For further information or a free brochure, please contact us at:
Ulverscroft Large Print Books Ltd.,
The Green, Bradgate Road, Anstey,
Leicester, LE7 7FU, England.
Tel: (00 44) 0116 236 4325
Fax: (00 44) 0116 234 0205

SOMEDAY WE'LL TELL EACH OTHER EVERYTHING

Daniela Krien

It is the summer of 1990. The Berlin Wall has collapsed, and Germany is preparing for reunification. Away from this upheaval, young Maria moves in with her boyfriend on his family's farm in the sleepy countryside of the East. A chance encounter with an enigmatic older man ignites an improbable affair. Henner is damaged and unpredictable, yet Maria is uncontrollably drawn to him. As the summer progresses, keeping their passion a secret becomes ever more difficult. A bold and powerful love story ensues, where violence and desire are inextricably entwined, painting a portrait of a community in flux.

PROMISE TO OBEY

Stella Whitelaw

When Jessica is charmed by Lucas Coleman into accepting a job at grand Upton Hall, she is not expecting to have to provide full-time care for his autistic son, asthmatic daughter, and the sharp-tongued Lady Grace, who is recuperating from hip replacement surgery — and she certainly did not expect a marriage proposal from her employer. But where is the children's mother? Fighting her attraction to the beguiling Lucas, she is determined to keep her head. A disastrous affair with a London doctor has put her off men; but when he descends on Upton Hall, determined to win her back, Jessica's life is thrown into turmoil.